THE PRISONER'S WIFE

THE PRISONER'S WIFE

GERARD MACDONALD

THOMAS DUNNE BOOKS · ST. MARTIN'S PRESS ✻ NEW YORK

This is a work of fiction. All of the characters, organizations, and events portrayed in this novel are either products of the author's imagination or are used fictitiously.

THOMAS DUNNE BOOKS.
An imprint of St. Martin's Press.

THE PRISONER'S WIFE. Copyright © 2012 by Gerard Macdonald. All rights reserved. Printed in the United States of America. For information, address St. Martin's Press, 175 Fifth Avenue, New York, N.Y. 10010.

www.thomasdunnebooks.com
www.stmartins.com

Design by Anna Gorovoy

Library of Congress Cataloging-in-Publication Data

Macdonald, Gerard.
     The prisoner's wife / Gerard Macdonald.—1st ed.
         p. cm.
     ISBN 978-0-312-59180-9 (hardcover)
     ISBN 978-1-250-01243-2 (e-book)
     1. Kidnapping—Fiction.   2. Intelligence officers—United States—
Fiction.   3. State-sponsored terrorism—Fiction.   I. Title.
     PR6113.A255P75 2012
     823'.92—dc23

                                                            2011050641

First Edition: May 2012

10 9 8 7 6 5 4 3 2 1

FOR JANET

ACKNOWLEDGMENTS

My thanks, for help, critique, and guidance, to Emma Healey; my editor, Brendan Deneen; his assistant, Nicole Sohl; Farheen Ahmad; Louise Doughty; Peter Buckman; Greg Dinner; Elisabeth Anton; Mary Hardin; Claudia Devlin; Anne Aylor; and Campaspe Lloyd-Jacob.

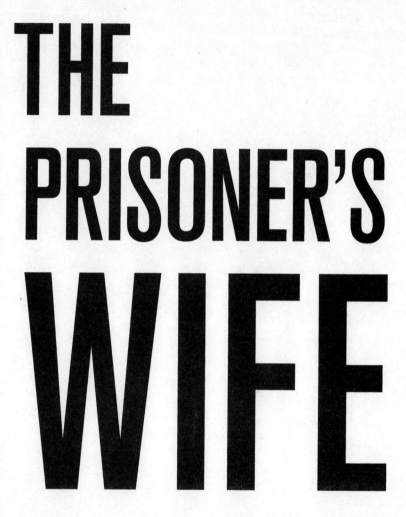

THE PRISONER'S WIFE

1

In the spring of 2004, Darius Osmani was disappeared.

In mid-April, in a black Volvo on the rue des Vieilles Boucher-ies, Hassan Tarkani and Calvin McCord, intelligence operatives, were talking money.

Calvin said, "You tell me what you get, I tell you what I get, one of us going to be unhappy. Trust me. That's the way it works."

They were parked without lights in the *quatrième*, between a shuttered café and a nineteenth-century apartment building. Streetlamps were already lit. In the rain, a pointillist halo sur-rounded the lights.

"Tell me," said Hassan, "for the same work, will a man from poor country, will he get less money than a man from rich coun-try?"

"Interesting question," said Calvin. As part of his training, he'd spent a semester at Michigan State, studying issues in moral belief. "We're talking ethics, I don't know what to tell you. We're talking practicalities, answer is yes. No question, rich guy gets more. 'To those who have, it shall be given and they shall abound; from those who do not have, even what they have shall be taken away.' That's the Bible, right there."

"This is Christian Bible?"

"That's the one," Calvin said.

Both Hassan and Calvin wore tight-fitting black caps, which were in fact ski masks, rolled to forehead height. Calvin, who had a low threshold for boredom, held a hip flask between his knees. He took a drink without making an offer to Hassan. By nationality Hassan was Pakistani; by religion, Muslim. Though Calvin had worked with Muslims who eased the pain with alcohol, his partner wasn't among them. So far as Calvin knew.

Hassan turned on the car's interior light to check a double photo—full face and profile—of a man in his late thirties. "What exactly has he done, this man?"

Calvin snapped off the light. "Nothing, far's I know. It's what he might do. Same as Iraq—preemptive strike. Lock up the ragheads planning whatever they're planning, what do we have? I'll tell you. Peace. Would you say God knew if you did take a drink?"

"Of course."

"I have this vision of your God," Calvin said. "He's sitting in front of like some infinitely giant flat-screen video monitor, keeping an eye on all you camel jockeys. He's pretty damn sharp. He'll be eyeballing some chick wearing makeup on this side of the screen, say the right side, or she got her head uncovered, whatever, then, same moment, he sees a guy like you, not you personally, out in left field, you sneak a little drink. *Gotcha,* says God, quick as a flash. Won't miss a trick, this guy. It's like a touch-screen he has up there, he just hits it with his hand and *bam,* blasts you. Do not pass Go. Get straight to hell. What's the road name mean?"

Through the rain-spattered windshield, Hassan peered up at a sign. "Old Butchery Street."

"Appropriate," Calvin said. "Something I wonder is, why the fuck you speak five languages and me—that's got more money and more rank and more education—I have trouble talking my own damn tongue."

"It has to do with color of passport," Hassan said. "If it is blue, you tell us poor people, 'Learn American, or we don't talk with you.' If you are sorry son of a bitch with green passport, you learn languages or you don't speak with any person outside of Pakistan." He touched the side of his wristwatch, illuminating numbers on its dial. "How long?"

Watching the apartments, Calvin said, "Long as it takes. He wants to get laid, has to come out sometime." He lifted the flask, resisted a moment, and took another drink. His hand shook a little.

In the darkness, his mind wandered.

"Global warming," he said. "You heard of this? Climate change? Sun getting hotter? Worries the shit outa me. I hate to be the one has to tell you, your whole damn country's going undersea."

Hassan said, "You're thinking of Bangladesh."

"The hell I am," said Calvin. "If I was thinking of Bangladesh I would've said Bangladesh, wherever the fuck that is."

Hassan considered explaining the subcontinent's geography and decided against it. He pointed to the now-opening door of the apartment building.

Calvin was peering through binoculars at a man who stood in the building's doorway, lighting a cigarette between cupped hands. The match glow lit up his face.

"Snap. That's our boy."

Moving as one, Hassan and Calvin rolled down their ski masks. They were out of the car, across the damp pavement, gripping the arms of the figure in the doorway. When the man yelled and tried to back into the hall, away from the black-masked figures, he was borne in the opposite direction, toward the Volvo. He shouted once. Something soft was pushed into his mouth. Though his arms were held, his feet were free. The prisoner had once been a soccer player, a fullback, in Iran. He kicked the black-masked man holding his left arm, kicked again, heard a muttered exclamation. Then something smooth and heavy slugged the place where the prisoner's skull joined his neck. At the same moment Hassan's fist hit the young man's gut, driving air from his lungs. The smooth and heavy thing hit his knees: first the left, then the right.

When his breath came back and his eyes opened, the suspect found his vision fading in and out of focus. Whatever was in his mouth made it hard to breathe. He tried again to kick, but his legs hung limp, like a doll's.

The masked men bundled him into a car's backseat.

Hassan followed the prisoner in, gripping his thin neck and binding his mouth with duct tape.

Calvin, in the driver's seat, pulled the car out, passing a soft-topped Peugeot. He did not turn his head. "Just don't do what you did with the last one, okay?"

Hassan paused in his work. "I did what, exactly?"

"Get out of here. You taped his fucking nose."

"Accident, right?"

"Tell me about it," Calvin said. "Just keep this one breathing." He made a sharp right turn. "I'm not flying out with a body bag."

He slowed for a red light on rue Rivoli, then accelerated through green. "Documents?"

Hassan cuffed the prisoner's hands behind him, bagged his head, then searched his pockets. The man made a sound that, through duct tape and hood, became a muffled groan.

Calvin now wore a black trilby hat. Adjusting it, shielding his face, he turned on the car's interior light, so Hassan could read.

"Hate to end up in Bagram with the wrong guy."

Hassan said, "He can hear you."

"That's okay," Calvin said. "He's not going to Bagram. Still want him to be the right guy."

Hassan had found the man's passport, which was worn and red. "We got him."

The man moaned.

"Planning to travel?"

"Pakistan. He has a visa. More than one."

"Won't be using them," Calvin said, without looking back. "Not anytime soon."

Hassan opened the backseat coffee-cup holder. From a plastic cylinder, he extracted a hypodermic.

"This won't hurt a bit," he told the prisoner. "It will relax you. Take away the anxiety."

"Understandable anxiety," Calvin said. "All things considered." At slightly less than legal speed he was driving down the boule- vards des Maréchaux, heading for the Parisian *périphérique*. "He must wonder what the hell's happening. I mean, I would." When his phone connected he called ahead for priority clearance at Charles de Gaulle.

Again, the prisoner made a sound. To ease injection, Hassan considered removing the man's outer clothing, then decided not to. Rule was, at destination, three thousand miles away, the prisoner's garments would be cut from his body and the bagged pieces flown to Virginia for testing. Till then, the guy stays dressed. That was the rule.

Through the prisoner's woolen jacket, Hassan administered a syringe-full of chemical relaxant. As the hypodermic's needle entered his arm, the man twitched like a rabbit.

Hassan patted the prisoner's duct-taped face. "Oh, come on," he told him. "Didn't hurt."

"Clean needle," Calvin said, from the front seat, "if that's what he's worried about."

"If he is worrying now," Hassan said, "soon he won't." He found the prisoner's pulse. "Relaxing already, this boy."

Passing a police patrol, Calvin slowed a little. "He might be worried if he knew where he was going."

"Fortunately," Hassan said, "he has no idea."

2

Three weeks after the disappearance of Darius Osmani, Shawn Maguire stood at the back of a Greek-owned coffee bar in a small English town. Night was falling; the bar was closed for business. Through a doorway he saw a neon-lit meeting room.

This was Addicts Anonymous. A broad church, it seemed.

Shawn had been stopped on his way in by Cody, a shaven-headed man whose flesh stretched thin on his bones. Cody had a dog, emaciated as its master. Thinking back, Shawn reflected that all the serious stoners he'd known had owned dogs. Thin dogs, every one.

The man laid a wasted hand on Shawn's arm, whispering, "What do you think? You believe these fuckers?"

Shawn had first met Cody a week earlier, at one of these meetings. Then as now, the man had his dog. He was strung out on horse pills and coke. To him, the assembled alcoholics were dead losers. "What is it, these guys?" he asked. "They do a legal fucking drug. Buy it on the main street, every second fucking shop. Come on. Tell me. What they got to bitch about?"

Breaking free of Cody's grip, Shawn entered the meeting room. Around its walls were taped messages directing troubled souls toward some higher power. HP, for short. On a central table were books, variations on the 12-step gospel.

Shawn guessed there were twenty people, twenty recovering souls, in the room that night. Around that number: In low light it was hard to see. One or two he recalled, without pleasure; the rest were new to him.

In that comfortless room, the addicts sat on plastic chairs, watching a young Anglo-Indian woman perch on the edge of a table at the front of the room. Shawn saw her eyes flick to him, as he took his seat. They'd met before, at one of these redemptive gatherings. He almost recalled her name.

She told the audience, "My name's Anita. I'm an alcoholic."

A ragged chorus from the plastic-seated gathering: "Hi, Anita."

The loudest voice belonged to a bulky guy with a mustache, wild off-white hair, and a jogging suit. Heart sinking, Shawn recalled the guy. Cedric Something. A man who craved attention and paraded his addictions. Both times Shawn had attended, Cedric had recounted an episode—maybe the same episode—in his long-running battle with addiction. Beat the demons one day at a time: That was Cedric's mantra.

"I'm clean," said Anita. She spoke slowly, tranced. "I mean, what I mean is, I was clean, like three months. Three months, four days. Five days. This time around I was, you know, counting. Marked them on the calendar, even. The days I was clean. I was just so happy." She paused. "Then what happens? I get a call from my ex. The things he said—I mean—I'm not perfect, I'm not an evil person—he was so—he was so—the things he said—like threatening—said he knows where I live and—he talked about—" She stopped, then said, "I was so, I was like so upset. Afraid. When I get that way, what I do—always—"

There were tissues on the table.

An older white woman in a floral dress, near the front of the group, said, "Anita, okay. Really. It's okay."

"Bullshit," said Shawn, to himself. "No way is it okay."

Shawn remembered this woman, the older woman. She'd shared in the first meeting he'd attended. Escaping, she said, the grip of prescription drugs. Watching her, Shawn believed the addiction. Wasn't so sure about the recovery.

"What I did," Anita said, "I'm so ashamed, I drove out to the country, found a pub on a back road, never been there before." She paused, then said, "I mean, no one knew me. Really, no one. Had log fires, this pub. I was going to have just one drink, just the one, make it last, you know? Eat some food, come home—"

Someone in the group—Shawn guessed it was Cedric—laughed, then turned a furious face to those who hushed him.

"I never know," Anita said. "Never know what it is. Happens every time. I never learn. Minute I have alcohol, somehow, I send out some kind of signal—I don't know, it's like turning up a thermostat. The heat. I don't know, I conjure up guys, wouldn't look at me if I was on the street, shopping, walking, whatever." She rubbed her eyes. "I know I wouldn't look at them. I had this double vodka, straight, rocks, that's the one I allow myself, I'm just sitting there in a dark corner, hiding away, not checking out anyone, this guy appears from nowhere. I mean, he wasn't even *in* the bar when I got to the place, don't think he was."

Shawn could see it right there. He knew the scene well. Tribeca,

Georgetown, Sussex—same sexual dance, same sad seductions. Now Anita. Even sober, even in go-to-work clothes, she had a darkness, a subterranean sexuality that got his attention every time. He'd spent years on that scent.

It was basic with AA meetings, rule one, they weren't pickup places. Shawn had never hit on Anita, or any other woman in the rooms. Then again, he was new to this recovery gig. He'd thought about a pickup. Of course he had. Down the line, maybe—but tonight?

Anita was weeping now. The room was quiet. "We were drinking," she said. "This guy. I took him home. I—we—I mean—" She stood, pushing herself up off the table. "And I'd worked so hard. Like, I'd been clean for months." Someone slid toward her the half-empty box of man-sized tissues. "That's, I mean, that's all, that's all I want to say right now, but thank you for—"

Another ragged chorus: "Thank you, Anita. Thank you for your chair"—an expression that had puzzled Shawn the first time he came to one of these coffee-bar meetings. Her *chair*?

Cedric, the man who'd laughed, stood on tiptoe, mouth open, ready to speak.

Instead Anita, her breathing slower, pointed at Shawn. "I'd like Shawn to share."

Snap. She remembered his name.

Cedric, put out, sat slowly down. Shawn bent his head. This was a moment he'd hoped to avoid. The three English meetings he'd been to, he'd listened to others tell their histories—alcohol, drugs, sex—all, it seemed, in miniature, scaled down for England. This odd little island.

He hadn't yet spoken, and hoped he'd never have to. Now they watched him. Waiting.

Anita found a seat at the end of his row. "Go," she said.

Shawn wouldn't, couldn't, stand. He said, "My name's Shawn. I'm American. I guess you hear that. Born in Alabama. Been living in England a while. Unemployed." That was the easy part.

Another chorus: "Hi, Shawn."

"I'm an alcoholic." Silence. Waiting. "I'm not what you call clean. I'm still drinking. Less than I did. Still, too much. You know what they say—eases the pain."

Again, silence, in which Shawn felt undercurrents of feeling. Among the saved, a soul impenitent; a man without strength.

"I'm also a sex addict."

In the shadows, someone sighed.

"I didn't know that term," Shawn said. "If I'd heard it a couple of years back, I would've laughed. I mean, I thought that's what you did. Like, excuse the language—I thought, if you're a man— survival of the fittest—you go tomcatting around, grab whatever tail's out there. Meet someone hot, a girl gets your attention, hey, do your damnedest, get her into bed." He paused, then said, "Actually, with me, not that simple. Looking back a couple of years, I'm telling myself, whoa, boy, enough already. I'd gotten married to a woman I always wanted to be married to. Took me twenty-some years to do it. When I put a ring on her finger, I figured she was all I'd need—why'n hell would I go chasing some other broad? But we're addicts here, you know how it is. I didn't stop. I slowed down, didn't stop. I guess—someone told me—that's what addiction is. You want to stop, and you don't stop. It's not easy. You do it that one last time, and it's never the last time." He was quiet awhile, then said, "Now, my wife's gone. I can't tell her

I'm sorry." He stopped, took a breath. "I think that's all I want to say."

A momentary pause, then the chorus: "Thank you, Shawn. Thank you for sharing."

Cedric was on his feet, taking his chance, telling the group he'd been eleven months clean. Shawn stood. Moving quietly, he left the room. He hoped no one would notice. As he crossed the darkened coffee bar he saw Anita had followed him out.

She said, "It's okay, getting out. Really. I know how you feel. Stupid Cedric—we call him One Year Clean—"

"Why's that?"

"New Year's Day," Anita said, "he relapses. Starts over. I hear that one more time, I swear, I'll physically—you know." She waited a moment, then said, "I'm glad you shared."

"Me, too."

"Must have been hard."

Shawn shrugged. "I guess, like lots of things. First time's the worst."

Anita was standing close to him. He could smell her perfume. No alcohol tonight. Patchouli, at a guess. His first wife, Lala, wore patchouli. At times, at home, it was all she wore.

"You were good," Anita said. "You know what they say—that's what helps. Speaking up."

He took her hands in his. "Works if you work it."

She said, "Can I buy you a coffee? Some place that's not here?"

Shawn thought it over. Considered the temptation. Knew how it would end.

After a few moments, he said, "Rain check?"

She nodded yes.

He felt a need to apologize. "I live—it's this, you know, village out on the hills—"

"Felbourne."

So she'd checked his address.

"—kind of a long drive back home. Cat to feed."

Eight bedrooms, all empty.

"Shawn," she said, "it's all right. It's okay. Another time."

Sober, single, sad, Shawn thought later, as he steered Martha's little Merc down unlit country lanes toward an empty rectory in an English hamlet. That's what he'd come to.

There were times—and this was one—when he wondered if that was all he had left.

3

On a late spring afternoon in West Sussex, a chauffeur, a Scot whose graying sideburns matched his skin, slowed his master's Lexus to avoid a flock of guinea fowl. Farther up the single lane of pitted blacktop he passed a sheepdog, three bantams, two cock pheasants bred to be shot, a skein of moorhen chicks, and islets of horse dung. He was not a man at ease with country roads.

The chauffeur parked on a verge outside the churchyard of St. Perpetua, where Shawn's wife and the village gamekeeper were recently buried.

Across the lane was a long-windowed mansion, its facade thick with jasmine and rambling rose. A weathered sign on its northern wall read FELBOURNE OLD RECTORY.

After exchanging words with the veiled woman in the car's backseat, a Pakistani businessman named Ayub Abbasi stepped delicately into the lane. Though the thoroughfare was empty, Abbasi looked to his left and his right, then back at the graveyard.

Middle-aged and plump, conscious of his appearance, he wore a dark Italian suit and Italian shoes, free of metalwork.

Down the lane stood the gamekeeper's daughter, watching. She whistled beneath her breath. Posh people.

Carrying a crocodile-skin valise, Abbasi entered the garden of the rectory opposite. There he paused, checking his watch, a Patek Philippe. His father, the high court judge, had once told him Rolex was for gangsters.

He inhaled a heavy scent that he recognized, with pleasure, as summer jasmine.

Moments later, the chauffeur heard, close at hand, first one rifle shot, then a second. By the time he was out of the car, looking into the garden, his employer was nowhere to be seen.

Within the grounds of the rectory, Ayub Abbasi pushed open a loosely hinged wooden door on which blue paint was peeling. He entered a walled garden and stood, his back to sun-warmed bricks, watching a tall American level a laser-sighted M-24 U.S. Army–issue sniper rifle. He aimed at a pear tree espaliered against the garden's far wall. His first shot had atomized a wasp-bitten pear on the left side of the tree, above the level of the wall.

Abbasi applauded discreetly. Though he himself carried no weapons, he appreciated expertise, in any field.

"Mr. Maguire," he said.

Shawn emptied a round from the rifle's chamber and came across the garden. He wondered, as he often did these days, if his visitor wore a wire.

"Abbasi," he said. "You found me."

Without speaking, Ayub Abbasi crossed the lawn to a slate-roofed summerhouse. He opened his valise and placed two bundles of hundred-dollar bills in the center of a cast-iron table, weighing them down with a chrome-plated garden trowel. "Down payment."

"For what, exactly?" Shawn asked.

"Don't spend it all in one place," Abbasi said. "I heard that somewhere."

"I won't be spending it anyplace, except the bank," Shawn said. He raised a level hand. "Debts up to here."

Abbasi surveyed the estate. "An odd place for a man from Alabama. A rectory. Last time we met, you were out of D.C., were you not? Manhattan maybe. Nowhere like this."

Shawn glanced at the money on the table, estimating its amount. It should clear some of his overdraft. It was like that all through the marriage. Martha had money; Shawn had debts.

He made a comprehensive gesture, taking in the rectory and its land. "Martha bought it. Came a time she wanted old England, not New England. A place in the country." He pointed. "Her grandmother was born down that lane. So she said. Poacher's kid."

Abbasi still considered the house. "Your wife lived here—she died here?" Shawn nodded. "I am sorry. You remember, I met her. Intriguing woman. Married to someone else at the time, was she not?"

"We both were."

"She was buried in Boston?"

Shawn pointed across the lane, beyond the Lexus, to the tree-shaded churchyard. "Martha's there."

For a time Abbasi was silent. Then he asked, "If it is not an awkward question, did your wife understand the business you were in? If she knew, did she approve?"

"Yes to the first," Shawn said. "No to the second. She never came out with it, but she hated the work. Spying, interrogation, all that shit. Made me rethink some things."

"She knew about, what do they call it? Terminations?"

"Not a place I want to go," Shawn said. "Put it this way. I have regrets."

Looking across to the churchyard, Shawn recalled Martha's energy. She was full of surprises. In Manhattan, he'd come home to find her ready to Rollerblade in the park or head for a gallery down among the meatpackers. She threw surprise parties for Shawn's daughter, Juanita, until Juanita was reborn, in a Berkeley church, as a Taoist of the seventh life. Juanita visited with her father and his new wife. She apologized for evil thoughts she might have directed toward them; she said there were many. She promised she would never, in this incarnation, trouble them again.

Martha had laughed and cried, driven her stepdaughter to Newark Airport, and kissed her good-bye. This was years back. Still hard for Shawn to believe that all Martha's energy—her laughter and her tears—was buried there, in the shadowy churchyard of St. Perpetua.

Outside the gate, the mustachioed chauffeur had turned the Lexus around. He stood by the car, bending his head, speaking to the veiled woman within.

"Your enemies, and your dead. Keep them close," Abbasi said to Shawn. "I believe in that." He stood by the slate-roofed summerhouse, scanning the walled garden. "So peaceful." He considered his host. "Your face. You lost a fight?"

"That was last week," Shawn said. "Skinny drunk kid. Thought I could teach him a lesson. I was wrong."

Abbasi said, "We all get old. You attacked one of your colleagues, did you not?" Shawn nodded. "Suspended from active service, I hear. No longer an American spy."

"They call it extended leave. I behave, take anger management class, they let me back."

Abbasi covered his mouth, disguising what might have been amusement. "You think?" His attention elsewhere, he asked how Mr. Maguire spent his time.

"You'll laugh," Shawn said. "It amuses people. What I ask myself these days—what I try getting my head around—is, what the hell was I doing out there? Last twenty-some years."

"What you were doing as a spy?"

Shawn nodded. "I mean, I know what I actually did, minute by minute, most days. Unless I was drunk. What I don't know is *why*. Why they told me to do whatever I did. Why I did it."

"Protecting America from its enemies, were you not? So Mr. McCord would say."

"Yeah," said Shawn, "right. It's what I tell myself. It's what I try believing."

He opened a bottle and poured two glasses of sparkling water. Abbasi, an observant Muslim, did not touch alcohol.

"My turn for a question, Mr. Abbasi. You employ people. A lot of people. Import-export, it's what I hear."

"In the past tense. I did employ. Like its owner, business is not what it was."

"I seem to remember offices, AfPak, Morocco, Kandahar, Miami. Am I right?"

"Sadly, Afghanistan, no longer. Nor Florida. But still, we are in Islamabad. Tenuously, in Fes. Also Peshawar, on the AfPak border. As you call it."

"So why? Why would you need me?"

"I have a problem," Abbasi said, looking around him. "A problem with your people. CIA, Office of Special Plans, CIFA—one or all. I never know. A problem with my people, too. My Pakistani, would you say, compatriots?" He pointed to a table and chairs midway across the lawn. "Might we sit over there?"

Shawn stood, moving out of the summerhouse. A cloud of white doves spread high through still air, planing and gliding in leaderless synchrony.

"I don't believe this. You're worried about bugs? Here? An English village? Do you want to pat me down?"

"If you would not mind. To be sure you do not wear a wire." Ayub Abbasi ran his hands over Shawn's body. "You are very fit."

"For your age," Shawn said. "That's usually how the sentence ends these days. I'm fifty-one. I lose fights."

"I know your age," Abbasi said. "I read the file. You are fifty-three. You still attract women."

"That," Shawn said, "I'm seriously trying to give up." He unpacked a new box of shells.

Abbasi eyed the rifle and the pear tree. "I know that you trained as a sniper. I had not realized you were such a shot."

Without looking down, Shawn reloaded the M-24. "I used to be good. Trying to get back there."

"For your own amusement? Or some other reason?" Abbasi seated himself at a wrought-iron table set on a mower-striped lawn. "You may know I also worked for your agency. Your former agency."

"CIA?"

"Indeed. I was, as you say, on the payroll. Liaison between America and Pakistan."

"Not Pakistan as such," Shawn said. "Liaison with Inter-Services

Intelligence, is my guess. ISI was always the target. Always the problem."

"For our purposes," Abbasi said, "and your purposes, ISI is Pakistan. You know, we all know, they are not just a spy service. Invisible Soldiers Incorporated, we call them. They take the dollars your Congress sends. They run my country, and much of Afghanistan, of course. Taliban is their creation. As is the drug trade." Abbasi smoothed his lightly oiled hair. "Sadly, now, those invisible soldiers wish to kill me."

"What can I tell you?" Shawn said. "I'm not a bodyguard." He glanced toward his sheep field. "These days, I'm a shepherd."

Abbasi made a dismissive gesture. "If I were hiring a bodyguard, I would not be here. You have heard of Nashida Noon?"

Shawn searched his now-fallible memory.

"I know the name. Prime minister of Pakistan, right?"

"She was, three years ago. Next month, she will be again, if our president fails to rig the election. He has a problem, poor man. A dilemma. When she takes power, Nashida will dismiss the invisible soldiers. Dismantle ISI."

"She'll try."

"She will try. If she succeeds, our president loses the people who keep him in power."

Shawn watched Martha's Persian cat, Miss Mop, climb a tree, tailing a squirrel. "You're telling me this because?"

"Because I had some papers, some items—e-mails between ISI and your CIA—which would help Nashida do what she plans." Abbasi looked around the deserted garden. "You have heard of Darius Osmani?"

Losing its hold on a branch, the cat fell into long grass. Shawn stood, to see if it was hurt.

"Quick change of subject there," he said. "Osmani." He thought for a moment. "Again, I know the name. I believe we had a file on him; not much in it. Memory's not so good, these days. Would you like lunch?"

Abbasi shook his head. "In five minutes, five or ten, I should leave. Osmani is, he claims, a research scientist. An archaeologist; a paleobotanist. Somehow, for some reason, he was among a group of Taliban fighters who overran the U.S. base outside Kandahar. These people also invaded my office. They took documents. None of them could read those papers."

"Except Osmani?"

"Except Osmani. Iranian. Graduate of the *grandes écoles.* Now, I very much need to know what Osmani knows. I need those documents. They are my insurance against being tried in my country. Or yours."

Shawn spent a few moments thinking this through. Unhurt, the cat skittered crabwise across the lawn.

"Mr. Abbasi, be serious. No one's about to put you on trial. Not in America. Even in Gitmo. We still have court records. Documents, no documents, either way, you'd be an embarrassing guy if you started talking."

From the arm of Shawn's chair hung a twist of paper on a string. On its hind legs, the cat reached up, paws batting the paper Shawn swung above it. Left, right, left, right came little cat blows. Back in his boxing days, Shawn would have given a lot to hit that fast.

"Remember Noriega? Dictator of Panama? When I was young," Abbasi said, "in those far-off days, I worked for Manuel. He was a son of a bitch but, as you people say, he was your son of a bitch. As we know, he, too, was on your payroll. George H. W. Bush, director of the CIA, put him there. The Agency knew Noriega was in the drug business, of course they knew—they protected the trade—but still, Manuel was useful. Arms go one way, drugs the other. So, as I say, all is okay. Until Congress outlaws the contras. Until George H. W. Bush becomes president. Until the canal must be returned to Panama. Suddenly, Noriega is no longer useful. What happens? America invades Panama. Thousands killed. Manuel is captured and tried. What comes out in court? Nothing. Do we hear of CIA drug-running? Not a word. CIA supporting Noriega? Paying Noriega? Of course not. Simply, he is a bad guy. Lock him up, throw away the key."

Shawn scooped up the little cat and cradled it on his lap. "He was a bad guy."

"Indeed he was. And President Bush, your forty-first president, the accomplice? The man who paid Manuel? Kept him in power?"

On Shawn's knee, the cat stretched upward, claws out, clutching at azure-winged dragonflies. "Okay," he said. "Point taken. You don't want to go to trial. Or jail. You want me to find this Osmani guy. You want your papers back. Why would you think I can do that?"

"Because," Abbasi said, "you have friends. In the world there are two databases containing a great deal of useful knowledge about these things. One belongs to Mossad, the other to your friends in American intelligence."

"Main Core?"

"Indeed. Main Core. I have no contacts in Mossad. They would not help me if I had. However, I know you, and you know people—"

"—who can access Main Core?" Shawn paused. "I do. One or two."

"Something else I know," Abbasi said. "You need money. A lot of money."

"Last time I looked," Shawn said, "it was illegal for U.S. agents to work for a foreign power. I take your cash, I'm out of intel for good."

Abbasi smiled. "Some would say you are already. There are many paths in life. Roads less traveled. Of course, there is also the question—do you have other ways of paying the rent?"

Shawn shook his head. He glanced back at the bundles of bills in the summerhouse. "Serious money. How do you know I won't take it and run?"

"You have many faults," Abbasi said. "I have never heard dishonesty was one of them." He made a comprehensive gesture, taking in house and garden. "Also, as they say in movies, we know where you live." His tone changed. "There is something else. When he was not riding shotgun with the Taliban, Osmani claims he was conducting an archaeological dig in Afghanistan. Excavating cellars in Ghorid ruins, somewhere on the Turquoise Mountain. Near Chist, I think. Now, whether he was doing that or not, he claims he found something of interest."

"Claims how?"

"He called me from Paris. Before your colleagues picked him up. Some time ago." From his diary Abbasi took a handwritten note. "Osmani wanted money for information. A great deal of money. There you have the phone number. The address, in the *quatrième*." Abbasi paused. "I had a second call, from the same number. This time, it was his wife."

Shawn paid attention.

"Is that surprising?" Abbasi asked, noting the reaction. "The man has a wife?"

"It's a lead," Shawn said. "It's interesting. So tell me. What's Osmani claim he found? What does he believe you'll pay for?"

"A small nuclear device, a semiportable device, built under the direction of Dr. Qadir Khan. You do know of Dr. Khan?"

Shawn said, "I worked on his proliferation file. He's a problem for us."

"While for us, for Pakistan, a national hero."

"Well," Shawn said, "you got my attention. If I do take your money, where do I start?"

4

In early-afternoon heat, an olive-skinned man stood sweating in an ancient English beech wood, overlooking the rectory of Felbourne village. He was dressed in what he hoped would pass for pheasant-shooting garb: green multipocketed Barbour jacket, tweed cap, trousers tucked into thick woolen socks, and soft-leather ankle boots. He carried a borrowed shotgun and, for quite other reasons, a nine-mil Beretta in a shoulder holster.

Uncomfortable in these clothes, and this place, the watcher wiped perspiration from his eyes. He had never shot a pheasant; had never, to his knowledge, seen a pheasant. Resting the shotgun against the trunk of a beech, he raised binoculars, focusing on Ayub Abbasi, who sat at ease on a lawn where woodland ended and the rectory grounds began. Abbasi was on more than one American watch list, which raised, in the watcher's mind, several questions.

Among them, the puzzle of what the Pakistani might be doing here, talking with the blacklisted CIA agent Shawn Maguire.

The couple on the lawn were too far away for the watcher to hear their conversation. He knew, though, that Abbasi would, at some point, be kidnapped and questioned. In the watcher's experience most of the Agency's guests—even those initially reluctant to talk— eventually answered whatever questions their interrogators asked.

The watcher's reflection was interrupted at that moment by shouted greetings. Lowering his binoculars he saw, coming through the trees, a heavyset man dressed in shooting clothes similar to his own, though more worn.

To his dog the hunter said, "Sit, boy. Sit. Stay." Then, to the watcher, "Any luck, young man? Got a bird?"

The watcher, reluctant to speak, shook his head.

"Nothing down there," said the hunter, nodding toward the margin of the wood. "American chappie's place." He pointed in the opposite direction, to where woodland opened onto acres of crops. "Watch this. Take a bet—dogs'll put one up."

The hunter spoke incomprehensible words to the dog. Head down, nose to ground, it dashed for the nearest field. Moments later, in a whirr of wings, two dun-colored birds rose in arcing flight.

"What'd I say?" called the hunter. "Go!"

The hunter and the watcher fired at the same time, the watcher's shot passing dangerously close to the hunter. Lowering his gun, the man turned to stare at the watcher.

"My God," he said. "My God—could've killed me." He pointed to the watcher's double-barreled gun. "Tell me something, son. You ever used that thing?"

5

SUSSEX, EARLY AFTERNOON, 18 MAY 2004

Two shots came in rapid succession, and a high, clattering bird call.

Abbasi stood, tipping his chair. Then he knelt, bending low on the lawn, as if in prayer.

Shawn extended a hand to help him up. "Shotgun," he said. "My neighbor Justin, shooting birds."

Abbasi dusted his clothes and righted his chair. "You are sure?"

"I don't have many areas of expertise," Shawn said. "Weaponry's one of them."

Abbasi sat back in his chair, breathing slowly. "I forget," he said, when he could speak, "about the English. The things they shoot." After a time he raised his head, scenting the air. "Jasmine. You know, do you, the men you call Moors built palaces to match their gardens—not the other way around?" He shed his jacket, showing the gold links fastening his shirtsleeves. "Returning to business, Mr. Maguire, you know that Dr. Khan, in my country, created nuclear weapons for other Islamists? Including, perhaps, al Qaeda."

"No evidence," said Shawn. "I mean, no evidence they got to al Qaeda."

"Not yet." Abbasi stood to check that his car was still parked in the lane. "Still, Abdul Qadir Khan spreading the word of God through nuclear fission—"

"Through ISI."

"Elements in our intelligence service. Yes, indeed."

In Manhattan, Shawn had worked on proliferation.

"This device Osmani claims he found in Afghanistan—if it exists—would be shipped from Peshawar by our friends the invisible soldiers."

"I've gotten more plausible tales," Shawn said, "out of fortune cookies."

Ayub Abbasi stood and stretched his arms. His double-cuffed shirt was striped, with a starched white collar. "Your payment, Mr. Maguire, is structured like this. We double the amount of the deposit if you find Osmani."

"Alive?"

"Preferably. The same amount again if you supply a precise location for Dr. Khan's device. Which you doubt exists." Abbasi began to walk toward the garden's gate. Shawn, setting down rifle and cat, kept pace. "You may know, Nashida Noon is now the most popular politician in Pakistan. Odd: Attractive young woman, Oxford educated, wishes to rule a Muslim country. A failed state. Or close."

"She'll win this election?"

"No question." Abbasi was looking across the lane, trying to locate his driver. "If she lives—a real question, of course. If she lives, she will be prime minister. When she dismantles ISI, she will remove our president."

Shawn could see the driver. He was in the churchyard, under an oak, near Martha's grave.

"Langley won't like that. President's on the payroll. Our boy in Islamabad."

"This," said Abbasi, "is one reason why Nashida wants to be rid of him. Also, of course, there is the fact that he hanged her father."

He waved. The driver came slowly from the churchyard. Holding open the passenger door of the Lexus, the chauffeur said to Shawn, "Beautiful place you have here, sir."

"Full of ghosts."

Abbasi was listening. "Go to Paris, Mr. Maguire. Find the wife. Find Osmani. A change will do you good." Half in and half out of the car, he took Shawn's wrist between thumb and finger. "The fact is, the truth is, my friend, I am running for my life. I have bad dreams. Reality is no better." Shawn tried to see the young woman sitting in the car's backseat. He wondered if this might be Nashida Noon. Her covered head was turned away from him, toward the graveyard. "If I may say," Abbasi added, "take care of your own life, Mr. Maguire. I hear a former colleague looks for you."

"Do we have a name?"

"It is all gossip," Abbasi said. He left open the car's bulletproof window. "As ever. Although I heard mention of Mr. McCord. Mr. Calvin McCord."

Shawn watched the driver start the Lexus. In these last weeks he'd had the sense of being watched—though who in this village would watch him, he had no idea.

"One more thing," he said. "Where would I look for Osmani?"

"That," said Abbasi, "is the problem. Osmani disappeared. Or was disappeared." He began to raise his window. "Start with the wife."

When the Lexus had gone, Shawn walked across the lane to the churchyard, to where Martha lay. Forget-me-nots blossomed blue on her grave.

"I've done it now," he said. "Taken his cash. I could be tried for this."

At times, since Martha died, he'd heard her voice. Now, in the shade, she lay quiet.

"Tell me this," Shawn said. "What do I do about Abbasi?" He waited a moment in silence. Then he asked, "And Calvin McCord?"

6

Shawn first met Calvin McCord at the turn of the century, which was also the turn of the millennium. The meeting was the moment Shawn's career began its path downhill. This was not something he knew. At the time, he had more immediate concerns.

Working for the Agency, Shawn was living alone in New York, overdrawn, drinking too much, sharing himself among three women, hearing radio chatter, convinced his country was about to be attacked by Saudi fanatics. Calvin McCord was the least of his worries.

Hugh Rockford, Shawn's supervisor, took him aside on a day when he, Shawn, had a whisky-related migraine. Rockford pointed out a man with a small mustache and brilliantined hair, leaning against an office wall, looking cool. Shawn guessed that he and the stranger were of similar ages—forty-something—though this man looked somehow young. Maybe just unformed. He was thin. He carried a brown hat in a hand that shook with a barely perceptible tremor.

"Calvin McCord," Rockford said, pointing. "He's yours, son."

Shawn stopped making notes on his PDA. "He's mine? Meaning what?"

"Meaning you're going to be a good daddy. Think Papa Bear. Think Goldilocks. You housebreak the guy, train him, make him a useful specimen, whatever he's useful at."

"What *is* he useful at?" Shawn asked then, genuinely curious. "Does he have analytic skills? Foreign contacts? Does he know languages?"

Rockford was losing interest in this conversation. "What I hear, he don't know diddly. Doesn't matter. He has local contacts. Daddy's Claiborne McCord. Name mean anything? Claiborne, the chicken hawk? Used to run this place? Kid's got Pappy. What else does he need? Go say hi, Shawn. Make nice, why don't you?"

Calvin was given a desk next to Shawn's. His hair was thinning; his left leg twitched. He wore a hat until he was told to take it off.

Making conversation, Shawn said, "Guess they call you Cal?"

"They call me Calvin," said Calvin.

After that, conversation languished. From time to time, Calvin produced a string of beads, counting as his lips moved.

Shawn paused in his own work to watch the new recruit. "Some sort of hippie trick you got there?"

Calvin checked to see if Shawn was serious. "It's a rosary. Five decades of prayer."

"I don't want to seem intolerant," Shawn said, "but maybe try praying on your own time."

Calvin slipped the beads into his breast pocket. "God has his reckoning," he said, "and his own time. God knows who is a patriot, and who is not."

This was more information than Shawn could deal with, given the way his head felt just then. He went back to tracing the itinerary of the nuclear peddler A. Q. Khan. However, his next confrontation with Calvin came less than an hour later. Making early-morning calls to his mistress and to Martha, whom he wanted to marry, he noticed the aroma around Calvin's desk.

"Son," Shawn said, "go pick yourself another perfume."

Calvin's face contused. He rubbed his still-new mustache with the back of his hand, thinking that through. "It's called aftershave. It's expensive."

"I believe it," Shawn said. "Find something else, or go without. If you're sitting this close, I need to like the way you smell."

After that, Calvin went pale and worked away quietly. Shawn discovered that he was, at his daddy's suggestion, drafting a position paper estimating Iraq's nuclear arsenal. Shawn, who didn't believe Iraq had such an arsenal, killed the draft before it could be circulated.

Calvin argued that everyone had a right to his own opinions.

"True enough," Shawn had said, "but not his own facts."

"You shouldn't dis me," Calvin told him. "Down the line, you'll find it's not a good idea."

Despite the way his head felt, Shawn laughed and went back to work. In later years, he would have cause to remember the comment. Beyond that one exchange, there was little conversation—apart from a disagreement over invading Pakistani tribal areas—until budget day. Calvin worked long hours. He seemed to have no life outside the Agency: no women, no whisky. Shawn had an unwise interest in both.

Things changed on budget day (the tenth of each month) when

Shawn found there had been no transfer of funds to his operating account.

He checked with Rockford.

"It's okay," Rockford said. "You got the budget. McCord's holding it."

Shawn was silent a few moments. Then he said, "You lost me. Why in hell would McCord be holding my money?"

"Tells me he's good with figures. Which you're not. Least, not on a bank statement." Rockford searched through a pile of papers. He came up with copies of credit card bills, some of which Shawn had not seen in the original. Rockford pointed with a pen. "You say you can handle money? There, the red print, see? With the minus sign? Current expenditure. A lot of it, I notice, bar checks in places you can't afford, 'less you got some private income I never heard about."

Shawn's voice was quiet. "You're telling me, if I need operating expenses, I have to go ask the little dipshit sits next to me? The snotty kid smells like a whorehouse?"

"For the moment," Rockford said, "this is exactly what I'm telling you." With the nail of his left index finger he pried dry flakes of skin from the arid plane of his right cheek. Pausing this operation, he said to Shawn, "Word of advice. You want to go easy with McCord."

"Because?"

"Because your daddy's name's not Claiborne McCord. Because all the time you've been here, Shawn, you've had woman trouble, which, I notice, it's not getting better. Because you drink too much. Because McCord don't do any of the above. Because he's on promotion track, Maguire, and you're not."

This last sentence made Shawn feel he'd been sucker-punched.

He felt nauseous. There was a perceptible time before he spoke. Then he said, "I was, last time I looked. I was on promotion track."

Rockford produced a pocketknife, a gift from a recent security conference on a Swiss ski slope. Using the smallest blade, he began cleaning beneath his nails. "That was then," he said, suggesting to Shawn that the meeting, interview, whatever it was, had ended.

7

Not quite four years after meeting McCord, and three days after meeting Abbasi, Shawn Maguire rode through Paris with his buddy Bobby Walters, his overweight brother-in-arms. They were in the backseat of a lengthened Maserati, driving down rue de Bretagne. The car had a smoked-glass screen between them and Alfred Burke, a South London fixer currently on loan to the CIA, the agency for which Bobby Walters still worked. Being, by Agency standards, an older person, he called it the Company.

Unlike Shawn, Bobby had stayed on salary. His life was a mess. He was three years away from retirement and, God willing, full pension. By then, in regard to the Agency, he'd be KMA. Kiss my ass. These days, though, he wondered if he'd make it to the wire.

One of Bobby's reasons for doubt was the fate of his companion. Shawn had also worked for the Agency until the day he was dishonorably discharged. Canned, in fact. Fortunately, Vice President Cheney—then planning to invade Iraq—was out of love with the CIA. Despite the spies' best efforts at telling him what he wanted to hear, the VP established other, more docile, networks. The good news for Shawn was that one of them—Counterintelligence Field Activities—struggled to find people who were even halfway competent at manufacturing the kind of data the VP wanted. CIFA employed the aging misfit Maguire.

That was when the good news ended. CIFA later suspended Shawn while internal tribunals investigated his record of inappropriate violence and failures in anger management.

"Shawn," Bobby said in the car that day, "did you ever tell me why they put you on hold?"

Shawn was looking through a darkened window as the limo turned into rue Charlot. "CIFA? Suspended me? No."

The driver made a sharp right turn.

"No, you didn't tell me?" Shawn nodded yes, that was correct. "Are you going to?"

"One of the guys I worked with had a knee replacement."

Bobby thought that through. "Which affected you because?"

"I'm not proud of this," Shawn said. "I was why he needed one."

"Jesus," Bobby said. He checked his watch, an aging Tissot. "You kneecapped an agent? No wonder they're pissed. How much time have you got?"

"On leave or right now?"

"Right now."

"Four, five minutes. Why?"

"Something I need to tell you. Calvin McCord's unhappy."

"With?"

"You."

Shawn stared. "McCord? He's unhappy with me? Why do I keep hearing this? You know what McCord did?"

"I do," Bobby said. "Believe me, I do." He knew the tale by heart.

"Son of a bitch. Tattles to teacher. Rats me out to Rockford."

Bobby nodded. "I remember. Night you lost your laptop."

"Right." Shawn tried to keep his voice level. "Screwed me with the Company. Got me canned. Listen, bottom line here, McCord took my job. It's how I got in debt."

The driver slowed to let a girl in a brief pink dress run across the road.

"Shawn," Bobby said, "please. Getting in debt, that's not McCord. That's Jack Daniel's. You were up to your ass in bar bills way before McCord. Going out with what's-her-name."

"Ellen."

"Ellen Reynolds, am I right?" Bobby shook his head. "Big-ticket chick. I have to tell you, that's a problem McCord doesn't have."

"McCord's a eunuch."

"Looks like a horse with one horn?" said Bobby. "It's maybe why he's working and you're not."

"What's the subtext here?" Shawn asked. "I don't have a woman problem. I was fine with Martha."

Bobby laughed.

"Meaning what?" Shawn asked.

"It means give me a break," Bobby said. "You've never been fine, Shawn, not with any woman. Even Martha. Whoever you're with, you want someone else. Story of your life." He swiveled to look at Shawn, turning something over in his mind. "Ellen," he said. "Man, was she ever out of your league. Never figured—how's a guy like you meet a piece like her?"

"Party in the Apthorp," Shawn said. "It's not a happy tale, any way you tell it."

Shawn met Ellen Reynolds when he was stranded in Manhattan at the turn of the millennium, without a woman.

Martha—dismayed by the new president, out of love with her native land—had left the States to live thousands of miles away in the English village from which, she said, her grandmother began the journey to America.

Shawn, abandoned in New York, went to parties. He met Ellen at one that, he knew, was out of his weight and class: a fling in the Apthorp, a heartbreakingly expensive apartment building on the Upper West Side. It was not a place Shawn would have considered had he not been lonely and tired of eating takeout pizza.

The apartment where the party was held, which overlooked the river, was the size of a small airfield—an airfield with mirrors and waiters and tapestries and crystal chandeliers. The place belonged to a banker who invited Shawn only because he believed that Martha, who had once been a colleague, was still in town. There was just-visible dismay when Shawn arrived alone, and comparable disappointment on his part since, while a few men registered his presence, none of their overgroomed women gave him more than a glance. Smiling, chatting, lightly hugging, air-kissing, women edged around him as if he were a misplaced chair.

Though obviously single, Shawn gathered not one but two tastefully tinted cocktails from a passing waiter and escaped to a balcony. He planned to ease the pain by drinking both and going back for more.

Ellen, who followed him out, took one of the frosted glasses from his hand. "Kind," she murmured, drinking deeply. "I'm Ellen." Then she said, "Dear God, what do we have here? Rubbing alcohol? You may need to carry me home."

Shawn didn't answer. He scanned her undernourished body. Young and skinny, Ellen looked coldly edible, white meat on a cooked chicken. Her clothes, at a guess, represented a couple of months of Shawn's current salary. He searched for something to say. "So," he said finally, "what are you doing here?"

"On the balcony?" she asked. "Same as you. Getting out of there before I died of boredom."

She finished her drink and looked through the glass door, hoping to snag a waiter.

"I meant," he said, "what are you doing at this party?"

She stared. "You're asking me? God, we always come to these things. I have a husband somewhere. Robertson. You know? Owns half the city. I was wondering who invited you. You look like you're going to a football game."

Shawn, who spent more than he could afford on clothes, could find no adequate reply. Rather than searching for words, he moved forward, pushing Ellen along the balcony. At the time, he wasn't sure why he did that. When she was against the far railing, holding it to stop herself falling into the river, and when he figured they could no longer be seen from inside the room, he kissed her, bending her backward, like a drinking straw, over the ironwork.

After a shocked moment, she kissed him back.

When she freed her mouth and looked at him, she said, "Wow. That was nice. I mean, yum." She shifted her jutting hips. "Forget about the football game. Where are we going?"

Shawn, who hadn't known they were going anywhere, shook his head.

"Listen," she said, "here's the deal. I go in. I head for the bathroom. You wait like three minutes. You come in, have a quick drink—I mean *quick*—then you go to the bathroom."

Though it was mid-June, Shawn felt suddenly cold. He hadn't bargained for this. "What are we doing in the bathroom?"

"Don't be coarse," she said. "I don't fuck in bathrooms. Not even in the Apthorp."

"So?"

"So, we take the elevator to the lobby. The doorman gets us a cab. You tip him, like a serious tip, so he forgets he did it."

Shawn was short of cash. He said, "I'm a bridge-and-tunnel person. I don't live in Manhattan."

She put fingers first to her lips and then to his. "I do," she said.

In Paris, in the Agency's hired limo, Shawn said, "Bob, that's a hell of a thing to say about a buddy. I had a woman problem? The way you talk about me and girls, it's like I'm the only one. Remember, I've known you a long time. I was in the house when Carly killed herself."

"If you had any decency," Bobby said, "you wouldn't remind me."

"You mean you forgot her?"

They drove on in silence through the narrow streets of eastern Paris.

Finally, coming into the *quatrième*, Shawn said, "Bob, moving on, two things you can do for me. Number one, check on Main Core. See what comes up for Darius Osmani."

"Spell it."

Shawn did. Bobby made a note. "Are you going to tell me why?"

Shawn shook his head. "Has to do with me needing money."

"As ever," Bobby said. "That's one thing. What's the other?"

"Tell McCord, he wants to know about unhappy, I've got news for him. Tell him to come talk with me."

"Now," Bobby said, "careful. I'm telling you, don't mess with McCord. You still think Calvin's the sad little guy you trained, back in the day. I'm here to tell you, he's not. He's all grown up. Takes no prisoners. Go easy with the guy."

Shawn tapped the smoked-glass screen. When the car stopped, he checked that he was at the right end of the rue des Vieilles Boucheries. He looked at the sky. It was going to rain.

"I really hate eating alone," Bobby said. "When you've done whatever you're doing, come have lunch. By then I might have something for you."

"Lunch is where?"

"Ma Bourgogne. Place des Vosges. They talk English, kind of. Ask someone. Two P.M., local." There was thunder close by. Bobby glanced upward. "You should stay in the car, my friend. It is going to piss down."

Shawn waved to his buddy, climbed out of the car, and closed the door. The driver, a stocky man, glanced at him with some interest, then turned his attention back to the street. The Maserati was still in sight, heading south, when the rain started. Shawn backed under the awning of a deserted grocery store that was once, the sign said, a Spar Mini-Super. More mini than super. Its sticker-covered window displayed three matchboxes, a newspaper, and two burst packets of fine-ground couscous, plus a potpourri of mouse droppings and dying flies.

A young woman in a summer coat and pink dress dashed under the awning to huddle against the store's cracked glass. Shivering, she glanced at Shawn. He reached out to pull her into the doorway with him, farther from the rain. For a moment, she resisted, then relaxed. It was a while since he'd touched a woman. Rain fell as if God had opened a fire hose. In moments, gutters filled; water spouted from drains; puddles formed; the streets ran like snow-melt rivers.

For some time the store's awning held fast, bellying under a weight of water until, strained beyond bearing, the canvas tore apart. A small ocean fell suddenly to the sidewalk, showering Shawn.

"Jesus Christ," he said.

The girl leaped back against him, as far as she could get from the flood.

"This is not France," Shawn said. He peered at the streaming sky. "This is the goddamn tropics."

The girl, too, was scanning the sky. *"Il va passer."* She considered him; she was trying not to laugh. She said in English, "You are *so* wet."

"I'll tell you something for free," Shawn said. "Wet is what happens when you get a hundred gallons of water dropped off an awning."

She shook her head, not following. As abruptly as it had started, the rain eased.

"Voilà. C'est fait." She checked the time, checked the sky, freed herself, waved, and left, running down the drenched street.

It's always a pinprick of pain, a death of possibility, a girl who waves good-bye.

8

Shawn edged slowly out from under the awning. He didn't trust this city. Truth was, these days, with his country's reputation heading south, Shawn didn't really trust any place outside of America, and not every place inside. He needed a drink. He surveyed street numbers, climbed three stone steps, and rang a bell.

Moments later, a female voice spoke through an entryphone. *"Oui? Vous voudriez?"*

"Shawn Maguire," Shawn said. "American. I'm looking for Darius Osmani."

There was a pause. Then, "Third floor, apartment five," she said in English.

A buzzer sounded. Shawn pushed the metal-lined door and went inside. Before him was a tiny open-grilled gold-painted Parisian elevator, which Shawn was not inclined to take. He'd met these things before. He guessed they dated from the days before Otis: evolutionary ancestors of real elevators; primitive machines only the French would use.

Switching on a dim, timer-controlled light, Shawn climbed narrow stairs that spiraled around the elevator shaft. Stairs like these—any stairs, in fact—made him feel his age. Once again, he resolved to stop drinking. By the time he reached the third floor, there was an ominous beat to his heart. Shawn waited awhile, until his breathing slowed, before he knocked at a door that bore a hand-painted figure five. Below the number was pinned a snap-shot of the Buddhas of Bamiyan. Someone in this place, Shawn reflected, traveled the Silk Road before the Taliban dynamited those giant effigies.

Something moved inside the apartment. There was a spyhole in the door: He was observed. When the door opened, he saw a thin and beautiful Afghan hound. The woman holding its collar was also thin and beautiful. Late thirties, he guessed. Her hair was clipped back and coming loose. Her breasts barely disturbed the fabric of her shirt. She was barefoot, wearing boot-cut jeans with a broad belt. Shawn knew women—Ellen, for one—who wore belts to minimize width of hip. With this girl, no need.

She said, "I am sorry. My husband is not home."

Her accent was French, with American undertones. Exactly where in America, he couldn't have said.

"Your husband is Darius Osmani?"

Still holding the dog's collar, she nodded. "He is. And you are?"

"Like I told you. My name's Shawn Maguire."

He could see her thinking. Police? Intelligence? Feds?

"Can we talk inside? I know some things you should maybe know."

She considered him, assessing. Free of makeup, her eyes were an unusually pure, unflecked green, showing the entire circle of pupil. She might, he thought, be wearing contacts, to achieve that quality of color. He'd need to get closer to be sure.

Making a decision, she edged the dog aside and let him in. "Danielle Baptiste," she said. "I kept my own name. Come in the kitchen. Coffee?"

He would have preferred a drink. "Coffee's fine." He doubted she'd have fresh milk. He knew the French and their so-called refrigerators. "But make it black."

The kitchen was long and narrow. She swept off the table a volume of Ibn Warraq's Koranic commentaries. A window looked out onto the brick wall of a light well. On the walls were detailed interiors of the Alhambra. Shawn remembered Martha, on her way back from Andalusia, poring over similar shots. He had to squeeze past the woman where she stood by the stove, lighting gas with a match from a hotel matchbook. He sat on one of three wooden chairs set around the table. Sighing, the dog lay beneath it, head on paws, frowning and watching the woman.

"You are what?" she asked, not turning. "FBI?"

"Uh-uh," he said, "I was an intelligence agent. Currently, I'm suspended. I may be retired."

Now she looked around. "That's an active verb? Like disappeared?"

He thought about it for a moment, then nodded. The coffee-maker was in two metallic halves, screwed together. It gurgled and made digestive noises. "Is that thing safe?"

"I guess," she said. "If you screw it tight. Otherwise, they explode." She pointed at the ceiling, which, he saw now, was coffee stained. "Sitting there, you're pretty much okay."

On a high shelf was a history of America's funding of the Nicaraguan contras: a well-organized criminal enterprise in which

Shawn had played a small part. After a time, Danielle brought the coffee machine to the table. She set out cups and sugar cubes from a parrot-pictured packet.

She thought for some moments, then spoke. "Let me tell you this," she said. "It may save time. I've not seen my husband in a while. He is an academic. A researcher. As far as I know, he was in Pakistan, then Afghanistan, researching what he calls"—she paused a moment—"the Ghorid civilization? This is not a thing I have knowledge about."

"Me either."

"You should know, Darius never phones. Not when he's working."

"Why? Pretty wife—why wouldn't he?"

She considered him, appraising. "Not everywhere is America. Sometimes Darius has no network. Clearly not on the Turquoise Mountain." She shrugged. "You know what they say. No news is good news."

"You came here, though. Because he asked you?"

She shook her head. "It was a woman, Catherine Someone. Parisienne. She said Darius was staying with her. I thought that meant *petite histoire*, maybe."

He shook his head. "I'm American. It's all I speak."

"An affair. For a moment, I was, what's the word, jealous. Then I thought, maybe not. Why would she phone me, if she was bedding him? Anyway, she said Darius disappeared. Went out and disappeared. If I want to come to Paris, I can take this apartment. She was leaving for a weekend. A long weekend. She is back this evening. She left a key." Danielle bent down to touch the Afghan. "All I must do is feed the dog. If I can't, I call the concierge."

He poured himself another cup of coffee, wondering how much

of this he believed. She had the kind of body that got his attention. A body like Ellen's.

"You're worried."

"I told you, not greatly. A little, of course. Would you not be, if it was your wife?"

"I don't have a wife. Did he go away, or was he taken away?"

"Darius? How would I know?"

"You could ask. Does this place have a janitor?"

"I told you. A concierge."

"Can I mention something?" Shawn asked. "I mean, I still think you seem, what would you say, kind of cool? You know? Your man missing and all." He made air quotes. "You're a little worried?" He was watching her. "If it was me, I'd be calling people. I don't know. Doing stuff."

She was quiet for a time. Then she said, "It is you who thinks he is missing. I think he is maybe doing what he always does. Working over some patch of desert in Afghanistan, looking for artifacts." She got up and came back with biscuits for the dog. Her loose shirt made it hard for him to tell the shape of her breasts. Ellen had smallish boobs. Shawn hadn't minded that; he'd never gotten off on top-heavy porn.

"Okay," he said. "Okay. If that's what you think, we'll ask the janitor, concierge, whatever he is. Those guys, they snoop. It's what they do in life, pretty much. Don't miss a lot."

"It's a woman, the concierge. Tell me, why are you interested in Darius?"

He thought about how to answer that. "I'll be honest with you." She smiled.

"I know," he said. "I know. You think that means I'm going to lie. Well, I'm not. I'm just working on a need-to-know basis." Maybe not lying; just not telling the whole truth. He was not yet ready to mention Ayub Abbasi, his paymaster.

She brought her knees to her chest and wrapped her arms around them. *"D'accord.* Okay. Tell me what I need to know."

"Far's I recall, we tracked your husband. Tracked him through the North West Frontier, Wana, Miranshah, Khyber, into Peshawar, then back to Afghanistan. He got to meet some people we know about."

"You thought he was doing something he should not?"

Shawn shook his head. "He didn't act that way. Satellites, Predator drones, these days, over there, we see pretty much anyone that's not hiding underground. We see where they go. Your man must've known that. So if he's out in the open, we figured he was doing something else."

"He was doing research. I told you. That was his job."

Was?

"Could be," Shawn told her. She had Ellen's musky aura, like a woman in heat. He wanted to touch her. "Let's say I believe that. We were listening to his phone traffic. Maybe he didn't call you. He called other people."

She stood, brushed past him, opened a window on the light well, and sat down again. "Is that a crime? Making calls?"

"Depends who you're talking to. Anyway, my agency lost interest. I didn't. I'd still like to talk with your man." He paused, then said, "I find him, I get paid."

She walked her fingers across the tabletop toward him, the way you do with a child. "You said you were suspended."

"What that means, I can do what needs doing, long as I have cash. Don't have to do what some Yalie fuckwit tells me. Excuse my French." He stood, putting his hands lightly on her shoulders as he squeezed behind her. "Come and have lunch, meet a buddy. We'll talk to the janitor on the way out."

She hesitated. "I can't leave the dog too long. Where would we go?"

"Place des Vosges. How far's that?"

She shrugged and pointed. "Seven minutes, maybe eight, that way."

He hesitated, wondering whether to say what he was thinking of saying. "I guess people tell you you're beautiful."

She nodded. "Some do." She pulled on boots, then a coat. "If we're going, let's go." To the dog she said, "Artemis, *reste. Je vais revenir. Promis.*"

On the stairs, when she'd locked the door, Shawn said, "You don't sound American. You sound like you've lived there."

"I went to school in Connecticut. New Haven. One of the fuck-wits." She went out onto the street, turned, and ran down another flight of steps, descending to a shadowy pit, below pavement level. Shawn followed, more slowly. Steps were beginning to bother him. Oil-stained water pooled below.

"People live down here?"

She knocked on a cracked glass door embossed with tiny stars. "Don't be provincial."

To the squat and ageless person who answered the door, Danielle said in French, "Madame, I am looking for my husband." She showed a photo: one taken for a passport, then enlarged. "He calls himself Darius Osmani. I think he was staying in this house."

The concierge had piled her hair in a shock the color of straw. Her mustache was bleached to an approximate match. She wore a flowered cotton dress but did not look, at first sight, like a woman. She glanced back at a dark-skinned younger man who sat at her kitchen table. With rapid, concentrated movements, he spooned a thin gray soup to his mouth, splashing a little. His shaven head was bent low to the plate.

The concierge scratched in the region of her waist. "You?" she said to Danielle. "Woman like you? French? You married an Arab?"

"In fact, he was Persian. Not Arab."

Wincing, the concierge stopped scratching. She flexed her finger joints. "Arthritis," she explained. "*Un cafard.* It's living in this cursed marsh." Danielle translated. The woman gestured into space. "He's gone, your man. Arab, Persian, whatever he was."

Shawn had understood this. "Ask where he's gone."

Danielle glanced at him. To the concierge she said, "Madame, how exactly did my husband leave?"

"He was, I am sorry to tell you this, mamselle, your pretty man was criminal. A crook."

The man spooning up soup said, *"Terroriste, non?"*

"Cops came," said the concierge. "The CRS, I think, they have taken him. They hit him, bof"—she struck the side of her own firmly coiffed head—"they put on cuffs"—she showed veined wrists—"a thing in his mouth, they put on him a bag, the head, you understand, then in a car. The back of a car. Pouf. Gone."

"In which direction?"

The concierge pointed east.

"What kind of car?"

The concierge shrugged. "Black."

Without looking up from his plate, the man at the table said, *"Suédois.* Volvo."

"Darius was kidnapped," Danielle told Shawn. "Or someone was. Cuffed, bagged, gagged. Driven away."

"Okay," Shawn said. He wondered about the words she used.

"If that's all this witch knows, tell her thank you. We have a lunch date." He put a hand on her arm. "It's okay. Don't be like that. We'll find him."

Danielle looked at him, expressionless. She thanked the concierge.

"Who does he say is a witch?"

"You speak English?"

"*Elle, un peu,*" said the man at the table. "*Plus que moi.*" He'd finished his soup and was eating a dry baguette while reading a racing page. He marked something with a pencil.

"Good luck with your Arab," the concierge said. "It's true, not all are thieves. But most."

"You need to feed the dog," said Danielle.

She led the way back up to street level. "Could have been anyone," she told Shawn. "The man kidnapped."

In a gutter still full of water, a pigeon struggled to breathe. One wing was torn off, leaving a bloodied stump. The other wing flapped. Shawn bent to wring the bird's neck.

Danielle pulled him back. "Don't."

"Come on," he said. "It's in pain."

"You think pain ends with death?" Ignoring the handkerchief he offered, she wiped her eyes with the back of her hand. "Leave me alone. It's okay. I can find him without you."

"Not if the Agency has him. He could be in any one of a dozen countries. You'd never even find the damn jail. We have them all over—like, seventeen countries." He pointed his right thumb downward. "No chance, Danielle."

It was the first time he'd said her name.

She took a deep breath, thinking that through. "Who is this lunch date? Who do you know in Paris?"

He was reading a text on his phone. Wondering, too, when he

might share a bed with this girl. How much that might set back his recovery program.

He said, "Bobby Walters. That's my buddy. Based at the embassy." He paused, then said, "We grew up together."

"In America?"

"Mmm. Alabama. Turkey Forge. Neighbors. Bobby was one of those fat, sad kind of kids. People used to hit him, on principle. He didn't play sports. First time he's left off the team, right there on the field, starts crying. After that, no one used his name. He wasn't Bobby anymore. He was the kid who cried." Shawn paused, thinking back. "Used to walk him to school, you know? Stop guys beating up on him."

"And you," she said. "Of course you were, what is the word? *Sportif*?"

"Played football," Shawn said. "I was on the team back then. Hard to imagine, I know."

Danielle led the way into the traffic-free rue de Béarn.

"Yet this sad, fat boy," she said, "he is the one who has work."

"Moral in there, someplace," Shawn said. "That's why we're meeting him. Bobby has access to a database, Main Core. Just don't cry on me if you don't like what you hear."

She was walking fast now, down rue Saint-Gilles.

"I wouldn't cry in front of you. Tell me again, the proper name? Your friend?"

"Robert Hamilton Walters."

"Will I like him?"

Shawn said, "Will you like Bobby? Who gives a damn? It's not what matters."

"So? Confide in me—what *does* matter?"

"We want to sound him out. See if he'll help find your husband."

She glanced up. "I still don't know about you, Mr. Maguire—why you look for Darius."

"Told you," Shawn said. "Full disclosure. I find him, I get paid."

Ahead lay the ordered beauty of the place des Vosges.

"You are paid to track him? Darius? Who would pay for that?"

"Who'll pay? Pakistani guy. Businessman, in a little trouble. Name of Ayub Abbasi."

"Why?" she asked. "Tell me, why does he pay?"

From the north, they entered the *place*: the old city's oldest square.

"You're asking me why?" said Shawn. "Why Abbasi wants your husband? Long story. Not sure I even know it all." He pointed toward Ma Bourgogne. "We meet Bobby, you'll hear some of it."

9

PARIS, PLACE DES VOSGES, 21 MAY 2004

Like a couple, like lovers, Shawn and Danielle walked together down the rue de Béarn, on the north side of place des Vosges and entered a cloister on the square's perimeter. An old woman in a patterned headscarf played a violin, small as a toy, the music a slow, haunting dance. She'd placed a man's hat, holding five coins, on the tiles at her feet.

"Be honest, now," Shawn said. "The concierge—"

Danielle shrugged. "Come on, Mr. Maguire. The man she saw—"

"—being kidnapped—"

"—he could be anyone. Woman like that, she will think any dark-skinned man is an Arab. What she calls an Arab. *Les beurs.* Of course, all are thieves. Maybe it was Darius. Maybe not." She paused, then said, "Let me tell you, we have a strange marriage, I

and Darius. All the time I've known him, he's been disappearing."
She turned to look at Shawn. "If I don't hear in the next few days,
okay, I shall be worried. More. Now, not so much."

Beside them, the old woman played her slow music: a waltz.
Danielle spread her arms. "Do you dance?" she asked. "Darius
would dance."

Shawn shook his head. "Never learned."

Stopping, glancing at Shawn, Danielle dropped coins in the
old woman's upturned hat. "I thought everyone could dance. Really? You never learned?"

"I was in school," Shawn said, "they made me go to dance class.
I'm talking small-town Alabama. Turkey Forge." They were walking westward now, along the cloister. "Boys and girls, Sunday-go-to-meeting clothes. In a parish hall, this was. Cured me." After a
moment, he added, "That's where I met Martha. My wife."

She stopped in the cloister, facing him. "You met—you met in
dance class? It's true?"

"Well," he said, "sure. I met her there—she wasn't my wife
back then. We were kids. Three other wives before Martha, but
she was the first I met. Last one I married."

"You told me you don't have a wife."

"I don't. Martha died. Cancer." He took her arm. "Come talk
with Bobby Walters."

10

Watching the street outside Ma Bourgogne, Bobby Walters believed, for a moment, he'd found again the girl he'd met on the boulevard Haussmann: the one who told him all was for sale, except love. Then he saw that this girl, though different, was another of the women he wished to meet. Not cover-girl cute, but cool. Confident. Unaggressive, he'd guess. (His second wife, the actress, had displayed all the female aggression he could suffer in this life.) Thick, shoulder-length hair, this girl outside in the *place*. Minimal ass, wide mouth in just the kind of feline face Bobby fancied. Wearing jeans, and boots with heels. Looking elegant with it. They could do that in this town: low-rent elegance.

Inspection finished, Bobby checked out the girl's man. By definition, this kind of arm candy needs a male arm to be the candy on.

Bobby saw that the arm here belonged to his buddy, Shawn Maguire. Absorbing that fact—knowing that Shawn was three years older, and, for Christ's sake, a human train wreck—Bobby felt fate had dealt him a losing hand. He'd thought this before, in connection with Shawn and women. He leaned across the table and pulled out two chairs.

Outside the restaurant, Shawn had paused in the square's cloister. "You still have not told me what you do."

"In your trade," Danielle said, "I thought you would know. You have knowledge about my husband. I'm still not sure how."

He shook his head. "Don't know about you. Tell me."

She spread suntanned arms. "Art historian, *moi*."

"There's a living in that?"

"There is, if you do what I do. I tell rich men whether or not they're buying fakes. Suppose you're a hardware guy from Atlanta about to spend fifty mil on El Greco. Trust me, I'm a cheap date."

"Are you right? About the artworks?"

Danielle checked the time. "They'll never know, will they? I mean, who can tell?"

"You must think you can."

"I think I can. Some of the greatest paintings in the Prado are forgeries. We cannot prove it, one way or the other. Will they let me examine the canvas? No way." She moved toward the restaurant entrance. "Come. Let's meet this friend you say might help."

Following Danielle into Ma Bourgogne, Shawn held out a hand to his childhood buddy: the man who'd been his partner in three covert actions. For a moment, he recalled heat, intolerable heat; a burning building in Peshawar where both men, locked in a cellar, came close to incineration.

"Mr. Walters," he said, "looking good."

"You mean fat," said Bobby. "I'll tell you something. Thinner than I was when you saw me this morning." He wasn't looking at Shawn. "You planning introductions here?"

"Danielle Baptiste," Shawn said. He took a chair. "Robert Hamilton Walters. You don't have a drink."

"I'm not drinking," Bobby said. He made hushing signs. "Please. It's not like it's a virgin birth." He spread his hands. "What's so strange? I'm on a diet, same as this lady."

Danielle, seated, considered Bobby. He wondered what she saw. "*Non, pas moi, monsieur.* Not I. No *régime.*"

Bobby was still staring. His recall of bodies was better than his memory for faces. "Do we know each other?"

Danielle shook her head.

"Damn," he said. "I've seen you somewhere."

She bit a breadstick, smiling, saying nothing.

"TV? Magazines?"

"Underwear," she said. "You must be one of those people who sign up for catalogs. It's okay. Really. Men do."

"Bobby," Shawn said, "shame."

"I was young," she said. "Doing my degree. I was persuaded. Three catalogs. Victoria's Secret. I hear they still use the pictures."

Bobby took two breadsticks and edged the glass away from Danielle. Grissini did nothing for a man's hunger, but right now that was all he could see to eat.

"Knew it wasn't just your face I remembered."

Danielle slid the half-full breadstick glass right across to Bobby's side of the table. "Mr. Maguire says you are based at the embassy. How is that?"

"How is that, or how is Paris? Paris is full of beautiful thin

women who don't fancy overweight Americans. So I'm learning."
To Shawn he said, "Apropos, what do you think of the mustache?"

Shawn considered. "Might look good, on a different face."

"That's what you get from friends," Bob said to the woman.
"Honesty. Can we please order some food? Something with fries?
These days I'm always starving. That's diets for you. Shawn, I need
to talk."

Shawn spread his hands. "This is me."

There was silence. Danielle beckoned a distant waiter, threading his way between tables.

"Okay," Bobby said finally. "What I want to know is, how do
you deal with it? Being out of work, I mean. Like, retirement."

Danielle watched the two men.

"Years back," Bobby told her, "anytime I screwed up, I'd think,
damn, it's not that bad. Next time, I'll get it right. Last year or
so—" He stopped and waved at the waiter.

"Time runs out," Shawn told his friend. "You and me, we're
getting to a place, there's no next time. Pass five-oh, Bob, that's it,
pretty much. No second act. Not in the Agency."

"My God," said Danielle, "you two. Whistling past the
graveyard—is that American?"

"It is," Bobby told her. "I'll have steak and fries. You order. You
look like you talk French."

"Here, Bourgogne, they talk English. It is a tourist place."

"Yeah, right," Bobby said. "Tell them steak well done. Fizzy
water, not Evian. Salty, that stuff. Like drinking brine. Plus, we
need salt. Pouring salt, you know? Not that flaky stuff. You notice,
they never put salt on the table, these days? What are they doing—
they think it's unhealthy or something? Tell them mustard, not
French. Ballpark mustard. Big jar of ketchup. Heinz, if it's all
they've got."

"Mr. Walters," she said, "this is Paris. They will not have Heinz. They will not have ketchup."

"Get out of here. Everyone has ketchup. Tell them extra fries on the side. Crispy. Extra thin."

"Alumettes."

"If you say so. Nothing green." Bobby turned to Shawn. "Okay, talk to me. Fess up. What's it like on the outside?"

Shawn felt the phone in his pocket vibrate. Sound was off.

"You're thinking of leaving? You'd do that? Quit the Company?"

Bobby glanced at Danielle. She was speaking with a waiter who looked like an art student. He lowered his voice. "Last month, Rockford says to me, 'Bob, you ever think about leaving the Agency?' I say, 'Mr. Rockford, that's all I think about.'" He picked two more breadsticks. "When you and me went in, you know? We thought we were doing something that was, like, worth doing—"

"Back in the day."

Bobby moved his hand toward Danielle's hand. Just touching.

"Shawn, I'm serious. I have a problem here."

Danielle moved her hand away. Bobby was sweating a little. He saw that the girl, finished ordering, was paying attention. He wondered what it would take to pry her away from Shawn.

"Off the record," he told her. "You're not hearing this."

"Or not understanding."

To Shawn, Bobby said, "You're free and clear. You could say what's happening."

"With intel?"

"You could tell it. Tell them it's a clusterfuck, excuse my French."

"Not the right expression," Danielle said, "when you are in France."

Bobby ignored her. Sex was sex, business was business. To

Shawn he said, "I have access, up to a level. I can give you background. You're out of the heat. You can publish." He finished the
breadsticks. "Make me feel I did something worthwhile."

Danielle checked through texts on her phone.

Bobby stopped talking while an overelegant waiter set out cutlery, then began again, speaking to Shawn. "Your field, son. Remember? Before Twin Towers—you told me, AfPak, that's the threat.
Not goddamn Iraq. You said ISI built the Taliban. Set up 9/11."

"You mean," Danielle asked, looking up, "Pakistan? Planned
9/11? Not bin Laden?"

Bobby was startled to hear an underwear model ask a question
of this caliber. "I didn't say that. Bin Laden exists."

"You said—"

"Listen," Bobby told Danielle, "do the math, girl. No secret—
this was a big operation. Twenty, twenty-one guys in place on the
U.S. mainland—these are camel jockeys, right? Don't know squat
about the place, don't speak the language, don't know New York
from New Year. You got to support them, train them to fly, get the
timing right, all the planes in the air the same time, heading
where they should be heading, God help us." Bobby glanced
around. It seemed no one was listening. "That's an intel operation.
Not a trick you do solo. Not if you're some Saudi God-freak sitting
in the boonies."

The waiter brought three steak frites. Absently Bobby started
eating Danielle's fries.

"So," he said to Shawn, "do it. Publish. Let the world know.
Maybe we won't lose this war."

Danielle smacked away Bobby's hand. "Eat your own frites.
What war will we not lose?"

"Afghanistan. Where d'you think? Day two, day three, we lost
Iraq."

"They say—"

"Sure. We say. Like we say we won Vietnam. Mission accomplished." He shrugged and went back to his food.

Shawn looked out to the square, thinking it through. He said, "Bobby, we have a different question. You pick up on Darius Osmani?"

"My husband," said Danielle.

Bobby was chewing his steak. Steak was one thing America did a whole lot better.

"Tried this morning," Bobby said to Shawn. "It's an access issue. The level I have gives me Osmani's dead file. It's tagged, by the way, as read by you." He noticed the woman was paying attention. "A year back, something like that."

"No indication where the guy is now?"

Again, Bobby registered the quality of Danielle's attention. "Can't tell you. There may be. My access won't let me in."

"Let's say," Shawn said, "just hypothetically, let's say folks from the Agency pick up a person on a Paris street. Let's say those same guys don't want to put him on trial, but they do want to question him. Enhanced interrogation. Where would they take him these days?"

Bobby paused, his fork halfway to his open mouth. "Bagram," he said finally. "Amman, Fes, Rabat, Poland, Syria, or—why the fuck are you asking? You just said, you don't even know we have him."

Shawn nodded at Danielle. "She has her doubts. I think your boys lifted the guy. I don't want a geography lesson. I just need to know where he might be now."

Danielle watched Bobby. He was eating again. He shook his head, waiting until he'd finished chewing. "Not in the loop," he said. "You could ask McCord."

Shawn grinned, without amusement.

"Okay. Talk to Ashley. She gets copied in on renditions. SCI clearance." He looked at Danielle. "Sensitive compartmented information. Don't repeat that."

Danielle asked, "Who exactly is Ashley?"

"Friend of his." Bobby pointed at Shawn. "Based in London. Wants to marry him."

He watched the girl react.

"Is this true?"

"It's true she's based in London," Shawn said. He had history with Ashley. "Plus, it's true she could tell us where a detainee—a particular detainee—gets himself rendered. Least, it's what I hope."

Danielle pushed her plate aside. She'd eaten very little. "How is she going to tell us?"

"She has access to Main Core," Bobby said. "Database. Like I told you, she's that grade." He held up a cell. "Use the phone. Call her."

"We'll talk to Ash," Shawn said. "We're going to England." He was pushing his luck with this woman he hardly knew. "Nothing more for us here."

Thoughtful, Danielle considered him. "Us?"

"Us. You may not think so, girl, but you want to find your husband, believe me, I'm your best shot."

"Probably true," Bobby said, though he wished it were not.

A voice in Shawn's mind asked if it were wise to invite this unknown woman into his life, but the voice was small and quiet, too subdued to hold his attention.

"If your man's been rendered," he said to Danielle, "I told you, you'll never know where he's gone, not until he turns up at Gitmo. If he's a frequent flyer, that could take, I don't know, years."

"Frequent flyer, I do not understand. What is that?"

"Detainee gets moved from jail to jail. Country to country," Bobby told her. "We have jails all over. Off of home base. Can't do enhanced interrogation on the mainland. Against the law." He snagged Danielle's unfinished meal. Eating what was left of her fries, he recalled the desolation he'd felt in class when—in any sport you like to name—he was last to be picked for a school team. Any goddamn team. Always the last; chubby kid standing by himself, sweating in the southern sun, pretending not to care, trying not to fucking cry. Failing. Now, thirty years later, here was his buddy about to leave the country with this desirable woman, while he, Robert Hamilton Walters, had to pay for female company if he were not to eat alone.

Not for the first time, Bobby felt that someplace he took a wrong fork in the road.

Shawn was standing, ready to leave. He said, "Tell me, Bobby, why not you? Why don't you go public with this stuff?"

Danielle watched Bobby smooth down his hair and mustache.

"Three reasons." He counted on short pink fingers. "One, mortgage; mortgages, plural. Two, alimony. Also plural. I have wives."

"More than one?" Danielle asked.

"Three. All ex. Strong, high-maintenance ladies. Cost me a fortune in waxing bills. I ever stop paying, trust me, these chicks'll show more body hair than that Wookie in *Star Wars*."

Danielle said, "What was the third reason?"

Bobby thought for a minute. "Someone might shoot me," he said. "Been done before."

By you, Shawn thought.

Bobby glanced at Danielle and dropped his voice. "Shawn? If anything happens—"

Shawn took the fat man in an embrace, surprising them both. "You're not going to die," Shawn said. "Not in Paris."

Bobby freed himself. "Not Paris. They're moving me. Red level posting. Peshawar again."

"Oh, man," Shawn said. He had an arm around Bobby's shoulders. "Someone up there don't like you. Listen, if you need me, call. You know I'm living in this little village? In England?" Shawn removed his arm, and passed Bobby a scrap of paper. "Use that cell. It's not traceable to me. Or her."

Bobby turned toward the door. "Got to go. Have a meeting. How are you guys traveling?"

"Train."

"You serious? Didn't know those things still ran."

Bobby shook Shawn's hand, then kissed the girl's mouth before she could turn away. He felt strange, kissing a woman like this, with his new mustache.

"We'll talk," he said to Shawn.

Through the window, Danielle watched the spy climb into a waiting vehicle. There were two men in the front seats. They did not look around.

"What kind of car is that?"

"Volvo," Shawn said. "Swedish automaker. Now owned by Ford. If you were going to ask what color the car was, the answer's black. Wouldn't you think that's a coincidence?" He left on the restaurant table more cash than a New York tip.

He said, "I know I would."

11

For a while, traveling through Normandy, when rail ran alongside road, Shawn saw from the TGV that even the fastest cars—the Astons and Ferraris—were left behind. In the train's dining car, sitting across from Shawn, Danielle rearranged misplaced cutlery and pointed out an empty wineglass to a passing waiter.

Shawn was used to choosing wine for women. "The merlot. Napa Valley merlot."

"*Absolument pas,*" Danielle told the waiter. "*Nous prendrons le vin de Cairanne.*" When the man set down menus and turned away, she said to Shawn, "You think, in France, we will drink this California *pissat d'âne?*"

For a while then, she was quiet, watching flat Norman fields unroll beside the train. He asked what she was thinking; saw that she was weighing her words.

"I was thinking about you. You say you were a soldier? A sniper?" He nodded. "I wonder why you left."

"I can tell you." He thought back. "Nineteen eighty-something, Special Ops, we're in Afghanistan. Hiding in a valley, waiting for dark. Had us a bunch of Stingers for the mujahideen."

"Stingers?"

"Shoulder-mounted ground-to-air missile. Heat-seeking. So the muj could bring down Russian choppers. The gunships."

She shook her head. "You gave these things to mujahideen? To the Taliban? The men you are fighting?"

"Weren't fighting them then. Later, we had to buy the damn things back—the Stingers."

The waiter brought wine and let Danielle taste. She raised a finger; he poured.

"Anyway," Shawn said, "we're in this little valley, old guy comes past, on the ridge—he's got this herd of goats. Lieutenant tells me, waste him. I say, sir, what do you mean? This guy's not fighting. He's old. Take a look. He's a goddamn goatherd. Lieutenant says, can't risk it. He'll tell the Reds we're here. Lieut takes my piece—sniper rifle, nice sight—blows the head off this old hajji. Lucky shot—guy never was that good with a gun. Anyway, end of story, I'm out. Disobeyed a direct order."

"You were, what do you say? Unemployed?"

"Uh-huh. It was a bad time. Next year, my buddy Bob—the one you met—he gets me this intel gig. Which I needed. Paid the rent, paid off some debts. Didn't save my marriage."

Danielle sat, thinking. When she looked directly at him, Shawn felt the same sexual shock he'd experienced when he'd first seen her, in the Parisian apartment.

"I was asking myself," she said, after a time, "why I would agree to come with you. Why will I go to another country, with a man I hardly know? A man who takes cash to find my husband. How to say—a hired hand." She sipped her wine. "Why would you do it? Take money for this? To find Darius?"

Shawn was thinking how to answer when the train dived into darkness, deep beneath the Channel.

"You want to know why I'd take money?" he asked, speaking against the blackness. "I'll tell you why. I need it. Right now, I'm out of work again. My wife had money, I have debts. I owe every son of a bitch out there. Him and his dog."

"You said she died."

He was quiet for a time.

Danielle said again, "Your wife—you said she has died?"

He said, "She did. I told you. Cancer. She left me a house. No money."

She placed a hand over his. The first time she'd touched him.

"Bottom line," he said. "I'm not proud. Can't afford to be. I work for anyone who pays."

The waiter brought a basket of bread and a bowl of olive oil.

Danielle turned, looking out to the dark. "You could sell the house, no?"

He moved the basket of bread. "This basket—that's the house." Inches away, he set down the bowl. "This—it's the churchyard. Little lane there, in between." He pointed. "Here's where I live." He moved his hand. "Here's where Martha's buried."

The train was out of the tunnel now, running through a barbed-wire-and-concrete welcome to England.

"This woman, this Martha. You loved her?"

"Took me half my life to work it out," Shawn said, "but sure. She was the one."

After the waiter had taken their order, Danielle said, "Tell me. It has to be legal, this work? The work you will do if you are paid enough?"

Shawn paused. "I won't kill anyone, if that's what you mean."

"But you have?"

"Have I killed? Weren't you listening? I was a sniper. I mean, damn, that's what you do." He poured a second glass of wine. "Like I said, it was a long time ago. Different now."

"Supposing I paid," she said. "If I paid what you want? Would you work for me?"

"When I find your husband," he told her, "I'll be out of contract. Then we can talk."

"If you find Darius," she said, "who knows if I will still wish to talk with you?"

Shawn raised his glass to her. "Not now," he said, "but sometime, when we know each other better, you can tell me what you mean."

"You mean, when you have got me into bed?"

"No," Shawn said. "No. What makes you think that?" He sat back, holding his wine, watching her. "Believe me, that was not what I meant."

12

Escorting the prisoner's wife, Shawn left the Paris–London Euro-star at the Ashford station in Kent. Since they had come into Kent, Danielle had been silent, withdrawn, keeping her distance. When Shawn tried probing her past, her answers were so brief and dismissive that, after a time, he stopped trying.

In silence, each aware of the other, not touching, they went to find his car.

Still uneasy on English roads, Shawn drove back to Felbourne, through greenlit tunnels and tree-hung lanes. To the hamlet that was now his home.

As they crossed the county border from Kent to Sussex, Shawn glanced at his companion. She'd turned her head, brushing away what might have been tears.

He couldn't be sure.

"I begin to think," she said, apropos of nothing, "I begin to think you may be right."

"About what?"

"About Darius. Disappearing. I have left so many messages on his phone—"

"And?"

"And nothing. *Rien du tout.* No word. Now even the phone is dead." She paused, watching light flicker through coppiced woodland to the left of the road. "If your people do have him—you think they will hurt him?"

Shawn wondered how much truth she could stand.

He said, "Possible. It happens."

She was quiet, then said, "If they do? Your friend told me some die. Some prisoners die."

It started to rain, just a little, then. A polite, English rain.

Shawn tried to find the right words. "What can I tell you? Believe me, no one's meant to die. Handbook says, detainee dies, we're doing it wrong. Body bags don't talk."

"This should make me feel better?"

Now a light mist blew across the Five Ash valley. Shawn switched on the wipers. The car was Martha's, the little two-seater Mercedes—a toy for cash-rich, child-poor couples. The car had computer-controlled options Shawn had not yet mastered.

He accelerated down the Broyle, the route's only straight stretch: once a Roman road.

"If the prisoner," she said, "if he is not a terrorist? If he has nothing to say?"

A rabbit dashed out of a clump of cow parsley, onto the road.

Eyes wide, body quivering, it turned to run back the way it had come. Shawn braked and swung the car around it.

"Believe me, they all have something to say. Those places, black jails, you just want to stop whatever the hell's happening. That's why we use them. Waterboarding, they tell me—takes like ninety-some seconds before the guy talks. Bad feeling, being drowned. Trust me, they all talk."

Danielle was looking out the car's window, not watching him. Shawn wondered if she was a woman he could live with. Physically, sure. The rest, who knew?

Always assuming she no longer had a husband. Part of his addiction recovery involved staying away from married women.

They were passing the open door of a busy smithy. Tell me, Shawn thought, in the twenty-first century, what kind of country still has working blacksmiths?

"Maybe it's lies, what they say. What the prisoners say."

"No question," he said. "That's a problem. Always. Maybe they're lying. Right after 9/11, we had what we called a high-value detainee. Al-Libi. After they waterboarded him, he talked like he was on the news. Helped start that little war in Eye-rack. Only trouble, the story was bullshit. Soup to nuts, fiction. Damn raghead, trying to stop what we did to him."

"You still got the war."

"We still got the war. Which, in a small way, we helped to start—me and Robert Hamilton Walters." He glanced across at her. "This business, you kiss a lot of frogs. You know what? Most of them, they stay frogs."

They were driving through villages where farm laborers' cottages stood for sale to city people. To commuters. They were the ones with money.

She was quiet again.

To break the silence, Shawn said, "Tell me something, Dani."

She said, "Danielle."

"Okay, Danielle. If I'm traveling with you, if we're going to find your man, I need to know some things. Like exactly where you met Osmani. What he was doing. Tell me the story."

Now the day had cleared. Frost, though, still lay in hillside hollows; tree shadows lengthened on hoarfrost fields.

Her reflection hovered on the window glass, distracting him.

"Not a secret," she said. "I had a commission." Her voice had lost its life. She was either lying, he thought, or recalling something she wished to forget. "That's how it started. How I met Darius. This American came to me. He'd bought a van Gogh. An authenticated canvas. It was called *La Grenade*. You know? The fruit, red, a little bitter?"

"Pomegranate?"

"Exactly. Pomegranate. In French, *grenade*."

"Like the explosive?"

"I suppose. This guy that bought the canvas, he asks me, is it right? Was it, in fact, van Gogh? He should have asked before he paid the money. I had a sense this one, this work—you know, it looked good, quite beautiful—but in truth I thought it was fake. Sometimes one gets that feeling. Though Vincent mentions such a canvas in his letters."

"You told the buyer?"

"Of course. He was called Lamar Grant. A man from Atlanta."

"Young?"

"He was older than me. Forty. Something like that. Good-looking, you would say, conservative, right wing, far too much money. Family money. Not enough to do in life. He thought he was smart. Smartest guy in the room, he called himself." She laughed. "A babe magnet, too. To me, not at all magnetic."

Unlike her.

"He didn't believe he'd bought a fake?"

"No. Not for a heartbeat. He told me, come on, you think that, so prove it." She shrugged. "With van Gogh, you know, proof is hard. If you are faking, if you are professional, you can search around—you still buy nineteenth-century painters' canvas, if you wish. In Arles, even. And stretchers, the same age. We prove nothing from that. The age is right, it will check right; too recent to be wrong. The first time I went to Arles I even talked with Jeanne Calment. When she was a girl, in a shop there, she remembered serving him. Remembered serving Vincent."

In his mind, Shawn did the math. Martha had talked of van Gogh.

"Come on," he said. "Don't give me that. Even a peasant like me knows dates. This woman, she'd be, what, hundred fifteen? Give or take."

"Give. When I met her, she was a hundred and twenty-one."

He glanced at her face, in profile. "Jesus. That's a healthy life."

"Smoked until she was ninety. All her life, drank wine." She watched him watching her. "Then," she said, "you know, with a canvas that might be a fake—you're not sure, of course, you're guessing—it's just a sense—you check the pigments. We know exactly what paints van Gogh used for each canvas. Most of the time he couldn't afford to buy colors, where he was, in the south; he had to write and ask his brother to buy. His brother Theo, in Paris. We have the letters—like I say, in one of them, he mentions *La Grenade*. He spells out the paints he would need. So, if the pigments are right, if the canvas is right, how do we prove a fake?"

"You lost me."

"We check the provenance. We talk to the former owners—the ones who are meant to have had the canvas. The first I went to see was an old woman in Aix. They said she bought *La Grenade*—or her father, I think, had it—from a Nazi collection. Always doubtful, those so-called ex-Nazi works. The woman lived on the Cours Mirabeau. Such a beautiful avenue. I booked a room on the Cours; next day I was going to visit. I was getting ready for bed when Lamar—this guy who is paying me—he comes right in my room."

"You had no clothes on?"

She made a gesture that could have been contemptuous or could have been rude.

"I had clothes on. He started pulling them off me. He drank too much, that man, did a lot of coke, but God, he was strong. I knew he was going to rape me. I had a vision of my father doing this thing. With my father, I don't know if it's true or if I imagined that. When I asked my mother she said of course it was all imagination, I was stupid, and anyway, she told me, it's nothing. Most girls, she said, most girls get raped."

He was driving faster now; way too fast for these roads. "There's a thought. What did you do? I mean, in the hotel?"

"I screamed. The door was half open—he'd left it that way. He was a careless man. Darius came in."

"Then what?"

"It was the first time I met him. The next thing, Lamar is on the floor. On his back." She flipped a hand. "Just like that. Of course I had no idea, but Darius was a judo brown belt. I think brown, is that right? Lamar didn't know what happened. He was much bigger, much heavier, than Darius. Stronger, too. He stood up and went for him, he was hitting out like this"—she punched the air, a feint more masculine than feminine—"then, bof, he is on the floor again." She laughed. "Lamar, down on the floor, looking up. Not knowing how it happened. Three times he went down, and I was hurt a little—he had hurt me, bruised me—but I was laughing. At the same time laughing, I couldn't help it. Lamar was so angry—he was humiliated—he ran out the door. Except he misses the doorway. Hit his head on, what do you call? The doorpost."

Shawn went into a sharp bend, accelerating: the way he'd been taught in the SEALs. "Guess you missed out on your fee."

"Of course—but I sent round an e-mail to the galleries, saying *La Grenade* was almost certainly a fake. When Lamar tries to sell, that will cost him, I don't know, twenty million? Something like that. Just then, I was thinking of Darius. Strange—it must have been erotic, in a way, what Lamar did. What he tried to do. Or what I imagined my father did. Who knows? Of course I don't want rape but I was, you know, so hot just then. You'll laugh. I wanted to bear his children. Darius's children. Five, six—more maybe."

"So?"

"Well, that evening I seduced him. Really, I couldn't help myself. Darius, he took my breath away." She looked at Shawn. "You don't expect great sex. Usually I don't come. Not the first time with a guy."

He was constantly surprised by the things she said, and didn't say. "It was? You did?"

She nodded.

"Then you married him? Bore his kids?"

"No kids. He didn't want. Marriage? Two years, that took. Great sex is not a reason to marry. You know? I have to feel I trust a man."

He turned directly toward her, looking away from the road. "Do you trust me?"

"I'm not sure," she said. "Right now, this moment, with you here, no. Please, just watch the road. I am not sure why I said I will come to England."

"Your husband," Shawn said. "Tell me, was he ever in Waziristan?"

For a moment Danielle was silent, her mouth half open. "*Salaud*," she said. "You son of a bitch. You do think he is a terrorist."

"It crossed my mind."

Turning off the highway, he drove up the half-paved lane to Felbourne village. The hamlet. She was silent, looking around her; shifting in her seat, uncomfortable, or uneasy.

"You live here?"

He said, "I do now. It's where my wife bought a house. Why'd she buy this place, you ask? My question, too. She had a grandmother, born here. Left for Ellis Island, hundred years back."

"Stop a moment." Danielle was looking from side to side, seeing trees and fields. "Okay, you live here, but why should I come to this place? You said we would look for Darius."

Shawn pulled the Mercedes onto a grass verge in front of Felbourne Grange, the manorial pile that bordered his own property.

"This country," he told her, "they have a saying about needles and haystacks. Where in hell do we start looking? Last time I was copied in on classified mail, we had twenty-some black prisons. Seventeen countries, Poland to Pakistan. Your guy could be in any one of those jails. What do you want me to do, Danielle? Toss a coin?"

She leaned back against the door of the car, away from him. "So? What will you do?"

"Only thing I can," he said. "I'll talk to the lady you heard about in Paris. Ashley Caburn."

"Why her?"

"Two reasons," Shawn said. "Number one, she has high-level security clearance. Likely she knows what we want to know. Second reason, she still talks to me. Not so many people do."

For a while, Danielle didn't speak. Stretching her arms tightened her white cotton shirt against her body. "Your house," she said finally. "How many bedrooms?"

Shawn glanced at her. "Enough that we don't have to share, if that's what you mean."

A lean man dressed in knee socks and green tweed knickerbockers emerged from an avenue of lime trees. The flesh of his face had thinned, limning the skull beneath. He carried a Purdey Woodward shotgun, which, Shawn knew, cost roughly the same as a ranch house in California.

"Justin," he said, "how are you, my man? How's Piglet?"

Justin pointed the engraved gun toward his neighbor in the car. His voice, when he spoke, was husky, close to a whisper. The voice, Shawn thought, of a throat cancer patient. "We need to talk," he said. "About your war."

"At this range," Shawn said, considering the shotgun, "that thing could do some damage. You mind pointing it away from us?"

"Not loaded," said Justin. Turning away, he demonstrated, touching the gun's bob-weight trigger. Pellets scattered new leaves from a weeping lime on the far side of the lane. Birds flew yelling in the air. Danielle dived downward, her forehead touching Shawn's knee.

"*Now* it's not loaded," Shawn said. Gently he lifted Danielle's head. "Let me introduce you guys. Danielle Baptiste, Justin Roxburgh Hallam Fox. Piglet's his wife. Did I get that right, Justin? What exactly do you want to talk about?"

Justin peered briefly into the car, considering Danielle. "Bit soon after your wife, I would have thought," he said. "Afghanistan. Durand Line. Gulbuddin Hekmatyar."

"You are both quite crazy," said Danielle.

Shawn restarted the car. "Here's the deal," he told Justin. "You stop shooting my pheasants, we'll get together, sort out the war."

"Pheasants in this village are mine," said Justin. He was reloading his shotgun. He pointed it beyond the churchyard. "My gamekeeper breeds them."

Shawn put the car in gear. "Justin," he said, "your gamekeeper's dead. Buried next to Martha."

Justin raised the weapon in salute. Danielle lowered her head below the level of the car's shotgun seat. Shawn drove slowly past the churchyard and made a right into his own driveway.

He reached across Danielle to open her door.

"This is it," he said. "We're home."

13

Late that night, in his own house, under a full moon, Shawn woke, naked. It was four in the morning—that was a guess. On his bed, Martha's little cat stood, arching its back, hissing at something unseen, in the moonlit dark.

Shawn listened. Somewhere in the house, someone was moving. He pulled on sweatpants. From under a pillow he took the loaded Makarov that, when he was still in the business, he'd managed to carry out of Peshawar. Without switching on lights he walked barefoot down the upper hall of his house. Behind him, the cat mewed. He was alert, waiting for sounds from the floor below, when hands grasped him from behind.

Danielle whispered, "Shawn? What is happening?"

"Jesus," Shawn said, "don't ever do that to me. Don't ever grab me in the dark. Could have put a bullet in you." She was wearing one of his T-shirts with a towel tied around her waist. "What are you doing out here?"

She held his unclothed arm. He could feel her shivering. "Someone came in my room. The door—it has opened—"

He slipped off the safety on his pistol. "You saw this person?"

"Just the door. It opened."

"Draft," he said. "Gust of wind."

"Feel," she said. "There is no wind. Someone stood watching me. After a time, the door closed. You think the wind does that? Opens and closes?"

He led her back toward her room. "Could have been Martha. This is her house. I feel she's still around. Checking you out, maybe."

"Martha?" she asked. "Martha, your wife?"

"She loved this place. Hard for her to leave, someone said."

Danielle stopped still. Moonlight fell through high windows, blanching her tanned skin. She nodded toward her room. "I can't," she said. "Can't go back there."

Shawn shrugged. "It was your choice, that room."

"I know. Now, not."

"Okay," he said. "There's two beds in my room. How's that sound?"

"Better," she said. "First, please, unload the pistol." Moments later, at the bedroom door, she said, "One more thing. Don't try making love with me."

The next time Shawn woke, it was morning. A depression in the single bed showed where Danielle had lain. For a moment he pictured her sleeping, then the image went.

Shawn lay a while, drowsing. He was slipping back into sleep when he heard his wife's voice in the room. As ever, it was nothing profound. Martha just said, "What about the sheep?"

Shawn looked around what had been her bedroom. Through an eastern window, rays of the rising sun came over the hills, dazzling him. Even without the sun, he doubted he'd see Martha. Since her death he never had, though, in his mind, he'd heard her voice several times reminding him of things he hadn't done.

She didn't make a big deal of it. In death she seemed amused by his domestic troubles.

"Are you surprised?" Shawn asked. "I was raised in Alabama. Hogs we had. Sheep, never."

She had started life among the pinewoods of Coaling County. It was true, though: He'd been meaning to check the sheep—their hooves. Till he came here, he hadn't even known sheep had hooves that needed tending.

Martha's voice was gone. Mornings, Shawn found, she never stayed long. He checked the time, then called Ashley in London. Her phone was off. Not surprising, really, given the hour and her nighttime habits. She was the one of his circle who could still drink like she did at twenty. Suffered the same way.

Shawn swung his legs off the bed and sat for a while, shivering a little. The bedroom was huge and cold. He'd learned that Brits don't believe in heating. If he stayed here—he wasn't sure he would, but if he did—he'd rework the system, with the balance of Abbasi's cash.

The initial installment was already gone.

Shawn asked himself, not for the first time, why would he stay? He thought about places he'd lived: Turkey Forge, Tuscaloosa, Peshawar, Queens, Manhattan, D.C. Who knew what came next? Paris, maybe, with Danielle. That was his kind of town. What the fuck was he doing here: a hamlet with twenty-three inhabitants? Twenty-two, with the gamekeeper dead.

It was about Martha, mainly, staying in Sussex. If he turned around and looked through the sash window, Shawn could see St. Perpetua's churchyard; could see her grave. Besides, she was still here, still in the house, still talking to him. He still heard her voice, at times she chose. The only woman he'd loved, really. If he moved to Manhattan, how would she take his going? Leaving her grave?

He had unfinished business here.

Right now, Shawn wasn't ready to think of leaving. He stripped off his sweatpants, dumped them on the floor, and went naked to the shower. That was another thing he'd learned: Brits know shit about showers. The tall Victorian contraption in this vast chilly bathroom had only two settings: COLD and TEPID. Shawn had laughed out loud when he first saw that TEPID. He wasn't laughing now. When he moved to the rectory and started using the shower, he found tepid was right on the money. Tepid was good as it got. He decided, for this morning, to take a bath—something he hadn't done since he left Turkey Forge and found the pleasures of showering.

The bath here was a standalone cast-iron claw-footed Victorian monstrosity; its water supply—though meager—seemed, for some reason, hotter than the lukewarm trickle from the shower. While water ran in the tub, Shawn stood naked at the window, stretching muscle, considering the tended expanse of his garden. Amy, the gardener's daughter, was out there, stocking a bird feeder in a steeply listing pear tree. Henry, her father, once tried teaching Shawn the names of English birds: mistle thrush, jackdaw, jay, fieldfare, greenfinch, bullfinch, warbler, woodpecker, blackbird, robin, wren. Some he got. The little colorless guys—linnet, dunnock, siskin—those were beyond him.

Shawn climbed into his half-full bath and lay back, his body adjusting to the switch from chill to lukewarm. Growing up, he'd had to follow his daddy into the family bath, pretending not to stare at the sturdy apparatus between his daddy's legs. In time, he'd watch the evolution of his own cock as it floated on the surface of a cooling bath. Which took him back to Turkey Forge—to teenage boys, talking sex. They knew then, sure as you could know anything, that true happiness came with a Hollywood model. It took Shawn two marriages—both to beautiful women—before he began doubting that truth.

For some moments, in cooling water, memories enmeshed him: the first time he came inside his first girlfriend, on a narrow bed in a shotgun shack—a climax so long and hard Shawn expected his body to deflate, like a spent balloon. Thinking now of Danielle's body, he climbed from the tub, toweling dry his own softening torso.

Shawn dressed fast. Needing air, wondering about his guest, he left the house. Minutes later he was in his field, running, breathing hard, jumping fallen trees, chasing Wallace, his Shetland ram.

Shawn wasn't in great shape for speed. These days it was hard, even for him, to believe he'd once been a Crimson Tide quarterback. Wallace, on the other hand, was quick: a goaty little beast, dark, curly fleeced, ill-natured, with short sharp horns. Fast on his feet.

Shawn's height was part of the problem. Short-legged, low to the ground, Wallace could turn on a dime; twice he left Shawn flat on his face in nettles and clover.

The second time Shawn stood, testing his limbs, he saw Danielle. Today she wore oversized shorts, cinched in at the waist and turned up at the cuffs, and a hunting shirt—all borrowed, he guessed, from someplace in the house. She made this unlikely outfit look good. She leaned on his field gate, laughing, the fears of the night forgotten. Seeing her took Shawn back to meeting her, falling for her, in a Paris apartment. Seemed longer ago than it was.

Limping a little from his last fall, he walked to the fence. "This is amusing?"

"Mmm. It is. Don't stop." She had her hand over her mouth now, trying not to laugh out loud. "Myself, I bet on the sheep."

"Come to the house," he said. "I'll make breakfast."

"When I'm done." She was back on the bridle path, ready to run. "Good luck, catching her."

"Him."

"Sorry." She shrugged. "I have trouble with sex."

She waved and moved away, loping through long grass.

Moments later, she was on the hill, climbing toward Shawn's beech wood. He opened the gate and watched Danielle scale a leaf-strewn slope, moving at an easy pace.

The warm air chilled. For an art historian, he thought, this was one remarkably fit girl.

Shawn guessed he could match that pace for a quarter mile, not more. Once, he'd run for miles without breaking a sweat. In the marines, it was part of his training. No longer. Time catching up. He should start jogging again. In Virginia, in the Agency, he ran every morning. Not here; not now.

Heading back to the house, thinking of Danielle, Shawn found Martha's cat bouncing through the grass beside him. It was the first time he'd owned a cat. He kept an eye out for Miss Mop's enemy—a ginger tom, a mangy barrel-chested beast.

Last winter, the tom came nightly through the cat door. It sprayed the curtains, ate Mop's food, found the little cat in her basket, and attacked her. For days afterward, the little cat was sad and still, refusing to play.

Shawn was alone that season, the first time in his adult life. He unpacked a hunting rifle and sat all of a summer evening by the attic window. In his last job, as a marksman, he'd been in the top percentile: one shot, one kill. He reckoned he could still take out a moving cat, but that didn't seem neighborly. Not for a man who'd recently moved to a small, close-knit English village. Shawn waited until he saw the tom edge through rushes and iris around his lake. He fired three times—one shot to the left, one to the right, and one over the tom's head. The shots came close. The cat skulked behind a bust of Venus and scanned the garden for gunmen. Giving up, it scuttled, belly to ground, for the cover of trees.

Shawn sent one more shot shaving the cat's left shoulder as it went over the flint wall skirting his wood. He didn't doubt there'd be another round. Like the Taliban, like the Terminator, this cat would be back.

Now Henry Thackeray, Shawn's gardener, stood at the kitchen door, waiting.

"Problem, Mr. Maguire?"

"Three problems," Shawn said. "Sheep. Washing machine. Hawks."

The hawks—magnificent birds—were killing Shawn's doves, which had until now lived peacefully in a whitewashed cote by the lake. That was before the peregrines came. These hawks hung over the hills behind the house, drifting, planing, circling on westerly winds, swooping at speed on Shawn's doves. They took the white birds on the wing, without pause, bearing bloodied bodies away. They killed one dove a day.

Henry sighted along his forefinger.

"Shoot the bastards." He meant the peregrines. "You could." Since he'd seen Shawn's target practice—picking pine cones one by one from a Douglas fir—Henry respected his employer's marksmanship.

"Isn't it against the law? Hitting hawks?"

"Up here, Mr. Maguire," said Henry, "you got no neighbors." He discounted the Hallam Fox clan. "Who'd know?"

"I'd know," Shawn said. "They're beautiful birds. I just wish they'd kill something else."

14

Shawn took the flowers his gardener had cut for Martha—blooms in a dozen shades of blue: nepeta, delphiniums, campanula, geraniums, gentian, iris. Blue was her color, always. The little cat ran behind him. He was heading for the churchyard when his cell phone rang.

A familiar American voice said, "Confirmation? You own a field? That's correct?"

"Bobby Walters," Shawn said, "why would you want to know this?"

Bobby, echoing a little, said, "I'm coming to visit with you."

"So soon," Shawn said. "There's a connection with the sheep field?"

Bobby said, "In a chopper. It's okay, buddy, relax. We have you in clear sight. Don't worry about it."

"I wasn't," Shawn said. "Just watch out for my sheep."

He wondered then why Bobby was not in Paris; wondered why the man would be flying over Sussex; wondered what he planned. For some moments, he stood in the lane, thinking over their history. His and Bobby's. For a while, they'd been like brothers, growing up together—sharing memories of Alabama, sharing women once or twice, until Carly died. They'd been close then: both sure they knew what America needed, if they could just get the intelligence through to the brass above. Then, at some point—Peshawar, maybe—they'd headed in different directions. Bobby was promoted; Shawn missed out. He was drinking and in debt. He had the feeling Bobby was moving away: He saw Shawn now as a liability. Not a fit associate for an agent on the up ladder.

If Bobby never went as high as he hoped, his buddy went no place at all. Shawn left the building, dishonorably discharged. No word, after that, from Bobby. So much, Shawn thought, for brotherhood. For looking after a fat, unpopular kid.

In the churchyard, he stood a while watching hawks circle the hills. He waited under the sycamores, holding the cat's vibrating body, considering Martha's grave. It was sixteen months since he'd buried his wife here, thousands of miles from her birthplace. On summer days, the churchyard seemed a haven where a body might rest; but, in the winter past, Shawn had grieved for his wife, alone in the earth. Rain falling on her face.

The grave was at the highest point of the churchyard, shadowed in summer by sycamore, ash, and oak: a gray granite stone lying flat among flowers. Its stone-cut inscription read MARTHA SEMEL, 1951–2002. That was all she had wanted. Frightened, facing death, she'd written the words in shaky capitals, on a day when she knew she had days to live.

Martha never trusted Shawn with practical tasks; he guessed arranging the carving of a stone counted as one of those.

"Managed that," he told her.

Suddenly there was noise, downdraft, a heavenly heartbeat. Shifting shadows on the grave. Leaves swirled across the church-yard as a black helicopter circled, rising, dipping, until, over the rectory, it dropped from sight. Landing, Shawn guessed.

He let the cat run and walked back though his garden, watch-ing the chopper make its final circuit, hovering, sideslipping, and setting down in his field.

Puzzled, uneasy, sheep huddled beneath a blackthorn hedge, eyeing the airborne intruder.

The helicopter pilot scrambled from the craft. He wore, Shawn noticed, an army-issue M-9 Beretta. Under still-rotating blades, the soldier made his way to open the opposite door.

From the cockpit, Bobby Walters waved, then beckoned.

Avoiding wasp pits, rabbit holes, and badger runs, Shawn jogged across the field to the helicopter. "Going up in the world, Mr. Walters."

Bobby sighed as he unstrapped his seat belt. "You mean the chopper? Not this boy. Laid on for one of the conference brass. Guy's tied up, so to speak, with a working girl. High-class ass. Misses his time slot. What do they do? Give it to me, so I bring you back."

Shawn thought this through. "Bring me back where?"

"Chastleforth."

"This should mean something?"

Bobby said, "Get in, I'll brief you. We have a twelve-minute meeting with Rockford."

Shawn shook his head. "Rockford? Hugh Rockford? Son of a bitch that canned me?"

Bobby sighed. "Same guy, different day. Now making you an offer you can't refuse. He'll take you back in the service. Sort out your pay. Update pension. I know you need it." He checked the time. "Like I say, you have a twelve-minute window, meet the man." He pointed behind him to an empty seat. "Come talk. Twelve minutes. How bad can it be?"

The pilot held open the helicopter's opposite door. Shawn glanced at the man's pistol, checking the position of the safety as he climbed into the Apache. Firearms and flying machines, he believed, made a bad mix.

"Fifty minutes," said Bobby, "you'll be back home. Round-trip, trust me. No one's going to know you're gone."

Shawn said, "Someone will. Okay, talk to me. What is Chastleforth?"

"Country house in Hampshire."

Shawn said, "Where the hell is Hampshire?"

The pilot lifted off and flew low along the flank of the downs. "Cute little hills you have, sir," he told Shawn. "Remind me of home." When no one asked, the man added, "South Dakota."

"Tell me something," Shawn said to Bobby. "In Paris, whenever it was, you're saying to me, go ahead, publish all the stuff you have. Pakistan, VP, nuclear ring, ISI, drugs—whole ball of wax. You know, I do that, it's a shitstorm. Company's going to hate it. Now, you tell me, no, no, no—make nice. Come buddy up with Rockford."

Bobby adjusted the shades he wore for flying. "Put it this way. I got talked to. They made me an offer. You know. Stuff happens. I changed my mind. You're wise, you'll change yours." He picked up binoculars and looked down at the hills below as the chopper looped over a woman, her hair wild in the downdraft. "Jesus God," Bobby said, "is that her? Damn, it is. That's the girl. The one in

Paris." Shaking his head, he turned to stare at Shawn. "How'd you do that? Just tell me how the fuck you do it."

Shawn leaned over, seeing Danielle on a hillside track. She'd stopped, shading her eyes, watching the low-flying Apache.

"I never did work out," Bobby said, "how you get these women. You're older than me. You're no better-looking."

The pilot glanced first at Bobby, then at Shawn.

"Thinner," Shawn said. "More charming. Better disposition." He watched as Danielle resumed her easy lope along the path toward his house. "In Paris, remember? I said I'd help look for her husband."

"The husband's Darius Osmani? The guy we talked about?" Shawn nodded.

"What I hear," Bobby said, "you were looking for Osmani before you ever met her."

The pilot turned. To Shawn he said, "Sir, you're asking where's Hampshire." He pointed downward. "That's it there. Hampshire." He indicated farther west. "Chastleforth."

Bobby looked at Shawn. "God's sake," he said. "You live here. Never heard of Chastleforth? Top honchos' meet-up. Think Camp David, for Brits. Cuter. Older. Like, three hundred years."

Looking down as the Apache dipped, Shawn saw a vast country mansion, its formal gardens and lawns encircled by ha-has, beyond which grazed herds of those Charolais cattle Martha once desired.

"Okay," Shawn said. "We have Rockford. Who else is meeting?"

Bobby thought for a moment, deciding what his companion needed to know. "Two-day talkfest. Brass from Langley. Some you might remember. NSC. OSP. CIFA. Whole alphabet soup. War on terror shtick. Plus Brits. MI5, MI6, so on. Got their panties in a twist."

"About?"

Bobby shrugged. "Same old, same old." He tried an effeminate English accent. "Are you fellows quite *sure* it was Saddam set up al Qaeda? Can we put this before Parliament? Is that kosher? Are you quite *sure* the man organized 9/11? He does have nuclear weapons?" Bobby shook his head. "Parliament, what can I tell you? Private school pussies. You know? Eight out of ten cats prefer being fooled." He gripped his seat as the pilot rocked the Apache, setting it down close to the ha-ha. "We gave them a present. Al-Libi's confession. Eyes only. Nineteen pages."

"I questioned al-Libi," Shawn said. "It was all lies."

"You know that," Bobby said, unbuckling his belt. "I know that. Let's hope the Brits don't."

Shawn climbed out of the helicopter to find himself in the sights of four black submachine guns, two held by British security, two by Secret Service men. He raised his hands. He had a long-established habit of treading cautiously with men who carried automatic weapons. He'd noticed that even a lousy marksman does damage if he's using an Uzi.

"What is this?" he asked Bobby. "Why Secret Service? Do we have the president here?"

"Heartbeat away," said Bobby. "We have the man who runs the country. The VP." With his hands in clear sight, he offered the senior Brit his security documents and nine-zero passport. The Brit nodded at Shawn; not, he thought, a friendly nod.

"Security cleared," said Bobby. "Doesn't have his documents right now."

Three men watched as Bobby and Shawn crossed the ha-ha. The fourth kept his weapon trained on the Apache in case its young Dakotan pilot proved to have jihadist sympathies. Under an arch of artfully pleached laburnum and Perle d'Azur clematis stood a biometric calibrator on a wheeled cart. When Bobby and Shawn had been fingerprinted and iris-scanned, they were allowed to cross the mansion's inner, box-hedged curtilage.

Bobby led the way down foot-worn steps to a stone-walled passage, deep underground.

Lighting was low. Shawn considered the size of the blocks. "Brits dug this thing?"

Bobby nodded. "Not recently. While back."

Shawn ran his fingers along stone slabs. A nice mortar-free fit. "Defensive?"

"Guess again," Bobby said. "It's for servants. Head honcho, Earl Whoever-the-fuck-he-was, back in the day, has a bunch of servants. Hates seeing these low-rent folk litter up the pretty garden. Answer? Put 'em underground." He stopped by a vast and empty hearth. "Up that chimney, you care to look, you see four fireplaces. One on each floor of the house."

Shawn doubted this. He bent to look upward. The chimney was square, four by four, he guessed. As Bobby claimed, it climbed through the floors of the house, clear and open to the sky.

"No kidding."

Bobby checked the time and pushed Shawn forward. "Move. We'll miss the window."

The tunnel narrowed and darkened. For a brief irrational moment, Shawn had visions of kidnap: of following Osmani to some black Moroccan jail. For reassurance, he touched the metal heft of his Makarov. Twelve rounds. If he went, he'd take one or two souls with him.

"Watch this," Bobby said.

He entered a passcode, threw a switch. Momentarily, the stone passage shone with brilliant light. A metal shield—not, Shawn guessed, installed by the lords of Chastleforth—slid aside. Bobby led the way to a low-ceilinged underground room, its oak beams studded with pothooks. Once, it seemed, the manor's kitchen. Now the room was full of communications gear, some of it, Shawn saw, newly installed. Secret Service, most likely. On the far wall, a CCTV monitor showed the front of the mansion, somewhere above their heads. It currently featured, in high definition, the head of the National Security Council in close conversation with the vice president.

On the far side of the former kitchen sat Hugh Rockford, his army-booted feet resting on a metal desk. He chewed at a toothpick. He looked older than Shawn recalled.

"Late," said Rockford. He checked the time. "We have nine minutes. Two things, Maguire. Number one, here's the deal. We now have an elimination unit. Reports direct to the VP." He nodded at the monitor, which still showed, above them, the head of NSC. "Bypasses those guys. Security Council. Condi Rice, so on, so on. Your name came up."

"Eliminating who, exactly?"

"You know," said Rockford. "Problem people. Problem people in problem places. Gaza. Lebanon. Iran. Syria. NoKo. AfPak."

"You got my attention," Shawn said. He was genuinely interested. "Reports to the White House? Do we have legal cover?"

Rockford nodded. "No sweat. Office of Legal Counsel—pen pushers. VP wants a law, these guys write it."

"We're talking assassination?"

"Not a term we use."

"My name came up because?"

"Because," Rockford said, "you're a top-percentile sniper. With security clearance. Uncommon cross-check."

"Okay," said Shawn. "That's number one on your list. What's number two?"

Rockford stared for what seemed a long while. It was, Shawn recalled, part of the man's inquisitorial tool set. Finally, he spoke.

"Give us what you know about Ayub Abbasi. Money, location, ideology, nukes. Sources tell us, what we're hearing, the guy's jihadi. Financing al Qaeda Web sites."

"In return," Shawn said, "you will what?"

"Think about reinstating you."

"While you're thinking," Shawn said, "I'll think about whether I talk to you."

Rockford swung his feet off the desk, his color high. He spat the toothpick. His buzz cut bristled. He brought a hand down flat and hard on the metal desk. The noise was impressive.

"Don't fuck with me, son. You're American. Ex-Agency. Damn, you have a duty, give me whatever fucking information I request. You familiar with the word 'treason?' "

"I've heard it," Shawn said. "Here's what I know. Ayub Abbasi's a Pakistani citizen. He was close to Nashida Noon, when she ran the country—when she was prime minister. Abbasi came to see me. Offered work."

"Which was what?"

"Find someone. Abbasi may have had Nashida in the car—I don't know. Never saw her face. The guy pays the rent with import-export business. He travels. Spends cash on clothes. Italian suits. Wants Nashida back into power. Wants her running Pakistan. Wants her to exit the president."

"Locations? Money?"

"Abbasi had business offices all over. Florida, Atlanta, Kandahar, Fes, Islamabad, Peshawar. I hear some of them closed."

"Jesus," Rockford said. With the blunt end of his toothpick he began to clean beneath his fingernails. "This I can get from Google. Talk about the nuclear connection."

"Is there one?"

On the wall monitor, Shawn saw the vice president turn his expressionless gaze on a CCTV camera. Deep underground, chilled by that saurian stare, Shawn was thankful for the distance between himself and the man who now ran his country.

Rockford checked the time. "You're looking for this Iranian guy. Osmani. Why?"

"Mr. Abbasi asked me to find him."

"Again, why?"

Shawn said, "Osmani has some documents, some information, Abbasi wants. Let me ask a question, Mr. Rockford. Who is holding Osmani?"

"Only one of us asks questions," Rockford said. "Right now, it's not you."

He checked the time, then stood, about to leave.

Shawn said, "What are you doing, Mr. Rockford? I mean, for me?"

Rockford paused. "I'll tell you what I'm doing," he said. "As of this meeting I'm revoking your clearance. Putting you on a watch list. Suspected terrorist sympathizer."

"You're *what*?" Shawn blurted. "You know what this means? Every time I take a plane I get some little pissant clerk dicking me around for two hours—"

"You start helping your uncle," said Rockford, opening a door on the far side of the room, "Uncle starts helping you."

Shawn stood. Moving fast, he went to the same door. He was stopped by a small British policeman with the pink-cheeked face of a choirboy. This uniformed cherub held a Glock 17. It was not, Shawn knew, a particularly accurate weapon.

Shawn was ill-tempered. "Sonny," he said, "I made a resolution, I won't take another human life. Not in this incarnation. But I tell you, kid, you even twitch, you're an exception."

"Believe it," Bobby told the tiny officer. He nodded at Shawn. "Marines' top shot."

The diminutive angel lowered his Glock.

"Good thinking," Shawn said. "Bobby, thanks a bunch. Totally wasting my morning. Getting me on a watch list. Let's go. Walk me back to the chopper."

Near the mouth of the stone-walled servants' tunnel, Bobby paused. He said, "Shawn, I've known you a long time. You're a patriotic guy. Why are you not worried about Paki nukes? We worked on this, did we not? It was your bag, your group. You tracked A. Q. Khan. Started NukePro. You were the go-to guy."

"I was," Shawn said. "For a while. Look how that ended."

Shawn's Nuclear Proliferation Group was born in New York, in the summer of 2001. It was a time when he found it hard getting out of bed; even harder getting to work in the mornings. His wife had moved to an English village. Martha left Shawn to decide whether or not he'd follow her. In Manhattan, Shawn's mistress, Ellen, was losing interest. When they'd first met—while her billionaire husband was out of town—Ellen magically shed her own clothes while, at the same time, undressing Shawn. She'd have them both naked in moments. That was then. Now, when Shawn wanted her, Ellen spent time in one of her several bathrooms, doing God knows what, while Shawn lay unclothed and horny in her husband's king-sized bed.

As if a wife and mistress weren't enough, Shawn had other concerns: anxieties that kept him awake. Money, debts, and work. Work in particular preyed on him. Though no one had yet spoken the words, Shawn knew he was slipping down the Agency's promotion ladder.

The trouble had started with NukePro. At first, it wasn't a group at all. It was just Shawn—middle-ranking Agency operative—who had a sense that someone, in one of the rogue states, was selling fission technology: selling plans, components, triggers, and certain other items of mass destruction.

After months of work, Shawn came up with documentation suggesting the trouble started in Islamabad and Rawalpindi. Pakistan was developing nuclear weapons and offering blueprints for sale to the highest bidder among the Islamic states. That year, the world came closer to nuclear war.

Shawn brought in his buddy Bobby Walters to work on the proliferation project.

Briefing Bobby, he traced the trouble back to Nashida Noon, in the nineties. "Remember?" Shawn had asked. "For a while she was prime minister."

"I hear she will be again," Bobby said. "If she lives."

"Don't bet the farm," Shawn said. "Anyway, last time, when she's running Pakistan, Noon sets up a nuclear program—puts A. Q. Khan in charge—"

"Who he?"

Shawn passed over a thin file.

"Read. It's not long. Abdul Qadir Khan. Trained as an engineer. He was working in the Netherlands, stole designs for centrifuges, took them back to Pakistan, started enriching uranium; making warheads. I mean, he made them for Pakistan, plus he had kind of a private scam going—garage business—selling nuclear kit compo-

nents. Do you believe this?" Shawn asked, showing a color brochure in Urdu and Arabic. "Had these printed in Islamabad."

Bobby said he didn't read Arabic.

"Brochure for fission weapons. That's what this is. Dr. Khan's
garage business. Guy's coining it."

Bobby, distracted, pointed at a new and cute assistant who was
crossing the office. "Did you talk to her yet?"

"How would I?" Shawn asked, looking at the new girl. "She only
started this week."

"Her name," Bobby said, "I believe she's called Carly. I think
that's it. I mean, *Carly*? What kind of a name is that? She went to
Wharton. That much I know."

"Not possible," Shawn said. "I never saw anyone that attractive
came out of Wharton. Come on, work. Concentrate. What's your
take on the nuclear thing?"

"That it's a wildly unlikely story," Bobby said. "I mean, color
brochures for nuclear weapons? Hello—but listen, if there's even
a twenty percent chance it's true, we give it to the boss. Right?
Hugh takes it up to National Security. Out of our hands. Let them
decide. I mean, that's what they're paid for, right?"

Hugh Rockford wasn't ready to take anything Shawn gave him
to National Security. He wanted more facts, more research. He
wanted a group. He liked groups.

"Maguire," he said, "we'll make it small. Nuclear Proliferation
Group. NukePro. Limited remit. You stay working with Bobby. Bring
Ashley over from London, if you need her. Talk to her, anyway. I'll
get Calvin to organize it."

"Let me get this clear," Shawn had said. "I spend months looking at covert nuclear proliferation. Looks like I've found a smug-
gling ring based in Pakistan. I find out who's selling secrets. I have
proof of Inter-Services involvement."

"What's ISI do?"

"Supports Khan. I know who they're selling technology to—Libya, for one."

Rockford paid attention. "Libya? How do we know this?"

"We know," Shawn said, "because I have a contact in Tripoli. An asset. He tells me he saw the bomb blueprints. He saw what they were wrapped in."

"Surprise me," said Rockford.

"Laundry bags, okay? Blueprints in bags from a dry-cleaning company in Rawalpindi. Where ISI lives. Libya's not the problem, though. Khan sold the bomb to North Korea—which I believe now has warheads and a missile—plus, he also sold to Iran. That's for starters."

Rockford made notes, thinking this through.

"So," Shawn said, "I get to this point—then you tell me I'm reporting to Calvin McCord. Is this by chance the same Calvin McCord, superpatriot—the guy who will, no question, take the credit for every bit of work I did—"

"We're not individuals," Rockford said. "We're a team—"

"You think Calvin knows that?"

Rockford brought his papers into a neat pile, indicating that the conversation was over. "Sorry to tell you this, Shawn," he said, "but Calvin's on the up staircase. You're on the other one. Take that aboard. Try to make nice. The guy could help your prospects."

"Be a cold day in hell," Shawn said, heading back to the corner office where Bobby Walters was waiting.

When Calvin came into the Proliferation Group, Shawn had to admit that the man had changed. He was no longer the undernourished, somehow furtive creature who'd joined the Agency three years earlier. Now there was a palpable confidence about him. Introduced by Daddy, he moved in high circles. Though his hands still shook, he seemed physically larger; more muscular, substantial. What upset Shawn was seeing that Calvin had somehow snagged Carly, the new assistant, fresh out of business school. She introduced herself, demurely, as "Mr. McCord's assistant."

Shawn had never had a personal assistant; certainly not one who looked like Carly.

When Calvin had reviewed the evidence Shawn and Bobby presented, he asked what they recommended.

"Pressure," Bobby said. "White House pressures Pakistan. We call Islamabad, tell the prez call off the army, reinstate Nashida Noon as prime minister, on condition she reins in Khan, closes down the Khan Institute. Nuclear fucking Central." By now, Bobby had read the files. "We tell the guy, break up ISI, or you're in deep shit. No more kickbacks. No more American aid."

"For the White House," Calvin said, "that's way low priority. They have other things on the burner. Don't spread it around. We're going to war with Iraq."

After this news there was silence for a minute or so. Then Shawn said, "Tell me—why would we do that—I mean, Iraq?— when we all know the threat comes from AfPak? Like, Pakistan, Afghanistan, the border lands."

"Threat comes from where the veep wants threat to come from. Right now, he wants it coming from places where there's oil. He's an oilman. Our job's proving Iraq has WMDs."

"Problem," Bobby said. "Since it doesn't."

"For Christ's sake," Shawn said. "We all know Israel's the only place in the Middle East with significant WMD capability. I mean, what are we talking here? Hundred fifty nukes underneath Dimona? More?"

"Now, now, boys," said Calvin gently, "something else we all know—Israeli nukes don't exist. Or if, hypothetically, they do exist, they sure as shit don't count. Message is, focus on Iraq. Prove it has WMDs."

"Whether it does or not?"

"Whether it does or not," Calvin said. "Pakistan—we keep that low-key. I'll tell you what we do. We kidnap this Dr. Khan. Run him through enhanced interrogation. Put him under pressure. See what he says."

"Kidnap how?" Bobby asked.

"How hard can it be? If you're right, the guy flies around the world, selling off nuke blueprints. We pick him up when he's changing planes, Schipol, de Gaulle, Dubai, Heathrow, wherever. We render him some place has no connections. Someplace poor and mean. Poland."

At the time Calvin said this, his group—what had been Shawn's and was now Calvin's group—met in a corner office chosen not for its view of the World Trade Center but because the air-conditioning seemed to work better there than it did in other parts of the building. Even so, the heat and humidity of a Manhattan summer were hard to bear. Only Carly, slim and chic, stayed cool. Bobby—who was at a low point with his weight problem—looked like he might not make it through the afternoon. Looking that way was particularly tough on him since he had particular reasons to look relaxed. Though he was twenty years older, Bobby was planning to ask Carly out on a date. He wanted to catch her before some other agent did. Unfortunately, the thought of asking was making Bobby nervous and physically uncomfortable. He sweated more than usual.

It fell to Shawn to point out problems with Calvin's kidnap plan. "First off," he said, "you may not know this, Calvin, but Dr. Khan is Pakistan's local hero. They feel about him the way some of us feel about George W. Protector of the nation kind of thing. Nashida Noon tells Khan—this is before the president sacks her—she tells Khan, let me know whatever you need, you've got it. So Dr. A. Q. isn't flying anyplace on scheduled airlines. He won't change planes at airports, like where the rest of us change planes. He wants to go someplace, he calls the intelligence guys. ISI. Inter-Services. Our friends in AfPak."

"Don't treat me like I'm an ignorant person," Calvin said.

Shawn stopped himself from saying what he thought of saying.

"Okay. So, here's what we have. Dr. Khan wants out, he makes a request—ISI provides a military plane. Most times, what I hear, that plane is full of army. Highly trained personnel. My guess, we'd need a squad of SEALs to get Khan off of a flight. We're basically talking Entebbe."

Calvin said, "Maguire, could you step outside a minute? I want a word."

Standing outside the corner office, Calvin lowered his voice. "Don't do that again. Do you get me, Maguire? You follow? Just don't do that again."

Shawn, not understanding, spread his hands. Do what?

"Don't contradict me in front of other people," Calvin said. "Not if you want to stay in this job." He came closer, until he was touching Shawn. His hands, his arms, were trembling. "Here's the thing. If I don't say it, someone will. Rockford asked me recently. He said, Calvin, be honest. Let me know what you think of Shawn Maguire."

In the heat of the afternoon, Shawn felt suddenly chilled, as if, in hermetically sealed Tower Seven, a sharp north wind were blowing.

Through the glass door of the corner office, he could see Bobby Walters trying pre-pickup lines on the attentive new assistant.

"I asked him," Calvin said, "I asked Rockford, do you mean what do I think of Maguire as a person or as an agent? He told me, start with, how's the guy as an agent?"

Shawn wasn't sure he wanted to know what came next.

"So you said?"

"I was honest," Calvin said. "I told him what I thought. I said, I like the man. He was my first mentor. I said, believe me, I have feeling for Maguire, but you want my opinion, as an agent—as an agent, he is over the hill."

Later that same day, Shawn began searching for a dignified way to leave the Agency, before the Agency left him.

Flying back from Chastleforth to West Sussex, the Apache pilot checked his bearings for Felbourne. He circled over the church of St. Perpetua. Shawn, looking down, saw a churchyard sapling bow low in the chopper's breathing wake.

"Real nice place you have here, sir," said the pilot. "You want back on the sheep field?"

"Sure," Shawn said. "Take care flying home."

"No problem," the pilot said, landing. "Believe me, they take real good care of the veep. Clear skies over Chastleforth."

Danielle was waiting at the field's gate. Machine winds fanned hair around her face. Watching the Apache lift off, she said, "You must be more important than I thought."

"Don't believe it," Shawn said. "What happened, I got demoted one rung further down. On a goddamn watch list."

She hooked her arm in his. Not counting last night, it was the second time she'd touched him. Together, they walked back toward the house.

"Now," she said, "you seem a little sad. Because of what has happened where you went?"

Shawn shook his head. "Uh-uh. I was thinking, if I'd met you when I was younger, you wouldn't have been married."

She was quiet a while, considering.

"You, though," she said, "a man with four marriages? You would have been."

15

Later that day, Shawn called London and spoke about Danielle to Ashley Caburn. By the time he was off the phone, Danielle had disappeared. Trying to find her, Shawn passed Kylie, the gamekeeper's orphaned daughter. Dressed in hand-me-downs, barelegged on a dry-stone wall, she watched Shawn's surviving doves. She reminded him of his daughter, Juanita.

At that age, Juanita had been a thin and anxious child who stayed in touching distance of her father—sensing perhaps that he'd someday leave home for good. As Shawn did. Years later, older and sadder, he tried everything he knew to restore that closeness, but that was a clock he could never wind back. Not now, not with his God-haunted daughter, now a novitiate in some West Coast ashram.

Down the village lane, someone had parked a late-model blue

Chrysler. As he passed, Shawn glanced in at the backseat. Turning, he asked Kylie if she'd seen the car's driver. Or a lady with long dark hair.

Without shifting her gaze from the doves, the girl nodded. "She's nice, that lady. Picked me up. Didn't mind I'm dirty. Gave me a kiss. Went down there." Kylie pointed toward the Grange. Moments later, she asked, still without turning her head, "She's pretty. You going to marry her?"

Shawn guessed Kylie had heard from her mother that he was now a single man. "I doubt it," he said. "I don't think she'd marry me."

"Yeah, well," said Kylie, watching the birds, "you're so old."

"Thanks for that, kid," Shawn said. "I need reminding."

He waved to Justin Hallam Fox, walking slowly up the lane swinging at nettles with a blackthorn stick. Sir Justin gestured toward Shawn. "Your popsy," he said. "Saw her this morning—on the hills, running. Damn silly sport."

As the old man shuffled on, Shawn entered the churchyard. For him, unbeliever that he was, this was a numinous place that drew him back. Even the trees, some of them, were centuries old. If this were Virginia, there'd be bus tours. Here, it was himself and Sir Justin Hallam Fox.

In their years of marriage, Shawn had never known what Martha believed. Over the time they'd lived in the hamlet, she'd crossed the lane to the church every Sunday, but what she worshipped Shawn never discovered and—he regretted it now—had never asked.

Skeptic though he was, Shawn first dated Martha after a church service in Turkey Forge. He was sixteen then, Martha a year younger. The pastor was the Reverend Jim Bob Newman. When God first called, Jimbo borrowed money from his brother Wade, who ran a low-rent gun-and-pawn-and-bait store on the road between Sugden and Shoat. With Wade's cash, Jimbo purchased a certificate of ministry from a Christian college in Tuscaloosa. Word of his sermonizing spread across the county: Foretelling the Rapture, denouncing the sins of President Johnson, Jimbo drew crowds from the pinewoods.

The other thing that made the preacher famous was the big hog. This wasn't just any big hog: It was the legendary Biggest Damn Hog in Alabama, a mythical monster, rarely seen, roaming pine plantations on the outskirts of Shoat.

Pastor Jim tracked that old beast for a year, until he pinned it down in pinewoods south of Sugden. When he saw the creature, Pastor said, he near to died of fright, Lord help us, the hog was that damn big. Jimbo stood dead still among the pines, staring at the thing, paralyzed, while the hog came, shaking the earth, heading right toward him. What saved the reverend was the fact that he had an illegal M-16 assault rifle, bought from brother Wade. Jimbo had the weapon on automatic but, the way he told it, that pig was near atop of him, more lead than meat, before the storm of shells took its legs out from under.

Sixteen-year-old Shawn traveled down through the pinewoods to see the body of the beast, before it could be moved on a lowloader or carved up for sausage. On the forest floor, he recalled, it was bigger than you'd believe. Not so big as a bus—the way early reports had claimed—but easy the size, he thought, of a recreational vehicle, if you could imagine an RV made all out of wild and hairy pork.

They never did get that hog on a truck scale, but the best guess at its weight was nine hundred pounds, plus change. Biggest hog ever, at least in the Deep South.

Another thing that was odd: Full of metal, breathing its last, the beast spoke to Pastor Newman. God, he said, spoke through the mouth of that hog. None but Jimbo heard it—it was just him and the pig there, after all—but the preacher swore blind that the creature gave voice, in tones like his mother's, only deeper.

The hog's last words were what brought Shawn to church; it was how he got his date with Martha. In the First Church of Christ Betrayed he heard the reverend reveal what exactly the hog had said, which, it turned out, was a brief injunction: "Love is all you need."

Like the Beatles, pretty much.

When the service ended, Shawn asked Martha out for vanilla Cokes at the Battle Flag.

"Yes," she said.

Shawn was confused. "Yes, what?"

"Didn't you just ask me out?" Shawn nodded. "Well," said Martha, "it was yes to that."

A breeze blew through Felbourne, carrying faint wind-borne scents of coffee. Looking around, Shawn saw Danielle. She'd appeared out of nowhere: standing motionless now by the oak door of the church, watching him. He came toward her, through seed-headed grass and sycamore leaves.

"I read the inscription," she said. "I'm sorry. What time of year did she die?"

"Martha? End of summer. Sixteen months back."

She nodded, silent. Shawn wished she hadn't found him here, by his wife's grave. It made him seem older, sadder, than he wished to be.

"Come on in. Coffee time."

Danielle hesitated, watching him, then nodded. The smell of

coffee was stronger now. There was no other house nearby; Shawn couldn't imagine where it came from. He let Danielle go ahead, across the lane, through the kitchen door. He heard her gasp.

"Who—?" Her question hung in the air.

In the kitchen—an L-shaped room—the washing machine still beeped. Miss Mop was in her cat basket, hissing, watching the visitors, fur fluffed up. Danielle picked up the cat and cuddled her.

A man Shawn knew was bending over his coffee machine. A man he didn't know was seated at his refectory table, tipped back in a bentwood chair.

"Calvin McCord," Shawn said. "All these visits I'm getting. Bobby Walters. Now you."

Calvin wore a suit of cerulean blue. He looked older than when he'd worked with Shawn, in the NukePro group, in Manhattan. He'd shaved his Zapata mustache; his hair was thin enough now to show the scalp beneath. When the espresso machine was adjusted to his satisfaction, he turned his attention back to Shawn.

"Tell me," he said, "what were you thinking? I mean, do you normally leave your door wide open? Any passing badass walks right on in?"

"Like you did."

"Correct," said Calvin. "Except, lucky for you, I'm not a badass." He pointed. "Laptop lying right there on the counter."

Considering his laptop, Shawn saw someone had unlocked the case while he was out. He could guess what they were looking for.

"This evil dude steps in," said Calvin, "this hypothetical scamp—collects that piece of gear, walks on out—tell me," he said to the man in the bentwood chair, "how many dollars we have to the pound these days?"

The man in the bentwood chair, olive skinned, wore a khaki shirt and matching cotton trousers. "Two bucks," he said, "plus change. You're in hock to China."

"Okay," Calvin said to Shawn, "let's just say the guy that's got your stuff, he's up four thousand. Profitable couple of minutes. How would you feel about that?"

"Ask me something else," Shawn said. "Ask me how I feel about getting visits from guys I don't want to see. Bobby Walters I don't mind too much. You, I do. Plus your friend there."

"Apologies," Calvin said. "I should have introduced you. This is Hassan Tarkani. I believe he's about to take his feet off your table. Thank you. Hassan, meet Shawn Maguire. Colleague of mine." He considered Danielle. "We don't, either of us, we don't know this lady."

"Ex-colleague," Shawn said. "I retired."

"Or was retired," Calvin said. "I have to tell you, man, something out there in the garden smells amazing."

Leaving his chair, Hassan walked across the kitchen toward the scullery. "Jasmine."

"Is that right?" Calvin asked. "Jasmine. Tell me, is that a tree or a plant? I could go for one of them."

"Not on the thirty-ninth floor, you couldn't," Hassan said. "You mind if I tend to your washing machine?"

This last question was addressed to Shawn. Danielle's wide-eyed attention shifted among the three men.

"That damn beeping," Calvin said. "Plays hell with your nerves. Isn't that right, lady?"

Danielle nodded. She was leaning against a beechwood bench, alert, watching both of the strangers.

Hassan pressed two buttons on the washing machine, then opened its door. The beeping stopped. Hassan felt the clothes inside the machine. "There you go. Clean undies. Dry as a bone. All you got to do now is fold them."

"See that?" Calvin said to Shawn. "These Pakis, smart as a whip, mostly. Nothing they can't do, except run their own sorry-ass country. Catch Osama."

Hassan said, "And get paid real money."

Calvin said, "Ma'am, I keep waiting. We still don't know your name."

"Danielle," she said.

Shawn left the room. When he came back, he had both hands in his jacket pockets.

Calvin considered him. "Now, now," he said, "I don't believe you would do that, Maguire." The coffee cup he was holding rattled against the saucer. "If we run a quick count around the kitchen, there's two of us here, me and Hassan there. Both of us holding. Then it's one of you, leaving out the nice lady, who I don't believe"—he scanned Danielle—"is carrying. Apart from which"—he made a comprehensive gesture—"you got such a pleasant home here."

"Plus the garden."

"Like Hassan says, plus the garden—which we truly thought was a treat. That jasmine, something else. Be a shame to get yourself run out of the country, Shawn. Which we could arrange. Undesirable alien. Look what you'd lose."

"Besides which," Hassan said, "you haven't asked us why we're here."

"That," Shawn said, "might be because I don't want to know."

"Let me guess," Calvin said to Danielle. "Baptiste? Would that be your family name?"

"You could earn cash," Hassan said to Shawn. "You could help us a little. More than you helped Mr. Rockford. You have something we need, apropos Ayub Abbasi. You told Mr. Walters, he spoke to us, you told him you want cash. We"—he pointed—"we have walking-around money."

"Besides which," Calvin said, "there's a war on. Next time they hit New York, you know, I know, could be nukes." He nodded to Shawn. "Courtesy of Dr. Khan. We're talking war. Good against evil. Christian against Muslim. Children of Darkness, Children of Light. White against black."

"White and brown," Hassan said, considering his own wrist. "White and brown against black."

Calvin looked from Danielle to Shawn. "Freedom under God, you know what I mean? There's a choice here." He looked from Danielle to Shawn. "Like the president says, you're not with us, you're against. Don't sit this out."

"What makes you believe," Danielle asked, "we might do that?"

Calvin shrugged. "Feeling I have. Plus, ma'am, you crop up here and there. You and your man. Entries on a database."

Shawn asked Hassan, "Another question. What makes you think I need money?"

Calvin smiled. "Are you serious? Long as I've known you, Shawn, you've been in debt. It's why you work for scum like Abbasi." He poured more filtered water into the coffee machine, keeping one eye on Shawn. "We checked. You have two bank accounts. Barclays and Citibank, am I right?"

"Both accounts overdrawn," Hassan said. "High five figures."

"Not counting credit cards," said Calvin. "Again, two. Platinum. Both maxed out."

Shawn waved Danielle away from where she was leaning on the worktop, watching Hassan. "Danielle," he said, "walk right over there, will you?"

Calvin moved fast. He put down his coffee cup and raised his hands—lightly tremulous—above waist level.

"Now, Shawn," he said, "don't do this. I was just in Cedars-Sinai. Knee problems."

"Runs in the family," said Hassan. "Next time, you know how it is, anything knee related, insurance won't cover Mr. McCord here. Preexisting condition. What can you do? It's in the small print." Hassan shook his head. "Charge like wounded bulls, those guys."

"Put your hands on the table," Shawn told him. "Don't push your luck."

Calvin had backed the length of the beechwood bench. "Don't be foolish, Shawn."

"We don't know how foolish I might be," Shawn replied. "Remember, I've done foolish things before. It's why Joshua Hoskyn can't walk straight. It's why I'm retired."

"Suspended," Hassan said. "We could fix that."

"Living a quiet life," Shawn said, "away from people I don't want to see."

"Oh, man," said Hassan, "that is unkind."

Watching Shawn, Calvin beckoned his colleague. "Son, say goodbye to the lady. Our friend believes we're outstaying our welcome."

At the door Calvin said, "I still have the same cell, Shawn, if you ever want to call me."

Hassan passed a card to Danielle. "Or you, ma'am. We could talk."

"Close the door behind you," Shawn said. "Do it gently."

At the window, Shawn watched his visitors depart. After a moment, he spoke to Danielle. "You know they were here for you?"

"No," she said. "I don't know. For me? What does that mean?"

Shawn pointed toward the lane. "Blue Chrysler out there. In the backseat, there's a head bag and hypodermics. I didn't see them, but somewhere there'll be handcuffs. That wasn't for me. It was for you. Bait and switch." He paused a moment, thinking it through. "Someone wants you back with your husband. Wherever he is."

16

WEST SUSSEX, 24 MAY 2004

Late in the afternoon, Shawn drove back from the Felbourne railway station with Ashley Victoria Caburn, a stocky, smiling woman
dressed in what she wrongly believed to be current fashion. Born
in Rhode Island of Anglophile parents, Ashley Victoria, schooled
in Cape Cod and Surrey, seemed more English than American.
Her official employment was at a high level of immigration control
within the U.S. Embassy. If she had in fact worked there, she
would now be part of her country's Homeland Security apparatus.
In practice, Ashley was a spy: a brilliant intelligence analyst. Had
she not been female, had she not been right about Iraq when her
superiors were wrong, had her sexual games been more conventional, she would by now have held some senior post in the CIA's
Directorate of Intelligence.

She carried flowers.

Glancing sidelong at this woman—his friend, and Martha's—Shawn reflected on the laws of attraction. A man of his age, he thought, should seek wisdom and judgment; qualities of mind, not flesh. To his shame, these were principles Shawn believed in but failed to practice. He couldn't imagine sex with Ashley. He wanted Danielle in ways that had nothing to do with judgment or wisdom.

In quite other ways, sex was Ashley's weakness. She was in long-running—and so far ineffective—12-step therapy for sex and love addiction. Her boss, disillusioned with his Brahmin wife, once took Ash to bed: an experience she did not enjoy. She doubted he had. Six months later, without further physical contact, she fell deeply in lust with the same man.

Go figure, she'd told Shawn. How do these things happen? Against all advice, she sent her boss inappropriate e-mails, called his Chelsea apartment, waylaid him at the watercooler, tried to get on his flights when he traveled. Only when she was briefly exiled to North Carolina did her passion dim.

Shawn's wife Martha had been Ashley's closest female friend; more than once, recipient of the spy's lovelorn grief. When Ashley came to Martha's funeral, she waited until the guests dispersed, then proposed marriage to Shawn. Now that he was single, she said, it was right they should settle down. She was lonely; she kept misbehaving; the clock was ticking. It was time she had a child.

Shawn had asked for a few weeks to think that through. He was fourteen years older than Ashley; he hadn't been planning on more children. Juanita had broken his heart more often than he cared to recall. Finally, he put the idea on hold.

"Can we go to Martha?" Ashley asked now. "I mean, before we hit the house?"

Shawn swung the car off the road, into his lane.

"We can," he said. He glanced at the flowers Ashley held. "Those are for her?" He edged the car around Justin Hallam Fox's border collie, rolling in roadside dust. "If I didn't say so, it's good of you to come down."

"Not entirely disinterested," Ashley remarked, gazing around her. Hawthorn hedges frosted with blossom; chestnut leaves unfolding their early-summer softness; moorhens leading their brood of sooty chicks across the unpaved lane.

"God, this is beautiful. I could live here, now she's gone." Ash shifted in her seat. "I'm hoping you'll see sense and marry me. I know you turned me down, but it was the wrong time to ask. At the funeral. Even I see that now." She paused a moment, considering him, then said, "I have to tell you this. It won't get easier, Shawn. Men think they stay sexy. You believe young women want you. Not true. Young women want young guys. Good bodies. Fifty plus, my friend, you're pretty much out of the game."

Shawn thought of what he might say, and decided not to say it. He parked in the lane opposite his house, at the churchyard gate. Ashley made no move to leave the car.

"Flowers?" he reminded her. "For Martha?"

She said, "I'm not finished. Inside information. There's been an official complaint. Something you did to Robertson Reynolds. You know? Property guy? Owns half Manhattan. He's unhappy, not to say royally pissed. He has influence. Big GOP donor." She turned to look at Shawn. "I never heard the details. What did you do?"

"I had a thing going with Ellen. His wife."

"Knowing you," said Ashley, "I could have guessed. There's also Calvin McCord."

"So I keep hearing," Shawn said. "Gets around, that guy. He was here, in my kitchen. Now what's he done?"

"Contacted all our agencies. All intel."

"All sixteen?"

"Uh-huh."

"About?"

"You," she said. "Heads-up is, hands off. Do not hire this person."

"Why would Calvin do that?"

"Three possible reasons," Ashley said. "First, he thinks you're insufficiently interested in the safety of our nation. Second, you're working for a jihadist. Third, he doesn't like you. These are not incompatible, one with another." She made herself comfortable in the car. "You know I love gossip. Tell me what went down with Mrs. Robertson Reynolds."

"Well," Shawn said, "what do you want? Young wife, old husband. He's out of town, buying up the rest of the world. Making more money than he'll ever spend. That's how it started."

"What's interesting," said Ashley, "is the finale. The last act. Tell me—how'd it end?"

Shawn's affair with Ellen Reynolds ended the night her husband returned early to his Park Avenue apartment. Robertson wasn't expected until the following day. Several million dollars richer than the day before, missing his young bride, he'd caught an early plane from Houston and arrived home while Shawn was in Robertson's bedroom at one in the morning, doing the kind of intimate things to Ellen that dismayed her husband as much as they pleased her. Shawn was in his undershirt, his face between Ellen's permatanned thighs, and moments later, there stood the property billionaire, at the door of his own bedroom, looking from his wife—now covered by a cream sheet—to the man perched on the edge of his, Robertson's, king-sized bed.

Shawn had a panicky moment, thinking the old man might be armed, while his own private-issue Glock was inside his pants, mixed in with Ellen's scattered underthings on the far side of the room.

Then he saw that Robertson would do no harm to anyone, except perhaps himself.

The old man was weeping; weeping clumsily, helplessly, as if it were something he'd never learned to do. His dark coarse-skinned face collapsed in pachydermatous folds. His breath came in long, sobbing sighs. He walked, stumbling, toward his wife, ignoring the man in his room. He knelt on Ellen's side of the bed, pawing her prone body.

"Don't," he kept saying, between breaths. "Oh, don't. Please. Please, Ellen, don't."

While Robertson wept on his wife's breast Shawn dressed, checked that he still had his pistol, and left the bedroom. At the door, he looked back. Ellen's naked arms were wrapped around her elderly husband, soothing him as the weeping died.

Shawn descended the mansion's marble staircase promising himself not to see the woman again; wondering why, right now, he felt such a son of a bitch. He'd always known Robertson was out there; always known how much it would hurt the old guy if he knew another man was sleeping with his young and nubile wife. Why should it be so much worse, now that he'd actually seen the man?

Now that he'd seen him dissolve in helpless tears?

Walking back across town in the warmth of a summer night, Shawn promised himself that from here on out, he'd be faithful to Martha. Nothing more on the side. Ever. It was then, at this penitent moment, that he knew he'd lost his office-issue laptop. For an instant—when he thought he'd left it in Ellen's room—Shawn wondered if he could face going back to the mansion. Then he remembered he'd gone straight to the bedroom, with Ellen and without the computer, which, back then, had been the last thing on his mind.

Minutes later he called the cell phone of his protégé, Calvin McCord.

"McCord," Shawn had said, "I know what time it is. I also know you're working for me, so get your ass out of bed, if that's where it happens to be. Go to Harlem, check these bars. They're closed, open them up. One of them has my laptop, I hope to hell." He listened, then said, "Of course it's got classified shit on the fucking disk. You think I'd be standing here pissing my pants if it didn't?"

Shawn confirmed that Calvin had a pen and something to write on, then gave the names of three uptown bars. As it turned out, he could have saved his breath. At 3:00 A.M., he found his machine where he'd left it, untouched, in La Cucina, still open in the Village.

"Which," Shawn said, "didn't stop the little mother telling Rockford I lost my laptop."

"Come on," said Ashley. "You were right about Afghanistan. Right about A. Q. Khan. That was enough to get you fired. You just made it easy for them."

"You know Calvin got my job?"

Ashley said, "Of course I know. Boy done good. Wrote the speech for Colin Powell."

This was news to Shawn. "You mean—*that* speech? United Nations? Why we had to invade Iraq?"

"That's the one."

"But," Shawn said, "Jesus God, it was fiction—end to end. I mean, please. Mobile labs? Armed nukes? Fucking fiction."

"What can I tell you?" Ashley asked. "Garbage in, garbage out."

In the shotgun seat of the Merc, with the door open, parked outside St. Perpetua's churchyard, Ashley was giggling.

"Shawn," she said, "Shawn, you can still make me laugh. Such a gift for screwing up your own life. Coloring way, way outside the lines." She shook her head. "Even by your standards, losing your laptop—that was a clusterfuck."

"I'd be amused," Shawn said, "if there was something I could do about it. My career, I mean. Something I could do to get back in the business. I guess that door's closed."

Ashley climbed out of the car, treading carefully across the lane to the graveyard.

"You guess right," she said. "As we speak, Calvin's locking it."

Ashley knelt in sun-dappled grass by Martha's grave, arranging the flowers she'd brought. Seven shades of blue. Though Shawn had worked with her since they met in Fayetteville, Ashley had been Martha's friend more than his. The two women came together when Ash was investigating a sophisticated system of money transfers that she believed (rightly, it proved) were financing terrorist cells. Martha was a highly paid money hunter, first for Kroll and then for other firms. She led Ash through the intricacies of financial migration: the tsunami of hot and cold cash washing daily around the world. The two women worked together for months until Ashley felt ready to move on the money laundry. When she did, her boss, of course, took the credit. It was, Ash said, no more than she deserved after the trouble she'd caused the guy.

When Shawn had his own troubles with the covert-action outfit he joined after being retired from the Agency, Ash offered a shoulder to cry on, as he and Martha once did for her. Now she stood by the grave, brushing dirt from ill-fitting designer jeans, a dampness about her eyes.

"I miss her, Shawn. God, I miss her." Sunlight through sycamores cast shifting shadows on the grass. "Such a beautiful place she's buried in. I'm sure she knows it."

"It's what she wanted," Shawn said. "To lie here. She told me that when she—when she knew, she kind of knew, I think, she wouldn't make it." Ash leaned over and kissed him then, this time a sisterly kiss. "I didn't—I didn't handle it too good." He thought back to Martha, alone in a white hospital ward. "Seeing her in bed. Those damn tubes in her body. Hickman line in her neck. Then"—he gestured around him—"you know, hearing her talk about this place. The churchyard. She just lay there, Ash. No illusions. Didn't listen to the doctors. Knew she wouldn't make it. Knew she'd die." He paused a while, then said, "You think—I used to think—death, it's final. One minute you're here, in life, next minute, gone. Well, it's not like that. It's slow, it's rough. Messy. Real hard to bear."

"For all of us."

"That's the truth," he said. "The ones who stay, the ones who go."

Ash watched him, wondering how to respond.

"You'll think I'm crazy—some days in the house I hear her voice."

"Martha's?"

Shawn nodded.

"That's not crazy," Ash said. "She loved this place. She won't leave easy. She'll be with you awhile."

They were silent then, one on each side of the grave, remembering the woman who lay between them. The churchyard was thick with wild cyclamen and flowering primrose. Late bluebells were still in bloom. The scent of jasmine drifted across the lane.

At last, Ash moved away. "I know you loved her. I'm sure you did. And yet—there's Ellen—"

"If you think love's that simple, Ash," Shawn said, "you maybe saw the signs, but you've never been down the road."

Ash was moving toward the churchyard gate, looking across the lane to the rectory. In Shawn's driveway stood a van that had painted on its side the words SQUIRREL MAN.

She pointed. "Does he have a name?"

"Squirrel Man? Another name? I asked him that. He said, call me Squirrel Man."

Ash shifted her gaze to the rectory. "It's so much her house. I can't imagine you living here. Not alone." She was watching him. "You came back, though."

"I was out of work. You know that."

"You would have come anyway. Martha could always beat out whoever you had over there." She turned her gaze to Shawn's cro-quet lawn, which spread to the right of the house. "Is that the current squeeze?" She pointed. "On the grass?"

Shawn looked where Ashley was pointing. Danielle was on the lawn, in a deck chair, reading in the sun. She wore a bikini top and shorts. It was the first time Shawn had seen this much of her body. He felt he was getting to know the girl in stages, like one of those kids' books where you fold down sections—head, torso, loins, leg—to create complete people.

Crazy, he thought, this thing with Danielle. He should quit. Let her find the prisoner. He walked through the leaf-strewn churchyard, toward the lych-gate.

"On the lawn? That's Dani. Squeeze, no. I'm trying to get her out of my life."

"Doesn't look like you're trying too hard," Ashley remarked. "She's staying here?"

"Not the way you think." He pointed to the rectory's east wing. "Separate bedroom."

"Because?"

"Her choice. She's married. Decent girl, she says."

Ash paused at the gate to the garden, by Squirrel Man's painted van. "What she's wearing now—does that count as decent?" She glanced sideways at Shawn. "You never learn, do you? It's always body—never brain."

"She wasn't raised by wolves," Shawn said. "Speaks in whole sentences. Come meet her. She's the reason you're here."

"Really?" Ash said. "I thought you liked my company. Maybe wanted to marry me."

"You're a wonderful friend," Shawn said. "Could we settle for that?"

"I have friends," Ash said. "More, I don't need."

On the rectory lawn, Shawn introduced these two very different women. "Ashley Victoria Caburn, Danielle Baptiste." Danielle unfolded herself from her canvas seat. Her skin was darkening in the pale Sussex sun. There was a narrow gap between her stomach and the belt of her shorts. "Ash works at the embassy," Shawn said. "She has some data, might help you find Darius."

Danielle shrugged herself into a denim shirt, which, Shawn believed, was one of his. She held a hand out to Ashley. "Enchanted." A comprehensive gesture. "How do you like the place? Or have you seen it before?"

The garden was at its most beguiling: stephanotis flowering, cherry blossoms lingering, iris around the lake, summer foliage unfolding. Chestnuts—their leaves like open hands—learning to be trees. Bumblebees staggering from flower to flower. A faint scent of wood smoke. Somewhere, the crazy knocking of woodpeckers.

Ash lacked interest in the natural world. Falling out of love, she ate too much. Overweight, she sweated lightly in the sun. "Shawn tells me you're worried about your husband."

"What would you think?" Danielle asked. "I mean, he is in Paris, one day he goes missing, we hear he is taken from the street. There is no word for a week. You believe I would not worry?"

Ash was impervious to anger. "You assume it's a Company heist?"

Danielle shook her head a little, catching up with this turn of the conversation. "Heist? It means—?"

"In this case, kidnap," Shawn said. "CIA kidnap." To Ashley he said, "Who knows? It has the marks. Foreign territory. Fast, efficient. Flown out of France, most likely. No airport record. Leaving aside whether they got the right guy."

"Modus?"

"Paris, *quatrième*. Two men in masks, we're told: cuffs, a sap, head bag. Black car, Volvo, in this case. Drives off, direction of the airport. Prisoner in back." He made a hypodermic gesture. "Injected, I guess." He pointed toward the house. "Come inside. Tell us where Osmani could be. Tell us about the jails. I have maps."

Walking across the mower-striped lawn, Ash spoke quietly. She said, "I know what you're doing, Shawn. You're looking for another Martha. You won't marry me. I'm not the body you want. Not that thin, not that sexy." She paused, looking back to where Danielle watched the cat leap at dragonflies hovering around the edge of the lake. "She's not the one. Whatever you have going with this girl, it'll end in tears." She pushed open the door of the house. "Remember where you heard it first."

In Shawn's front hall, at the foot of the stairs, a small man in overalls knelt in silence, perhaps in prayer. His skull was clean shaven, though his face was not. As Ashley entered, he stood, turned, and ran up the stairs.

"Squirrel Man," Shawn told his visitor. "Also a warlock, he tells me. It's why he prays before he kills critters."

"Like our president. Muslims, in his case."

Shawn watched the vanishing warlock. "Clears them out of the roof space." He pointed Ashley to her left. "This way. Books, maps, Pimm's."

Danielle, buttoning her shirt, caught up. "Warlock is what?" she asked.

From upstairs came the sound of furniture moving.

"Male witch. Don't ask what it has to do with squirrels. No clue."

In the drawing room, Ash, thirsty, poured from a jug full of greenery into a crystal glass.

"My," she said to Shawn, "aren't we English? Country house, lake, dovecote. Sheep. Pimm's." She considered her glass. "More like a marsh than a drink." She glanced around the room: the cornices, the murals, the chairs, the colors. "God, Martha had such taste. I could live here, if I was asked. Wouldn't change a thing."

Danielle was not drinking. "After kidnap, what then?"

Ashley said, "I don't know. Ship the guy someplace. Selected location. Post 9/11, we keep them offshore. Someplace they don't have Red Cross inspection."

Shawn poured more Pimm's. "But do have electrodes."

"Shawn, shame," said Ashley. "I see why Calvin has his doubts." With her refilled glass, she moved to one of the maps Shawn had set out on a cherrywood table. "Here we go. All this stuff's in public domain. If it's not on the Web, it will be. We have black prisons"—she moved a finger from place to place—"Poland, Jordan, Morocco, Belarus, Egypt, Libya, Pakistan, Syria, North Korea, Myanmar—"

"In the axis of evil?"

From somewhere on an upper floor came the sound of running feet.

"You know how it is," Ash told Danielle. "Evil's relative. Depends who's talking." She marked jail locations on Shawn's map. "These I can tell you. Some guy did an FOI on the Agency's flight plans. Seems we fly suspects in Gulfstreams—"

Shawn was listening to noise from the floor above.

"Gulfstreams?" Danielle asked.

"Executive jets from Georgia. Georgia, USA." Ashley moved round the room, examining paintings Martha had bought. "Nice way to fly, if you're not head-bagged, cuffed, shackled to a bed."

"When you have flight plans—what?"

Ashley was bored with this woman. She wanted to lie down, stretch out, talk to Shawn about marriage or, at least, living together in this half-empty mansion.

"We have flight plans, we know where the planes go. Where they go, honey, that's where the jails are."

Danielle was quiet then. She stood by a long window, looking out at the garden, her breathing uneven. When Shawn put a tentative hand on her shoulder, she shrugged him away.

Shawn saw Squirrel Man exit fast from a side door into the garden. He carried a metal cage and a package.

"A person is picked up in Paris. Like my husband. Where would they take him?"

Kicking off her shoes, Ashley lay back on a chaise longue: one that Martha had bought at a village auction. She, too, looked out at the garden. She'd been at a Mayfair party last night. Now she wanted to sleep, though not alone. She raised her head to drink.

"Where would they take him? My dear, it could be anywhere. We move them, country to country. Frequent flyers." She tried to focus on Danielle, on the girl behind the looks. "Your husband's Iranian?"

"Darius? Yes. He has a French passport, and Iranian. His research base was here."

"Why was he in Paris?"

Danielle said, "I can't tell. Maybe a girlfriend."

"Ahh." This was territory Ashley knew. "He had lovers?"

"Not that I heard. Of course, you know, wives are the ones who do not hear."

Squirrel Man knocked on a French window. He was trampling tender plants, standing in a flower bed Henry Thackeray had planted with Japanese anemones. When Shawn opened the window, the room filled with the scents of freesia and jasmine.

"Got three, Mr. Maguire," said Squirrel Man. "Little bastards."

Two squirrels crouched on the floor of their cage; a third stood on its hind legs, gnawing with rodent teeth at the imprisoning mesh.

On the chaise longue, Ash pushed herself upright. "Let them loose."

"Can't, ma'am," Squirrel Man told her. "Against the law."

"What law?"

"Tree rats," said Squirrel Man, changing tack. "Rats with tails, that's all they are."

"All rats have tails."

"Furry's what I mean," said Squirrel Man. "Furry tails. Let 'em go, little scamps, next thing, they be back up your roof space, chewing insulation off your wires. Dry's tinder up there, Mr. Maguire. Two bare wires, one spark, whooff, that's your house gone. Up in smoke." He offered Shawn the laptop case he was carrying. "You must've left it in the roof. Don't know what you was doing. Not a lot up there. Wires and pipes." He blew on the case. "No dust, hardly."

Shawn had never been in his roof space. He considered the little case, the name DELL imprinted on it. He started to open it; stopped as it grew suddenly warm. He paused a moment, then, moving swiftly, went through the open window, pushing past the startled Squirrel Man.

The rodent hunter turned to watch his employer race across the croquet lawn.

Ash reached out to pour herself another drink. Drops spilled on the cream chaise longue. "Full of surprises, our host," she remarked to Danielle. "Who knew he could move so fast?"

Danielle, too, was watching Shawn. "Or why."

On the far side of the croquet green, Shawn spun the satchel like a discus into a dense grove of laurels. He was already running backward as the bushes turned to skeletal shapes limned against a white and blinding sheet of fire.

In moments, the laurels were blackened sticks. Something sharp and acrid mingled with the smell of wood smoke.

"Oh my God," Ash said, entranced.

Leaving his cage and captives on the lawn, Squirrel Man ran for his van, arms arched over his head as if to protect himself from falling debris.

Shawn walked slowly backward toward his drawing room's open window.

"Jesus, Shawn," Ash said, "that thing was in your roof space? White phosphorus? Someone doesn't wish you well. Should we get out of the house?"

"I doubt there's anything else," Shawn said. He nodded at the smoking hedge. "That would have been enough."

"In the right place, no question," Ash said. "All the same." She stepped cautiously into the garden, opening the squirrel cage. "I feel better outside." She looked toward the roof. "Timer set. House burns. Electrical fire. Dodgy wiring. Squirrel damage. No questions; case closed. Smart stuff. Do we know who might want you dead?"

"Well," Shawn said, "assassination's a bit like Dani's theory on wives and affairs. The person most concerned is the last to know."

Danielle was still in the drawing room, at the window, listening. "May never know."

"Unless what you said in Paris is right," Shawn told her. "Death is where the pain starts."

They stood in silence awhile as the hedge burned down. Smoke drifted toward the Grange.

Ashley asked, "You have any visitors? People alone in the house? Anyone I'd know?"

"Calvin McCord," Shawn said. "Plus a sidekick. Pakistani. Hassan Someone."

"Well, well," Ash said. "Those boys."

"It could have been me," Danielle said. "I have been alone in the house."

"Sure, sweetheart," said Ashley. "You look like an arsonist. What would be your motive?" She nodded at Shawn. "You need this guy. Why would you burn his house?" To Shawn she said, "Will you follow up on Calvin and Hassan?"

"Tell the local cops?" Shawn asked. "Constable, I have no evidence, but I believe two intel agents tried to incinerate my house. Call D.C., will you? Ask them to extradite."

"Mmm," Ashley said. "Problem." She turned to Danielle, who was watching the fire burn out. "If I was starting, looking for your man, I'd try Fes."

"Morocco?"

"We have a jail," Ashley said. "Shared establishment—near Temara. Good start."

Danielle watched her. "If you have many jails, why this?"

Still considering the scorched laurels, Ash sipped the last of her drink. "Public knowledge," she said. "We pay people in Morocco. Lot of Gulfstreams go there. If your guy's a frequent flyer, that's his first stop."

"Fes?"

"Fes or Rabat. Temara. If you like, I'll check the file."

Which, Shawn thought, you've already done.

Where the hedge had been, there was only white powder.

Though it was still warm, Danielle shivered, thin arms wrapped around her body. "For an immigration person," she said, "you know a lot about rendition."

The breeze shifted, blowing sour smoke back toward them.

"Ah, well," Ashley said, "rendition. It's an area of interest. We all have things we're curious about. This happens to be one of mine." She touched Shawn's cheek. "As for you—from what I hear, my love, you should take care where you travel."

"Even in Morocco?"

"Especially in Morocco."

17

In a twin-bedded room of the Riad El Medina Hotel, Danielle Baptiste stood at an uncurtained floor-to-ceiling window, considering peopled streets in the old-town quarter of Fes. It brought back memories of childhood. Level rays of early sun warmed her. Closing her eyes, she unbuttoned her jacket. From a minaret somewhere, a muezzin called. On a mahogany chest of drawers, she'd put a monochrome photo of her husband, Darius. In the photo, the man's eyes were not on the photographer but fixed on some point, some distant point, beyond him. Though Darius was young, that detached gaze reminded Shawn of a suspect he'd once interrogated: an old man; a man who at least seemed old. With Arabs, he'd found, it's hard to guess at age.

That man—the prisoner—saw some person who was not, in truth, within the room; a being who was, perhaps, dead. Shawn never discovered who it was, or what it was, that the man saw. Until the day of his death, under extreme interrogation, the suspect refused to confess, or even speak. For all the interrogators knew, he might have been deaf, mute, or simply stubborn. It was hard to tell.

Without turning, Danielle said, "We're sleeping in the same room?"

Shawn unpacked a black leather bag, which was all he carried these days, going abroad. "We're doing a lot of traveling, looking for your husband."

She turned from the window then. "Tell me. You think that's a waste of money?"

"If I thought it was a waste of money, I wouldn't do it."

Ayub Abbasi's money had settled some of his debts. Not, by any means, all.

"What I know," Shawn said, "these days, I don't have a paycheck. I may never work. There's a limit, what I can afford."

He wanted to share this room. No reason she should know that.

"I have money."

"Okay," Shawn said, "okay, rich girl. You have money. Go buy yourself another room. What do you think I'm going to do in here? Rape you?"

She knelt down then, trying to make the air conditioner work. A slow-moving ceiling fan stirred the room's torpid air without cooling it. She pulled off a sweater, making her shirt ride up. Her tan was fading. She rolled her sleeves. As a child, she'd loved this warmth.

"It's happened before."

It took him moments to work out what she meant.

"Rape?"

"Rape."

"Come on," he said. "That was some asshole from Atlanta. I'm a sweet old guy from Alabama. I don't do that stuff."

Somewhere in this town, Shawn had found a half pint of good whisky. He checked the time. He filled a tooth glass he'd taken from the bathroom.

"I don't know what you do with women." Danielle pushed windows wider. "I'm curious."

"Ask me," he said. "I'll tell you the truth."

She laughed and then was quiet, fanning herself with a travel magazine. She could feel her temperature rising. Across the room, he folded clothes, squaring them up, retying the laces, stacking them in the only closet.

He was neat, she noticed. More than neat. Military, maybe.

"All right," she said. "We have time. Tell me how it started. First sex. First time in love."

"Why would you want to know?" He thought for some moments, deciding what to say; deciding how honest to be. "Okay. First sex—a kid called Ann-Mistique, if you believe that. Ann-Mistique Proffitt. She was fifteen."

"Even in Alabama," Danielle said, "must have been—"

"Under age? Sure. Long story. Sheriff involved." He thought awhile. "Then there was Venetia. Actress. After that, I married a stoner called Lala. I know. I know. Both mistakes. I thought, hell, that's it. I'm through with marriage."

"What happened?"

"Meeting Martha, meeting her again, that's what happened."

"The one who died?"

"Uh-huh." He looked across the room. "Are you okay?"

"Mmm. Not sure. I'm hot. Tell me about Martha."

"Jesus," he said, thinking back, "where to start? She was smarter than me. I didn't know girls could be that smart. First date was after church. Church of Christ Betrayed, in Turkey Forge. Back then I used to dream about her—teen dreams. I'd buy her a ring, we'd marry, find a house, have kids, settle down."

"You were how old?"

"Don't mock. I was nineteen. It's what people did, those days. Least, they did where I come from. Get married in church, buy a tract house, few hundred dollars down. Beds from the bed store. Move in, have kids. That's your life."

She was sitting now, knees up under her chin. It took him back to the day he'd met her, in a Paris apartment.

"But," she said.

"Yeah. But. Martha wasn't singing from the same sheet. Leaves Alabama—lights out for L.A. Broke my heart. She wrote a script, thought she could make a movie."

Danielle put a hand over her mouth.

"Laugh," he said. "Sure. We all did. Then it happened. Someone, some guy in that crazy business, he picked up her script. Blind luck."

"Maybe it was a good script."

"You still need luck."

"The movie was made?"

"It was. We all—me and my buddies—whole big gang—we all hit the theater. This is Turkey Forge. There it was, up on-screen: 'Script by Martha Semel.' I thought, damn, this isn't right. She's supposed to be back here, marrying me, having kids, not making movies in Hollywood." He paused for a moment. "Maybe would have made me straighten up and fly right."

Danielle was lying back now, listening, her face shiny with sweat. "She never came back?"

Shawn shook his head. "You're in Hollywood, why would you?"

He stopped talking, watching her, then leaned across and touched her forehead.

"You sure you're okay? You're hot."

She said, "I'm catching something. I felt it on the plane. Not serious." She watched him, her eyes a deeper green in this light. "You were telling me—what came next?"

"What came next? I told you—fell out with my daddy. Started drinking straights. Bad habit, so I found. Drove up to D.C., signed with the marines. That's when I married Lala. Great ass, meanest temper."

"Ohh," she said, "of course, not you? You were never wrong?"

"Don't start," he said. "You sound like her." Then he said, "No, take it back. Wasn't Lala so much, it was me. We couldn't ever agree what to do with Juanita."

"Juanita was your daughter?"

"Still is," Shawn said. "Except I never see her."

Thinking back, it's easy to see what went astray. Juanita was Shawn's darling. He raised her like a boy: taught her to hunt deer and dive for fish. Then other things took over his life: money, women, work, whisky. One day, around her fourteenth birthday, Juanita stopped speaking. She continued with her daily routine as if nothing had happened. Shower, dress, cornflakes, fruit, milk, take books, pack bag, walk to school down the block. She just didn't talk. As far as Shawn could make out, Juanita did her schoolwork, neatly, precisely, without speaking to anyone. Lala said to leave her be: Kid'll grow out of it, she said. Whatever it was. Shawn couldn't do that. The longer Juanita kept silent, the more he felt he'd failed. He cracked jokes, played tricks, drew cartoons, bought gifts Juanita didn't want. He blamed Lala for what was happening. Lala fought back, refusing blame. She fought in other ways, refusing sex. Shawn felt bad about his wife, worse about his daughter.

He would have done anything for Juanita. In the end, there was nothing he could do.

"Except," Shawn said, "it got worse. I split up with Lala."

"What happened with Juanita?

"She blamed us both. Me more." While Shawn spoke he was considering Danielle. Her eyes were unnaturally bright now: She glowed with inner heat. "You are catching something. Running a temperature. Get in bed."

"Okay," she said. "I think that's right."

She headed for the bathroom. He took a swallow of whisky and went back to unpacking.

"So," he said, raising his voice, "that was the first time I fell in love. That was the wife I missed back then. Martha. Took me twenty-some years to put it right. Find her, marry her. You wonder, don't you, how something like that might have changed your life. If you'd gotten the timing right."

Shawn freed his Makarov from its wrapping. Even for those with security-stamped passports, it was getting harder to move firearms through airports, even one as haphazard as Heathrow. He loaded a fresh clip of shells. It was quite some time since he'd used a weapon in anger. He wondered when he'd do it again. Whether he could still bring himself to do it.

Danielle came from the bathroom, heading for bed. She wore a T-shirt that brushed the tops of her thighs. The shirt was one of his. It read, in bold type, DOES NOT PLAY WELL WITH OTHERS. In bed, she lay facedown, half covered by a sheet. When she spoke her voice was muffled. "Tell me," she said. "Tell me about Martha. Tell me what happened."

"She died," he said. "I told you. That's what happened."

Facedown, like Danielle. That was how Shawn found Martha one morning in Sussex, when he came in from tending his sheep. Any other morning, she would have been in the kitchen, making coffee and toast, with the kitten beside her on the bench. Shawn was shocked to find her still in bed.

When she heard him come into the room, Martha said, "Shawn, I don't want you to worry, but something's wrong. I broke a rib."

He stopped in the doorway, filled not with worry but with mindless dread.

"You broke—what do you mean—you broke a rib? Did you fall?" Cautiously, he sat himself on the edge of the bed, touching her back. "Martha, what did you do?"

Facedown, her voice was indistinct. "I bent down. I was picking up a pillow."

"No," Shawn said. "No. You can't. You can't break ribs that way."

He wasn't a believer in portents, but now, from nowhere, a cloud hung over their future.

Martha said, "You know what? I bent down again—it happened again. I broke another rib. Shawn, I'm aching all over. Something's wrong."

The kitten that slept at Martha's feet had abandoned the bed. From a windowsill, it watched, eyes wide, fur fluffed. In the roof beams, some insect ticked like a hand-wound clock.

Later that morning, Dr. Reuben Gibb, portly and choleric, drove out from Chichester to the rectory in Felbourne. Plagued by heartburn, the doctor was not, by choice, a house-call man. He took Martha's temperature—which was normal—and a blood sample. Shawn had to help Martha to the bathroom so she could give the doctor a sample of urine.

Dr. Gibb thought the pain came from back strain. Maybe, he said, a slipped disk. He forced a smile. At our age, he said, all too common. However, not serious. He prescribed Tylenol and chiropracty and recommended a back-pain man, a good fellow, in Hazlehurst.

As he climbed into his veteran Ford, the doctor told Shawn, in confidence, that most of Martha's pains were imaginary. This was true, he said, of many women: illness imagined—hypochondria, stress, sexual dissatisfaction, menopause. Female problems. Say no more. It may be, whispered Dr. Gibb, gripping Shawn's arm, it may be something in the marriage. Not going well. No reflection on you, old man. Could be the time of life.

"You know how women are," said Dr. Gibb through the window of his car. "In the medical trade"—with his hands he made quote marks—"these women. Worried well, we call them."

"It's me that's worried," Shawn said. "She's unwell."

By then, though, Dr. Gibb had closed his car window and was struggling with the starter.

From inside the house, Martha was calling her husband. She stayed in bed that weekend. She said the pain seemed to move— seemed to move from place to place, around her body. "Which makes it sound like the damn doctor was right. It's just something I imagine." Her breathing was shallow then: To breathe deep was painful. "I'm not imagining. Believe me, I'm not."

Shawn, with the sadness of the condemned, said, "I never thought you were. Not for a heartbeat. It's not a thing you do."

He brought drinks—water, juice, vitamin mix—and made meals; didn't know what else to do. With the little cat, he went outside to pick lettuce and asparagus. He hulled broad beans for salads. He needed to stay active, needed to stop thinking about what might lie ahead.

Late on a Saturday afternoon, when he came back from tending his doves, Shawn found a beautiful dark-haired woman—in her late thirties, he guessed—standing on his stoop, breathing in the scent of the jasmine that grew around the door frame.

She held out a hand. "Mr. Maguire? I'm Dr. Haber. Susan Haber. I'm a partner in a practice with Dr. Gibb. You know? An older man. He drove out to see your wife."

"I do know," Shawn said. "Thanks for coming all this way."

"Well," said Susan Haber, "I fear you may not thank me. I'm not bearing good news." She pointed to a cedarwood seat on the edge of the croquet lawn. "Shall we sit?"

Shawn felt a chill, as if clouds covered the sun, though the sky was clear and the day still warm. He perched on the end of the garden seat, as far as possible from the doctor, as though she herself might be the bearer of illness: might carry some contagious and terminal disease.

"We now have a report on your wife's blood and urine samples," Susan Haber said.

"And?"

"We would have to do more tests," she said, "but immunofixation shows there is a high level of creatinine and an abnormally high level of paraprotein in the blood."

Dumb, he looked at her.

"Sorry about the language. It's causing what we call hyperviscosity syndrome. That just means her blood has thickened beyond normal viscosity."

He felt as if he were losing Martha. She was leaving him: vanishing in a deluge of medical jargon.

"Could we cut to the chase? What is all that? What's it mean? Is it bad?"

She was looking toward the lake, not meeting his eyes.

"It can be, Mr. Maguire. Over time, amyloidosis and hyperviscosity lead to organ—even mental—dysfunction. The real worry is, what's causing this? Where's the protein coming from?"

He said nothing for a while, thinking. "Okay. Tell me. What is it? What's causing it?"

"Those signs suggest multiple myeloma." She reached out to put a small hand over his. "It's a cancer of the bone marrow. With multiple myeloma, the patient starts producing quantities of abnormal plasma cells in his or her bone marrow. The cells grow and multiply uncontrollably. They invade adjacent tissues and organs. They spread—spread through the lymphatics or through the blood vessels. The bones themselves weaken."

"Would that explain cracked ribs?"

She tightened her grip on his hand. "I'm so sorry."

He wanted her to go. Wanted this visit not to have happened.

"Tell me," he said, after a time, "if it *is* this thing—" He'd already forgotten the word. His voice sounded to him like another person's voice, as if he were suddenly aged. He heard his father's voice in his own. "If it is this thing, what do we do? Is it curable?"

"Finally, no, it's not. Some patients go into remission."

"Some do?"

She watched him, waiting.

"If some do, you mean, most don't?"

She shook her head. "Unfortunately, that is what I mean. We should get your wife into hospital."

"Hospital? For incurable cancer?"

She said, "Mr. Maguire, there's always a chance it's not myeloma. There's always a chance of beating the odds. I told you, some patients do have a recovery."

"You said for a while."

"I'm so sorry, but that's what remission means. If you agree, I'll call her an ambulance."

"Please," Shawn said. He wasn't thinking clearly. "I know you're trying to help, but not now. Not now. Let me talk to Martha." He paused, then said, "She's always been the one who took charge."

The doctor sat still for a minute, watching him, her eyes wide, like the eyes of the kitten on the sill.

"Your decision," she said. "Just don't leave it too long. If we're right about the myeloma, your wife's time is running out."

In Fes, Shawn ran downstairs to the lobby of the Riad El Medina. A group of young Western women in flowing rainbow robes and headbands sat around a carved table, telling each other's fortune with packs of worn tarot cards, each illustrated with a somber woodcut. One of the women was black, Shawn noticed; up to that moment, he'd never seen a black hippie. This girl had prominent breasts, wide hips, and a narrow waist. Blue-painted nails. She brought to mind the Wanted posters of Angela Davis, back whenever it was: the time he'd joined the Agency. Three of the other girls—Americans, Indian and white—were smoking water pipes and giggling at the cards.

The black woman turned over a card that showed a graphic skeleton astride a dark horse. "Oh, my Lord," she said, crossing herself. "Death. Someone about to die."

Shawn spoke to a headscarved Moroccan woman behind the reception desk. "Do you speak English? My wife's ill. She's running a temperature. High temperature. Can I ask you to call a doctor?"

GERARD MACDONALD

For some moments, the receptionist was silent, considering him. She started to say something, then stopped. "The woman is not your wife," she said finally. "I have her passport. Today is our holiday. No doctor will come."

Shawn held hands clenched by his sides, telling himself to be calm. "Okay. Can you tell me where I could get a thermometer?"

The receptionist, still polite, said no.

"No, you can't tell me, or no, I can't get one?"

Someone touched him. Shawn turned to find the black woman standing close, her hand on his arm.

"Man," she said, "relax. Anger get you no place. Won't even make you feel better, most likely." She held out a hand. "Clemency."

"What does that mean?"

"My name. Clemency. I'm a nurse."

For the second time that morning, Shawn looked closely at her.

"I know," she said, "I know. But when I'm out of these trinkets, I have me a uniform. Chicago. Cook County Hospital." Watched by the silent receptionist, she moved toward the stairs. "Let's come see your lady. On the way, I go pick me up a thermometer."

They climbed stairs together. On the third flight, Clemency paused. "You don't mind me saying this," she said, "you-all not looking too good yourself. You really worried about your woman?"

Shawn nodded. He'd paused, holding the stair rail, breathing hard.

"You in love with her?"

Shawn, reluctant to answer, said nothing.

"She younger than you?"

"Thirteen years."

"Oh, man," she said. "Oh, man."

Shawn unlocked his room and watched from the doorway as Clemency went in to sit on the edge of the bed in which Danielle

146

slept. He was surprised by the gentleness of her movements. She touched her patient's forehead. "If it's okay," she said to Shawn, "I like you outside for a minute, with the door shut. What I have is a rectal thermometer."

Four minutes later, when Clemency opened the door to Shawn, Danielle was awake, covered by a sheet, and propped on pillows. Despite the damp cloth held to her forehead, she radiated heat.

"Hundred three, just over," Clemency said. "Kind of high. Food poisoning, maybe. Something she drank? But fever's breaking, is my view." To Danielle, she said, "Girlfriend, you keep yourself right here, drink a whole lot, don't eat much, canned soup maybe, sleep when you can. My guess, this time tomorrow, worst gon' be over." To Shawn, she said, "You need to go out, buy this girl a bunch of bottled water."

"Thank you both," Danielle said. Her voice was weak. "Can't remember the last time I was sick."

"Not your fault," Clemency said. "That's nature, doing that. Working on you. You just go get yourself well." To Shawn she said, "I'll walk downstairs with you. Sooner you have your woman drinking clean water, better she going be."

In the empty hotel lobby, when Shawn thanked Clemency, she said it was nothing. She gave him her cell number, just in case.

"I come in tomorrow, check on the lady." Briefly, she put her arms around him: a sisterly hug. "You take care of yourself, too. Looks like you should get some sleep. Girlfriend going to need you stay healthy." She waved, ran for the door, and was gone.

Later, watching himself in a clouded wall mirror, Shawn saw what Clemency meant. Maybe it was worry over Danielle; maybe something deeper. Whatever it was, he didn't look good.

———

In the dark hours of the following morning, Shawn woke, wondering what had disturbed him. The room was still and quiet. Turning, he saw what it was. In shadow, Danielle stood by his bed, holding a pillow. She wore his DOES NOT PLAY WELL WITH OTHERS T-shirt; the moon lit her damp and fevered eyes. She could have placed the pillow over his face. Shawn took it, then held Danielle by her upper arms, feeling the heat of her. He turned her around, led her back to her own bed, and covered her too-warm body with a sheet.

"Dani?"

She stared at him, wordless. Then her eyes closed.

Shawn went back to his bed. He lay there awhile, wondering if a slightly built sleepwalking woman would have the strength to suffocate an aging sleeping man.

If the woman were Danielle, he thought, all bets were off.

18

At four in the morning, Shawn woke again. Under a pillow, his cell phone vibrated. He left the bed, went to the bathroom, closed the door, and answered.

A man's voice said, "Mr. Maguire?"

He knew who was speaking.

"You will remember me? This is Ayub Abbasi."

"I don't know what the hell time zone you're in, Mr. Abbasi," Shawn said, keeping his voice down, "but where I am, it's four in the morning."

"The dark night of the soul," Abbasi said. "In fact, I am in your time zone, and your town. I am in Fes, where my office was."

"Was?"

"Was," said Abbasi. "I can tell you about that. Right now, I need to see you."

"As in tomorrow?"

"As in now. A man you might know is waiting outside your hotel. It is a walk, rather than a drive. Along the edge of the souk."

"What if I tell you I don't take meetings at four in the morning?"

"Then I remind you that, for the moment, you are on my payroll, and you are hoping for more money. Don't be long, Mr. Maguire."

Shawn broke the connection and swore. He dressed, checked that Danielle was asleep, took a key, and left the hotel room. The door locked behind him.

Outside the hotel, the streetlights—if any existed—were out. The moonlit street was empty save for a skinny dog, growling at some dark threat, and two lean cats, bodies tense, squaring off for a fight. Another cat—larger, this one—lay dead in the gutter. From somewhere unseen, Shawn found a thickset man standing to his right, uncomfortably close. That disturbed him: In this business, being blindsided shortens your life.

Recognizing his companion made Shawn feel no easier. Alfred Burke was a handyman: a paid killer, raised in some violent pocket of southeast London. He'd once told Shawn that on Saturdays he'd attend synagogue, when there was one nearby. There he made peace with his God. The rest of the week, he plied his lethal trade. Alfred undertook deniable assignments for anyone who could afford him. He knew his own value; he was not, he said, a cheap date. He specified cash up front, in American dollars or in euros, whichever currency was, at the time, more valuable.

Shawn knew of two recent deaths, both prominent men, both garroted, both murders informally attributed to the man beside him. Alfred had not been charged with either killing. Nor had anyone else.

"Alfred," Shawn said. "You get around."

Alfred said, "Paris last time, right? You was in a car with Mr.

Walters." With an unlit flashlight the handyman pointed toward the souk. "Right, my son, move. Time's short. We go this-a-way."

"Whoa," Shawn said. "Hold on a minute. Before I go anyplace with you, my friend, I want to know who you're working for."

"Mr. Abbasi, right this moment. He's paying me. Said he was calling you."

"He did."

Alfred glanced at Shawn. "You got a problem, don't you? Trust. You don't trust me."

"Not for a heartbeat," Shawn said. "Are you holding?"

Alfred spread his arms. "Pure as a virgin's tit. Search me, if you like. But you know, and I know, if I wanted to take you out, which I don't, but just supposing I did"—he held out short-thumbed hands—"this here, it's all I need."

He set off down a narrow lane between high and leaning buildings. Shawn hesitated for a moment, then followed. They were heading east. Here there was a single streetlamp. He kept three paces behind Alfred, looking around him, keeping clear of doorways. Shawn was of two minds about this procedure. At times, he thought the whole precautionary business absurd. Meeting in darkness, undisclosed locations—who needs this shit? Then he recalled three colleagues who decided to scrap the rule book; all died early, unpublicized, and violent deaths in foreign postings. So, for now, he took care, following several paces behind his guide until Alfred stopped, pointing down an alley even narrower than the one they were in.

"I hate these places," Alfred said. "I truly do. Still, that's where he is. The boss."

Shawn was inspecting the stonework of the building beside him. A cable set between stones took his attention. "Alfred," he said, "you go first. I'll follow."

The alley was darker here. Halfway along it, the thickset man knocked with his flashlight on a wooden door set three steps below the level of the lane.

Shawn waited but heard nothing.

Alfred opened the door and stood aside, gesturing at the void.

"You think I'm going in there," Shawn told him, "you think wrong."

"Not wrong, Mr. Maguire," Ayub Abbasi said from somewhere in the gloom of the cell, a darkness even blacker than the dark outside. "Come down. As a place, it is unpleasant but, trust me, quite safe."

Shawn looked around him. His guide had left as quietly as he'd arrived. Shawn had wondered on other occasions how so big and heavy a man could move so silently. He descended three stone steps, bending his head low to enter the cellar, which, he now realized, was not without light. Brick arches receded into darkness. Each arched aisle was, he guessed, lit with a single low-wattage lightbulb hidden by curves of brickwork. One of these bulbs dimly illuminated Ayub Abbasi, seated at a rusted metal table. That and two chairs were the visible sum of the cellar's furniture.

Shawn sat in shadow, waiting, and watching Abbasi. The man had lost weight. When they had met in Shawn's garden, three weeks earlier, Abbasi had worn an Armani suit. Now he was dressed in his native salwar kameez. He could have been a street trader from the souk.

"Times are hard." Shawn gestured around him. "This your new office?"

"It may be," Abbasi said. "The suite I had in this town was firebombed. If I had been working at the time, I would not be here. You know the quality Napoleon sought in his generals? It was luck.

You are looking at a man, Mr. Maguire, whose luck is running out. Or has run out. In that sense, we may be similar, you and I."

"Hey," Shawn said. "Thanks."

Abbasi pushed a bundle of dollar bills across the desk. Shawn took them and did a rapid count.

"This is not what we agreed on. I need money. It's not enough."

"It is not," Abbasi said. "However, it is all I can afford. In every sense, my friend, I am going downhill. In a few days' time, I may have less cash. Or none. Tell me about Osmani."

"Osmani," Shawn said. He worked through what he should say. "Not a hell of a lot to report. You probably know, I'm here with his wife."

"Osmani's?"

Shawn nodded. "Danielle. If you're going to ask, answer's no. It's not a sexual thing."

"You would be happy if it were."

"Maybe," Shawn said, "but it's not. What can I tell you? Agency's got a hold on Osmani. Picked him up in Paris. They keep moving him. I don't know why."

Abbasi said, "You know better than I—frequent flyer—is this not what they do?"

"Sure," Shawn said. "Question is why. Why he's a flyer—that's what I don't know."

"Your friends want what I want—those papers he took. Information about Qadir Khan's network. Proliferation. It is why I am here." Shawn waited. "You know," said Abbasi, "and *I* know, for the Agency, that could be embarrassing. Pentagon finances ISI. They, in turn, finance Dr. Khan, maker of bombs. Seller of nukes. This might come out if Osmani were freed. If he went public."

"Isn't that why you want the stuff?" Shawn asked. "Here's

another possibility. Let's imagine there's this businessman, Muslim, he's got offices in different places, one of them being Peshawar. Convenient site, right on the Afghan border. Now, suppose this person worked both sides of the line. Wanted to give the bad guys a little help with weaponry. A business like that, import-export, it would be good cover, right? Things come in crates—who knows what's inside. If this same imaginary guy got his hands on a small nuclear device, he could put his jihadi friends into a whole new league. The West has nukes, now jihadis have nukes. Ups the stakes. How's that for a scenario, Mr. Abbasi?"

"It makes me think, Mr. Maguire," Abbasi said, "you should perhaps retire—try writing thrillers. Maybe that will get you out of debt. Though I hear it is a competitive market, violent fantasy. Until then, if you wish to be paid, concentrate on finding Darius Osmani. I am running out of time, and patience. For me, this is, I don't exaggerate, a matter of life and death. I, too, have my sources. They say Osmani will not be kept here. The Agency will move him soon to Cairo. Egyptian special branch. Mukhabarat. Who may get more results."

"Than DST?"

"Indeed. Different techniques. Extreme interrogation. At that, they are masters, the Egyptians." Abbasi sighed again. "So I hear."

"You sound," Shawn remarked, "like things aren't too good."

"I told you," Abbasi said. "Last week, there was a firebomb in my office."

"Phosphorus?"

"So they say. I hear you had the same in your house. Two men have tried to murder me. My assistant was killed. Decapitated. They sent me the video—his head being removed—*pour encourager les autres,* as your *copine* Danielle might say. I was trained in mathematics, Mr. Maguire. The University of Chicago, which has a good faculty. I know the numbers. Unless something changes, the odds are I shall not be alive this time next year. Or next month."

"Take a vacation," Shawn said. "Cuba's nice. They don't like U.S. agents. Stay off the Guantánamo end of the island, you could be safe."

"My problem," Abbasi said, "I don't wish to lose. It is naive, I know, but still I believe there should be justice. I don't like what your country does to my country. I don't like what my country does to Afghanistan—the corrupt narco state that we Pakistanis, and you Americans, have created. I wish to see Nashida Noon as prime minister. She has many faults, but I wish to see her running Pakistan. I hope to be alive to help her."

"Will she make it?"

"If she lives, of course. You know of our election?" Shawn nodded. "Next week the votes are counted. If the president allows it—if the votes are not rigged, or not too much rigged—then Nashida will win. I want to work with her. We can break the power of ISI. Which, I told you, is one reason I need to know what Osmani knows."

Shawn stood and stretched. For himself, he wanted to be in his hotel room. To be near Danielle, to smell her scent. To be back with this sleepwalking woman who had, perhaps, tried to kill him.

"Your choice," he told Abbasi. "Myself, I'd be heading for someplace quiet, drinking Cuba libres. But I'll call you tomorrow. After I see Osmani."

"Inshallah," Abbasi said. "What are you looking at?"

"It's taken a while for my eyes to adjust," Shawn said, "but that box back there looks like a mainframe computer. That other box alongside it looks like a server. Odd things to have in a cellar." Abbasi looked in the direction Shawn was pointing. "Also I noticed, outside, someone's set a new aerial into the stonework. Not a thing you'd see, 'less you looked real close."

"Which you were doing."

"Which I was doing. I just wonder whether the person who bought the server maybe uploads al Qaeda's information to the Web."

Abbasi shrugged. "Who knows? I came to this pit looking for cheap office space. The equipment is not mine." He wrote the number of a disposable cell phone. "Call me tomorrow. Whether or not you see Osmani."

Shawn, making his way to the door, paused. "Are you okay here?"

"As safe as anywhere in Fes," Abbasi said. He pointed into the darkness of the cellar. "I have a man back there."

"Armed?" Shawn asked.

Abbasi nodded.

"Alfred Burke?"

Abbasi shook his head.

"An armed guy I didn't even know about? That makes me uneasy."

"If he is not there," Abbasi said, "it is I who feel uneasy." He stood, his back bent, holding the table to steady himself. "Follow the edge of the souk, Mr. Maguire. I wish you a safe walk home."

19

As the sun rose over Africa, Shawn was woken by Danielle's fingers on his lips. She was perched on the edge of his bed, wearing his T-shirt, her fever gone.

"You were crying in your sleep," she said. "Saying, over and over, that you want, I don't know what. So, tell me, what is it you want?"

He brought himself back to her, to the room of reality.

"What do I want? Come on. You know what I want."

"You Americans. Always now—you want it *now*—"

"Since I met you, actually."

She laughed. Her fingers on his lips, her voice a whisper, she said, "You have to wait. I will come to your bed. Not now. Not today. But soon."

No mention of the night's events. Of walking in her sleep.

"Now, Shawn," she said, "out of bed. Shower. Shave. We're meeting Younis."

She sat watching Shawn as he used a shaver. Years back, in Vietnam, he'd had a hell of a time shaving. Tough beard, tender skin, and no power in the DMZ. Since then, he'd gone electric, hadn't used a blade.

"Before you met your husband?" he said. "You never talk about that."

Danielle looked up from a hand mirror. "Relationships?"

"Must have had some."

Lip gloss in hand, she shook her head. "Plain girls don't."

Shawn switched off the shaver. "You were plain?"

"According to Maman. So competitive, that woman—beyond belief. For a time, you know, I hated her. Later, of course, she becomes a person to be pitied." She finished her Evian and tossed the bottle away. "Living in a world of her own, Maman. Hoping to make it as an actress, to work again—with Chabrol, maybe." She was silent a moment, then said, "After thirty, for a woman, it's hard. The camera, you know. It is not kind."

Shawn swapped shoes for sneakers. "Your father?"

"Papa?" She stopped, trying out what she was about to say. "God, he was so good-looking. I think, now, he didn't like women. Disappointed, having a daughter. When we were in Paris, he used to point out pretty men—never women. My mother said that meant he was faithful to her." She laughed. "I thought it meant something else."

Shawn took the pistol from his toilet bag and checked the loading. "Politics?"

"For Papa? Of the right, of course. Extreme right. *Algérie fran-*

çaise, imprison the leftists, deport the Arabs—*les beurs,* he called them."

"And you?"

"Naturally, the opposite. What can you do, with a father like that? Only react. I was a *soixante-huitarde,* a girl of 'sixty-eight, years too late." She began painting clear polish on her nails. "Then Papa left home. I saw him only if he didn't have to meet Maman— if I was in Provence, or Morocco. If I was here with Benoit—"

"Benoit?"

"My surrogate father. Benoit, he was—I guess now they'd call him a radical lawyer. He defended prisoners. Moroccans. He paid the price."

"He's dead?"

"He is." She made her fingers a pistol. "Assassinated." Danielle paused, then said, "This morning we meet a man who"—she made quote marks in the air—"worked with him. Younis. Another so-called radical."

She watched Shawn shed his shirt. Drinking less these days, he was back in shape. He changed to a clean shirt: the last he'd have until their baggage arrived.

Over the past month, he'd gotten near to his military weight.

"In the end," Danielle said, "my father brought me to America. Ivy League education—he thought it would make me a good conservative. Too late. I never wished to be near him."

"Uh-huh," Shawn said. "I've been there. What you learn, it's a circle. More you run, closer you get to home. Back where you started."

She spread her fingers, letting polish dry. He stood and checked his watch.

"We should go meet this guy—who is—remind me?"

"Younis Khreis. My godfather."

The morning was cool; she was still pale, pulling on a cashmere jumper.

"Background?"

"Lawyer. Pay attention. He worked with my stepfather. Benoit." From the doorway, she beckoned. "Come. It's a start. I mean, God, we don't even know Darius is here."

"I believe he is," Shawn said. "I talked to people."

"The woman in England? Ashley?"

"Her, yes, and others. My guess, your man's a frequent flyer, he may not stay. Right now, he's here."

They left the room then. Shawn double-locked the door, though he knew that anyone who wanted to get in would do it. He followed Danielle down a staircase on the hotel's outside wall. It led to the riad's interior courtyard, blue-and-white tiled, planted with fruit-bearing palms. At the courtyard's center, fountains filled a blue marble basin. In the water, fish, smooth, sinuous, and blue. Trout, maybe, though, in his years of fishing, Shawn had never seen a blue trout.

A fountain's soft plashing; a murmur of doves.

"Another morning," she said, "if we're still in this town, I'll buy you breakfast. Under the palms."

"You can buy me breakfast today. Just tell me where we're going."

"Café Maroc, in the medina." She glanced sideways. "What's wrong?"

He was following, trusting that she knew the way. "What you said about your life. Some things don't add up."

"Have you ever known a life where everything adds up?"

"Plus," he said, "makes me edgy, being with a person knows a place better than I do."

Danielle took his arm, amused. "Tough, no? Being alpha male." Her bare arm on his. Could she feel the acceleration of his pulse when she touched him?

From a side street came an old, robed man who gripped Danielle's fingers in a clutching, withered hand. With his good hand he held a girl, dark-haired, six or seven years old, Shawn guessed. The man spoke a language Shawn did not understand, though he'd heard it before.

Danielle hunkered down to run her hands through the girl's hair. The kid came close and whispered something. For a long minute the man spoke, low-toned; then Danielle ended the conversation. She kissed the girl. The man, his face hooded, hailed a *petit taxi* and was gone.

"You know that guy?" Shawn asked.

Danielle was walking on, toward the medina. "Mmm. From when I lived here. The girl's his granddaughter."

"You were speaking Arabic?"

"Maghrebi Arabic."

"I never knew you could do that."

She glanced at him. "Many things you don't know about me."

A vendor's cart, laden with herbs, forced them across the sidewalk.

She said, "This morning, you're not easy company."

"I'm never easy," he told her, "in places I might get killed."

He hadn't mentioned his nighttime meeting with the lethal handyman. Or with Abbasi.

Danielle turned to consider two women who sat beside of the road on hanbel rugs dotted with trinkets. Their heads were darkly covered. Without hope their eyes moved among passersby, Danielle, and the arrays of bright toys. They looked up at her as she bent to give them dirham notes. They murmured thanks, making no judgment and no attempt to sell.

She hesitated, deciding whether to turn left or right. She went left, into rue Ed Douh. "Remember?" Danielle asked. "Your little village in Sussex? Phosphorus in the roof of your house? It's not just Africa where they try to kill you."

He told her that was no help. He didn't want to die in either place.

Laughing, she stopped at a coffeehouse, considering a crowd of seated, suited men. "This is it," she said. "This is where we find Younis."

20

Danielle led Shawn into Café Maroc, edging a path through terraces crowded with seated coffee drinkers. All male; a mélange of sartorial styles. Some of the men wore Arabic garments, others Western clothes, favoring three-piece suits, double-cuffed shirts, and lightly tinted Ray-Bans. All were grave; none were young.

Above the seated men was a blue canvas awning, drawn halfway back, advertising Fanta in both English and Arabic. At this cool time of day, men chose to sit in the morning sun. Shawn had never understood it, the sexual balance in these countries. All men on this street; no women, save Danielle.

How did that work? He did know it wouldn't suit him, living here for long. Though he'd sometimes wished it otherwise, Shawn needed women. He learned that during his time in the marines—an all-male bunch then, all heterosexual. The unit ran on testosterone.

Shawn recalled waking in a hooch near Vietnam's DMZ. That night, deeply asleep, he'd seen with surprise that he was alive: alive and dreaming. At times, south of the Zone, he'd dreamed of women: narrow-hipped hoochgirls; girls like boys. Dream-women expect nothing, not even cash. These, though, were not frequent dreams.

Recurrent dreams were different. Worse. They came on hot nights when roaches ran down walls to pause above beds, bright, alert, shiny, antennae quivering: creatures that would one day inherit the postnuclear world. Meantime, they'd eat the skin from the soles of your feet so subtly you might not even wake. Old hands slept with socks on, inured to the smell of their flesh. In the morning, the boots—the FNGs, the fucking new guys—they'd swing off their racks and fall around yelling, trying to walk on skinless feet.

Men laughed. What could you do? Fucking new guys.

Shawn slept in socks, in swamps of his stink. Rather that than having to march across country with no goddamn skin on your feet. The nightmares were worse than the insects. From some dreams Shawn woke sweating and shaken, whispering aloud, his body rocked by the arrhythmic clamor of his heart. There were times when he woke in the echoes of error. Sometimes the mistake was aboveground, sometimes in Cong tunnels below. Always it was terminal, always incorrigible. Shawn's dreams were full of death. There were times he'd thank God for waking him to the sad damp heat of day; for dragging him back from his dreams of dissolution. In the end, though, when they blew away his buddy Charlie Slocum, days weren't much better than nights.

In the Café Maroc that morning, with the prisoner's wife, he thought back to this.

Danielle went ahead into the café, through glassed doors to inner rooms with mirrored walls and chandeliers and floors patterned in blue and white geometric tiles. When Shawn caught up, she was standing by two seated men. The older of the two wore a dark and shiny suit, plain black, with a thin black tie. He was small, almost bald, physically constricted, hunched in his chair. His left eye was infected, weeping. His remaining hair, combed across his skull, was dyed a light-absorbing black, though his sideburns and mustache were gray. His projectile breath took Shawn back to the silage smell of southern farms. The man looked exhausted; no, in some state beyond exhaustion. Through rimless square glasses, he considered his visitors.

"Younis Khreis," said Danielle. "This is the man I told you about. Shawn Maguire."

Younis did not rise or offer a hand. He said to Shawn, "You have been here before, I think. In Rabat?" He gestured to the giant beside him. "This is Tariq."

Shawn had been staring at Tariq: one of the biggest men he'd ever seen, Texans included. Tariq was not just tall—though, even sitting, he came close to Danielle's height—but broad as well. What intrigued Shawn was this: The guy was huge, massive indeed, but not fat, his polished skin underlain with smooth layers of, what? Subcutaneous muscle?

Whatever his composition, this was a man who'd break a neck like snapping a match. A man to treat with care.

Shawn could not shift his gaze from Tariq's dark bulk. He'd never seen anything like it.

Tariq looked calmly back.

Younis said, "Bodyguard."

Tariq shook his head. *"Pas seulement."*

"He is a student of art also. What you would call Moorish art, is that word right? The geometric and the calligraphic."

"Symbols of a single perfection," Danielle said.

"There, you see," said Younis. "My goddaughter knows. Once again, the divine harmonies. There is no God but God." To Danielle he said, "Your territory, I think." To Shawn he said, "Are we speaking English or French?"

"We started in English, let's keep it that way," Shawn said. "Plus, it's all I understand." He took a seat, still considering the taut immensity of Tariq. Danielle sat on the far side of the table, where, Shawn guessed, she could see the terrace and dodge her godfather's breath. "You know what we're like," he said. "Gringos. Lucky if we speak one language. Why do you need a bodyguard?"

Younis wiped his weeping eye. "I work for those in our prisons. Here we have our own little war. I think it does not make your press. We are not kind to men who go against the state. When I find them in prison, I offer legal help. Mostly unpaid, since their possessions, if they have such, are confiscated. It is not a popular thing to do, helping these men. Not in this place. My wife was, what is it? Carjacked?" He waved to a waiter, who held a small child by the hand. The child was a tiny plump version of Tariq, as if the man had been magically reduced to a hundredth of his size. "She was shot in the neck, my wife. Maybe for money, maybe not. Maybe for my sake, maybe not. Now she is crippled—paraplegic, is that what we say? I have three children, a sick wife. I am more tired than you can believe. If I knew how to stop my work, I would." He pointed to the terrace. Shawn watched Danielle move away from the slipstream of the lawyer's breath. "You said you speak just one language, Mr. Maguire. You should learn from your colleague there. He speaks many."

The waiter brought four small cups of coffee. Shawn willed himself not to turn toward the terrace. "Who is my colleague?"

"A man called Hassan Tarkani. Pakistani, but we believe he is an American agent. Intelligence agent, a spy, though of course he does not acknowledge this, and we ourselves are not supposed to speak of it."

"Pakistan," said Tariq. "ISI."

"Maybe, also," Younis agreed. "A busy spy."

The waiter returned with dishes of nuts and dried apricots. Danielle's gaze shifted between Younis and Shawn.

"Hassan Tarkani," Shawn said. He recalled the man sitting in his kitchen, his feet on the pinewood table. "Is he by chance with a guy called Calvin McCord?"

Younis said, "Ask him." He shifted in his chair. "I see him sitting out there, to the right. He came just after you arrived."

Danielle was visibly impatient. "They can wait. I need to know about Darius. My husband. Seven weeks now, Younis, I've not heard from him. Imagine what that's like—"

"Darius Osmani. Yes." Younis took two smoked almonds between thumb and forefinger. He considered them. "I have heard of Mr. Osmani. I am afraid they have him"—he pointed westward—"our police, over toward New Town. Ironic, they should bring him here, no? They delivered him the other day to Temara."

"Temara?"

Younis nodded at Shawn. "Your friend will know. South of Rabat. Near the zoo. Prisoners there hear the animals, caged like them, though not, we hope, tortured. Temara is our main, but not only, enhanced interrogation facility—is that not right, Mr. Maguire? State of the art, they say. Enlarged with American money. Used by American military intelligence. Now, I hear, they transferred your husband. He is in the jail"—he pointed—"here, in Fes."

Danielle sat for a while, saying nothing. When her breathing was easier, she said, "I keep asking—no one tells me—what will they do to him?"

Tariq, expressionless, said, "*Farruj*. Grilled chicken."

Danielle glanced at the waiter, who was out of hearing. She looked back to Tariq. "What does that mean?"

"No," Shawn said. "Leave it. You don't want to know."

"Don't tell me what I want. Tariq?"

Younis said, "Tell her, Tariq. You have done it, after all." To Shawn he added, "Art history is not his only talent."

Tariq, too, was watching the terrace. He spoke without turning his head. "Grilled chicken, you handcuff the *mec*, the prisoner, you cuff him behind his legs, like this"—he bent vast arms behind him—"you put a rod through here, you hang him upside down, the circulation stops. Then you beat his feet until the flesh is a mess. Sometimes electricity also. Next comes *falaqa*."

"Please," Shawn said. He was aware of Danielle, watching him. He didn't want her thinking badly of him. "Enough already."

"No," Tariq said. "*Falaqa* is easy. Just, you pour water on the guy, you make him walk across salt. That's all. I don't know myself, but they say it is painful, after the feet are beaten."

Danielle said to Shawn, "Did you do that?"

He shook his head. "I have seen it done." To Younis he said, "How do we get into the jail?"

"You still have a security clearance? Not canceled?" Shawn shrugged. If his clearance had been revoked, he doubted jailers here would know. "That, and money maybe," said Younis, "that will get you in. We might both go. There is one man, a client, so-called—once a month they let me see him."

Tariq moved surprisingly easily, for so large a man. He took the hand of a bearded coffee drinker at the next table and raised the man's arm until he hung like a doll, his feet high off the floor. The man screamed. His companions stared, motionless, expressions congealed like lard.

The waiter stood still. For some reason, the child ran to wrap his arms around Tariq's leg.

A nickel-plated handgun the bearded man was holding fell to the floor. It was small, a short-barreled thing, the kind Shawn preferred. Younis bent to pick it up. "A precaution," he said. "I hate it when they scream."

Shawn looked around, checking the room for other weapons.

Danielle threw herself against the mortal bulk of Tariq's body.

"Put him down," she cried, "God's sake, put him down, you ape! You'll pull his arm out! *Déposez-le! Vous allez déchirer le bras!*"

Over the bawling of the hanging man, Tariq said, "I am human. Don't call me ape."

"Pardon," she said. *"Mais lâchez-le! Lâchez-le!"*

Tariq lowered the bearded man. He staggered and whimpered; his freed arm hung limp from its socket. Shawn walked to the terrace and seated himself at a metal table, opposite Hassan Tarkani. The agent's presence in Fes made him uneasy. What, he wondered, brought the man to Morocco?

For a moment, there was silence: each watching the other, and the door of the inner room. "How about this?" Shawn said finally. "Last time we met, remember? You were in my kitchen with your feet on my table. You recall that?"

Hassan sat silent, watching a man who'd come from within the café. Turning, Shawn saw Calvin McCord, unshaven, unwell. He sat on a metal chair beside Hassan and put his feet on another. Shawn saw that the man's hands still shook with the slightest of tremors.

"I was just saying, Calvin, back in England, you guys moved into my house. Uninvited."

Calvin said, "We did apologize. Why would you bring that up now?"

"Someone left an incendiary device in my roof space. White phosphorus."

Calvin shook his head. "Hard to comprehend," he said, "the evil in the world. But hey, you're still with us. You survived. Any suggestion who could have done such a thing?"

"I think," Shawn said, "it might have been you." He glanced from Calvin to Hassan, who was attending to the conversation. "Or your sidekick there."

"Paranoia," Calvin said. "Did you fingerprint the device?"

Shawn shook his head. "Pay attention. White phosphorus. Burns to ash."

"There, you see. No evidence. No suspects. Be careful, my friend. In your position—making accusations you can't prove." He captured Hassan's coffee. "I have a question for you. How does it feel to betray your country? To work for a man like Ayub Abbasi? You know, high on our blacklist?"

Shawn thought about that. "Who put him there?"

"Not important," said Calvin. "Answer the question, Maguire. Your country's at war. You work for the other side. There's a word for that."

Hassan smiled. "We have faults," he said, "but we know which side we are on."

"How about we trade?" said Calvin. "You tell me what you know about Abbasi. About Dr. Khan and the nukes. We tell you what we know of Osmani."

Shawn said, "I don't want information. I want access. What exactly is he charged with?"

"Osmani?" Calvin shook his head, clicked his tongue. "Come on. We don't charge these people. You know that. Charge them, you've got lawyers, publicity, fucking court case. We wait until they confess."

Shawn thought back to a day when Martha gave him a book about a trial—a man on trial for unknown crimes. The prisoner, of course, admits his guilt. How could he not?

Watching Hassan rise and walk to the inside room, Shawn turned back to Calvin. "Confess what?"

"What they wish to confess," said Calvin. "You've seen it happen. We all have things to confess. You, for example. You call yourself a patriot, yet you steal classified documents. You work with people who have no love for America. Like the girl in there. Like Abbasi. Or"—he pointed—"that lawyer. Younis Khreis." Calvin touched his cup without lifting it. "You see? Crimes confession could extricate."

Hassan came back and resumed his seat. "Expiate."

"Ah, Jesus," Calvin said. His coffee cup rattled on its saucer. "Will you shut the fuck up? It's my language."

Hassan watched the giant Tariq, who now stood at the door of the inner room, surveying the street.

"Go after that boy," Calvin said, speaking of Tariq, "you better be loaded for bear."

Hassan finished a bowl of nuts and dried fruit. With his mouth full of smoked almonds, he said, "We are all mortal. In any body, hollow points make a hole."

Shawn imagined that Calvin these days had his own mortality in mind. His vital signs were not good. He guessed this was probably not known to those who might want the job Calvin himself had taken when Shawn was eased out of the Agency. To his own surprise he felt a moment of sympathy for this man who would struggle all his life to emerge from the shadow of his five-star father. He waved to Danielle, who emerged from the inner room holding the arm of her dwarfish godfather. The giant bodyguard followed them.

Leaving a bunch of dirham notes on the table, Shawn joined the group. They walked down the shaded side of avenue Abdelkrim al Khattabi, toward the New Town. The sidewalk was less crowded now, men, women, and animals retreating from the heat.

"You know I am here as bodyguard," said Tariq. "They will never let me in the jail."

Back in the café, Calvin watched the group around Shawn. "Off your ass, boy," he said to Hassan. "Someone needs to see where those guys are going."

Hassan didn't move. "We know where they are going."

Calvin picked up his phone, checked that he had a signal, and called an officer in Morocco's Direction de la Surveillance du Territoire. The DST contact was a man you could trust—silent and efficient, trilingual. He was a ranking member of Mossad, though neither Israelis nor Moroccans acknowledged the fact.

"It's that time again, my friend," Calvin told Levi. "We have us a body to move."

21

The stone-carved gateway in its outer wall was old and ornate, but, within that wall, the jail on the outskirts of Fes looked like a concrete office building. One in bad repair. Only metal shutters and machine gun–mounted watchtowers set it apart.

On the gate was a sign in three languages, forbidding photography.

"Old," Tariq said, referring to the gateway and its carvings. "Well worked. Marinid architecture."

From the desert came a warm wind, bearing sand.

"Which is what?" Shawn asked. He kept his distance from the giant bodyguard.

"Marinids ruled this place," said Younis, who, in hours he had free, studied the city's history. "This was up to the fifteenth century. They had unusual customs, these kings. Among them, burying men and women alive at each of the gates, to protect the city. Gates guarded by the living dead. Which, in the end, like all systems, failed to work. Death does have dominion. End of the Marinids." He stopped for a moment, considering the jail. "The building, of course, is a modern facade. Behind, all is old. Your people financed it. The facade, I mean, and the cells inside."

"My people? Americans?" Shawn considered Danielle, pale today in the African sun. "Why not *her* people? She has a blue passport. Why's it always my people when something bad goes down?"

"You can imagine," Danielle said, "there might be reasons."

Around the building, within the outer wall, was bare, packed earth. Not even weeds grew. A single twisted fig tree, heavy with fruit, stood on the eastern perimeter. Two men in uniform waited on either side of the jail's main door. Both were young and awkward; both carried submachine guns.

Shawn watched them closely. He distrusted nervous young men with automatic weapons. He'd known a few.

"There is also Israeli money," Younis said. "We owe a debt to Mossad. They train our people, when they are not killing them."

"Who interrogates these days?"

"Your military intelligence," Younis said. "At times, OGA."

Danielle divided her attention between Younis and the guards, "Excuse me?" she asked.

"OGA. Other government agencies."

"Basically, Brits," Shawn said. "They're not like us. Kind of shy of being name-checked, places like this."

Tariq, smiling, said to Younis, "Sir, I shall wait here. We know they will not let me in." Holding his son in his arms, he moved to a patch of shade beneath the solitary fig. Set down, the boy searched the ground for the green-black fruit, split with pink, that birds had missed. His father watched as Younis showed identification to one of the soldiers. Moving back a little, still uneasy, fingering his weapon, the man gestured toward the metal door. Younis beckoned Shawn and Danielle. All three entered the building. Moving slowly in the midday heat, the second soldier closed the door behind them. He turned a bored, expressionless gaze on Tariq. One burst of fire, he thought, would stop a man, even of that size.

The jail entrance gave onto a vast stone-floored courtyard. In the middle stood an Apache helicopter whose markings, if they ever existed, had been erased.

Opening off the courtyard was a stone-walled room, buzzing with flies. It was unfurnished except for a plastic desk, two broken chairs, and three filing cabinets, only one of which had drawers. On the desk stood a black dial telephone and a blank-screened, finger-marked computer, beige in color.

Shawn noticed steel hooks in the ceiling.

Behind the desk were two young men in uniform, about the age of the pair outside. They played cards. One had the insignia of a sergeant. Both wore dark glasses and, despite the heat, black gloves.

Pointing at Shawn, Younis said to the sergeant, "This man has worked with your people, in Rabat. In Temara. With Colonel Qasim Behari. You see he has a pass. A nine-zero passport. American."

The officers laid down their cards the better to examine Shawn's security pass and the documents Younis placed before them. They passed papers between them. One man switched on the computer, slapping its flank without apparent hope, and without result.

Moving with unexpected speed, the sergeant captured a passing blowfly. With an audible crunch, he crushed it in the palm of his glove. He said in French, "The men. Not the woman."

Danielle shrugged. *"Ça va."* She moved toward the exit. *"Je vais rester au dehors, à côté de Tariq."* To Shawn she said, "I'll be outside. You take care."

"Why?" asked the sergeant, in English. "What is she meaning?"

"If anyone offers you a ride back to town," Younis told Danielle, "refuse. We shall go together."

The sergeant said something in French to Younis, and both men laughed.

"What was that?" Shawn asked.

"He says that the woman has very beautiful green eyes, and breasts you could eat, like a mango," Younis replied. "He says you are a lucky old man, if you take such a chicken to bed."

"I wish," Shawn said in English.

"Now," said Younis, "he brings us down to the cells."

The sergeant led the way out of the stone-walled office, along a corridor, down timeworn steps to a basement. Here the air was damp, the walls gray-green and, surprisingly, wet. Low-wattage bulbs were trapped overhead in wire-mesh cages. Most were dead. Smells of piss and shit hung on stagnant air.

On each side of the passage, cells were numbered down one side and up the other, the numbers both Hindu and Arabic. Each metal door had an inspection window; all the grilles were unshuttered. From where he stood, Shawn saw that the cells had loudspeakers, and in each, he guessed, was a single, high-powered light in a ceiling recess: standard procedure, he knew, for disorientation. Noise and light to banish sleep.

Through the first inspection window, he saw a naked man, squatting above a pisshole in the floor. Flesh hung loose on the prisoner's bones; his penis drooped. He watched the doorway with the gaze of a trapped animal.

In the next two cells, diaper-clad men hung by their arms, one spread-eagled, as if crucified. From links on their wrist shackles, shining chains ran to bolts in the cell's stone roof. Though weak, the first man was pulling himself up, Shawn guessed, to ease the pressure on his wrists. He'd seen detainees who'd lost their hands when circulation ceased. These two, though, seemed physically intact.

Shawn recalled the hooks in the stone roof of the office above. Perhaps, he thought, there were times when the young, black-gloved solders filled in forms, or fought their lifeless computer, while the prisoners swung above them, turning in the breeze of the ceiling fan.

In the third and fourth cells, two more men hung from hooks. To Shawn, they seemed lifeless, though he knew it was unlikely. The CIA book of rules—standard operating procedure—recommends that dead bodies should be promptly removed, preferably for incineration. Absent crematoria, burial in lime.

The prisoners made no noise. Two were dressed in off-white women's panties that came from God knows where. Otherwise, they were naked. Their unwashed skin made it hard to tell whether or not they were Arabic. All—even the hanging men—were chained by their ankles to wall bolts. Drainage gutters ran across the cell floors.

From somewhere, a sound of machinery.

Shawn leaned against a damp-stained wall. He felt nauseous. He was too old for this. Across the corridor, Younis systematically checked odd-numbered cells. Motionless, the Moroccan sergeant watched, his weapon loosely held in a black-gloved hand.

From above came a louder sound Shawn could not, for the moment, identify.

Several minutes later, Younis returned. "Not on this side, your man." He held a handkerchief to his nose, against the stink. His eye still wept. He spoke in French to the sergeant, then in English to Shawn. "Sadly, my client has died and been buried. Once again, sudden death, it seems. Aneurism, hemorrhage of the brain."

Shawn was at the last inspection window. "Our guy's not on this side." He pointed. "That door there. The one without a window."

"*La sépulture,*" said Younis. "Do you say, sepulcher?"

"What's inside?"

Younis translated the question for the sergeant, then translated the answer. "They call that the grave. There is a human in there. He will never come out. Not walking. But he is not your man."

Shawn knew then what he was hearing: rotation of blades. Above them in the courtyard, he guessed, the unmarked helicopter was taking off.

To Younis he said, "I think we just missed our guy." He pointed upward. "Sounds like the chopper's gone."

Younis thought for a moment. Dabbing his eye, he led the way toward the stairs. "Frequent flyers." He shook his head. "Always hard. So hard to trace. You should take your woman, my Danielle, you should take her home to England, to France, wherever. She will not find her man."

Shawn shook his head. "I'll maybe take her home," he said, "but she's not my woman. And Younis, I'll tell you this—she'll keep looking."

When Shawn arrived back at his hotel room, his laptop was missing. Not a serious loss. Shawn had learned something from his last night with Ellen: from losing his laptop, his job, and her. Now secure data dwelled, encrypted, on a server somewhere near Amarillo. The FBI could, if they wished, crack the encryption. They'd gotten good at that. First, though, they'd have to find the server.

For form's sake, Shawn reported his loss to the local police. In broken English, he was told by a gray-haired uniformed sergeant, sorting papers, to come back during office hours.

"Which are what?"

"After ten in the morning,' the policeman said. "Not holidays, or religious festivals. Both of which occur, as it happens, tomorrow."

"If I leave Fes tomorrow?" Shawn asked.

The man behind the desk shrugged. What, he said, could anyone do about that? He advised Sean to forget the loss. "Go back to your hotel," he said. "Get drunk. Is that not what Christians do?"

Shawn did go back to his hotel, but not to drink. Pausing outside the door of his room, he heard sounds he hadn't heard since the last weeks of Martha's life—racking, choking sobs, then a cry, hardly human. Opening the door, he saw Danielle, half naked, on the floor, rocking, between the beds. She seemed not to hear Shawn close the door and softly leave. He'd known some weeping women; he never knew what to do, or what to say.

22

On the last day in Fes, Shawn was depressed, uneasy; a feeling that lay in his gut, without a cause he'd put a name to. In part, it was foreboding: a sense of something evil gestating, something ominous in the air. In part, it had to do with his feeling for Danielle—desire might presage disaster, even death. He sensed she was dangerous: He knew he should forget her, and doubted he could.

On that evening, their last evening, Danielle said she'd take Shawn to supper. Now she was beautiful. When Shawn asked, she said she'd wept awhile for Darius and was through with tears. Calmer, she said she'd find where her husband had gone, and follow him there.

One way or another, she said, they were through with this town.

———

Danielle led Shawn through crowded streets—to him, more like lanes—in the city's medina. From somewhere came a sound of quarter-toned music, a slower, sadder music than they'd yet heard. It matched Shawn's mood of unease.

From byways, doors opened to unlikely courtyards, carnations planted with pink-flowered trees, fan palms, cacti, set around fountains. In one water-haunted garden was a raucous party, a family celebration: tables set with food, women slow-dancing to a plaintive tune, fireworks punctuating the sound of argument and laughter. Shawn thought of the last time he'd partied in palm-shaded gardens: years back, it was. They'd been in Andalusia, celebrating Martha's birthday. A child of the Deep South, she'd fallen in love with southern Spain: cognac in the sun at breakfast above the blue and shimmer of the sea.

Another life. Since then, with Martha gone, there hadn't been much to celebrate.

Danielle walked faster now, threading her way through crowded streets. Taller than the men and women around her, she was easy to follow. Shops here were small and shadowy, cavelike metal-lined recesses where legs of lamb hung from hooks, the meat gray with age. There were dishes of offal, intestines like softened hosepipe; baskets piled with fresh-cut herbs; odors of sweat, grilled meat, and roasting spice.

Shawn's mind was on the prisoners he'd seen; on the nameless hanging men, their unseen inquisitors. He'd done it himself, such interrogation, and seen it done by others.

Captors and captives, both now invaded his dreams.

Here, in the souk, Shawn had the feeling he was being fol-lowed, but—looking back along the lanes—he saw no one out of place in those densely peopled streets. At his feet, he found a child: a little boy, crying in the dirt, chubby arms protecting his head.

Shawn stopped, blocking traffic. Like water around a rock, crowds flowed about him. He bent to lift the kid. The boy rested a small dark head on Shawn's shoulder.

Danielle made her way back to where they stood. She nodded at the child. "What are you doing with him?"

"Least I can do," Shawn said, "is put him someplace he won't get stepped on."

"Come," she said. "We can do that."

Minutes later, Shawn, holding the boy, followed her into what seemed to be a grocer's store. Shelves filled with jars of spice and herbs and preserved fruit reached to the ceiling. The floor was stacked with floury sacks.

Danielle spoke in brief Arabic to an apron-clad Moroccan behind a wooden counter. To Shawn, she said, "This man will take the boy. He knows the family."

Shawn set the child down. "You sure about this?"

"Of course I am sure. Here, they care about children."

The apron-clad man lifted the child and placed him on a high chair behind the counter.

"Could've fooled me," Shawn said. "Kid was on the ground, folks walking over him."

"It's a side of you I haven't seen," she said. "The good father."

"Didn't work so great with my daughter." He waved good-bye to the boy as Danielle thanked the storekeeper and set off toward the back of the shop. "This is where we eat?"

Danielle led Shawn to a narrow room, poorly lit, its walls hung with calligraphic tablets. In this claustrophobic cell, it seemed, food was served.

"My father," Danielle said, "Benoit, my surrogate father—he used to bring me here, when I was a child."

"This is the lawyer you talked about? Radical?"

"One of them. Sometimes I came with Younis—sometimes it was Benoit and me. Daughter and daddy, we were so close."

"You were lovers? You and him?"

Danielle nodded. "Of course. My introduction. It was part of the excitement. The city, too. The food, the music, the market—it all seemed strange. So different from what I knew in France. So sexy." Dramatically, she shivered. "Dangerous, I thought. I wanted to be a lawyer, then. Working for prisoners."

Shawn thought that over. He turned back toward the shop, trying to see what had become of the child.

A young man with the look of a Koranic student set out plates on the only uncluttered table. Above it hung an old-fashioned ceiling fan from which descended four metallic lights: iron molded in the shape of tulips. There was no menu. Danielle ordered in French, which made Shawn uneasy.

"Danielle," he said, "don't give me a hard time, but what the hell did you ask for? I should tell you, I'm not good with third-world chow."

She put her fingers over his, leaving them a little longer than she needed to. He could count on one hand the times she'd touched him.

"Shawn," she said, "it's Morocco, not Manhattan. I want to thank you for helping me." She pointed to the front of the shop. "And for that child."

"Which means?" he asked, with sudden hope.

"This evening, it is on me. You don't eat burgers. Or catfish."

"Don't knock catfish," he said. "My first date was Miss Alabama

Catfish. Cute as a button, that kid." He did the math. "She'd be fifty now."

Danielle shook her head. "Miss Catfish. Such a redneck. Tonight you have tagine"—she pointed—"cooked in one of those dishes, you see there? Conical?"

"Tagine? Made with what, exactly?"

"Lamb—lamb and prunes and apricots and honey. It's delicious. You don't like it, sue me."

When the food came, Shawn watched Danielle eating, considering this woman with whom he'd fallen in love, or lust. He'd never known which was which. He was about to speak—about to ask something intimate—when the light changed. Standing in the doorway, filling the doorway, stood Tariq, the giant bodyguard. He was silent, watching. For the second time that day, Shawn wished he had a handgun.

Danielle drew out a chair. The giant seated himself with care, unsure of the chair's strength. He sat for a while, taking in his surroundings. The man had, Shawn thought, an operative's eye for hidden threat.

It was Shawn who spoke. Tariq made him uneasy. "How did you know we were here?"

"It is smaller than it seems, this town," said Tariq. "If you are foreign, if you are American, it is hard to be out of sight."

The young man, the scholarly waiter, brought more food: dishes of some creamy concoction. Shawn tasted the stuff on the tip of one finger, testing for the heat of chili peppers. Tariq said he would not eat. For a moment Shawn imagined the Rabelaisian business if ever the big man were truly hungry: truckloads of bread, butcheries of meat, sacks of grain, barrels of wine.

He examined his own plate, checking its odd ingredients.

"Tell me something," he said to Tariq. "You know Calvin Mc-Cord? The CIA guy? He was in the café this morning?" Tariq nodded. "Give me your best guess. Why do you think he was here the same time as we were?"

"Here in Fes?"

Shawn nodded.

Tariq thought this over. "Maybe he is seeking the same thing you seek. To do with the bomb, perhaps. Your people worry about jihadists with nuclear weapons."

"Are you surprised?" Shawn asked. "Why Fes, though?"

"I would guess," Tariq told him, "it is to do with the man in prison. The man who was in our jail." He nodded at Danielle. "Her man."

That was Shawn's guess, too, though he still had doubts, about both McCord and Danielle.

Now she had stopped eating. "When you phoned, you said you had something for me."

It was the first Shawn knew of a call between Danielle and Tariq.

"Cairo," Tariq said. "Your man, the frequent flyer. Younis said I should tell you—maybe you know—he believes they have taken him to Cairo."

Shawn believed that, too. Danielle turned to him. "Do your people take prisoners there?"

Shawn finished what was in his mouth, the fruit, mixed with meat. It tasted strange; he could get to like it. "My people don't do that. Never."

"CIA?"

"The Agency? They do. Remember, in England—Ashley told you that. Plus Special Plans uses Cairo—the guys Bobby Walters works for. OSP does what the hell they want—veep's office, they're like the goddamn Nike ads. Just do it. They write laws. Whatever you do, if it's not legal today, it will be tomorrow."

Tariq said, "We know there is a Company facility—somewhere in Cairo."

Shawn said, "Sure. Shared with Mukhabarat."

"Tell me," said Danielle.

"Security police," said Tariq. "Good at what they do, they tell me. The jail is in Giza."

"Close," Shawn said. "Gaber Ibn Hayan."

"Okay." Danielle pushed her plate aside. "I know Giza. That's where we're going."

Shawn was still eating. He'd discovered he was hungry.

"Who's the 'we' in this sentence? I never said I'm going to Cairo." He tried a fine pale grain with his meat. "I have a home, remember? House, cat, five sheep. Maybe a lamb, by now."

"Fine," she said. "You have helped. It's okay. If you are gone, I'll go alone."

Tariq held up a huge hand. He leaned toward Shawn. "Before you leave this town, Mr. Maguire, there is a thing you can do for us, if you will. In return for the help of Mr. Younis. We would be grateful. Someone you might identify."

Shawn finished the food on his plate, enjoying it, and thought that through. He had the sense that this was an offer he might not refuse.

"You say someone? Where is this person? Why would you think I'd know whoever it is?"

"Three minutes' walk from here. Maybe four. It would help Mr. Younis." With surprising speed for a man so heavy, Tariq heaved himself to his feet. "If you will come with me?"

Danielle left money on the table. She followed the two men

out. The shop was empty, the child gone. They emerged in a still-crowded street through the souk. Shawn spoke quietly. "You know this town, hon. Remember what way we go. We could be in a hurry, getting back." He crouched against a wall as a young man on a motorbike rode at dangerous speed through the thronged market. He looked after the disappearing youth. "Son of a bitch. I hope he has life insurance."

Tariq said, "The person we are about to see had none."

Five minutes later, the bodyguard turned into an alley between two warehouses. There was a smell of something musty here—dry, decaying, not unpleasant. Flour-coated sacks of grain were stacked against each wall, leaving a narrow central path.

A wooden door opened into blackness. Shawn thought back to where he'd met Ayub Abbasi. Could this be the same cellar? The air here was cold and still. He saw no sign of computer or server. Somewhere in darkness, water dripped.

"What the hell's in here?"

Tariq produced a tiny flashlight, ridiculously small in his giant hand. "No one who can harm you."

Danielle followed Shawn along the cellar. Pillars—some wooden, some brick—supported its ceiling. Shards of stone lay about the floor. It was cold. Tariq closed the door behind them. He pulled aside a sacking curtain and shone his light. In the pencil beam lay what had been a young man: the body of a man who would never be old. He lay in pools of water, oil, and blood. Part of his shirt was gone. Part of his belly was gone. From the body cavity, guts flopped fatly to the floor.

Danielle turned away, choking, then walked into darkness. Shawn heard her retch, or maybe try not to vomit.

Shawn had a sudden sense that Danielle had recognized the body before him, although—given the dead man's identity—he saw no way that she could have. Considering the corpse, he remembered a tale Martha told him days before she died. To her, it was significant in some way he didn't understand. "In a busy Arab market," she'd said, "a merchant looking for his servant meets the figure of Death. Terrified, the man turns and runs. Later he tells his servant he will go into hiding, as far away as possible, in the distant town of Samarra. The next day, it is the servant who meets Death in the market. As frightened as his master had been, the servant drops to his knees. Death reassures him. 'Don't worry,' Death says to the servant. 'It is not you I seek. I am needed elsewhere. Today I have an appointment in Samarra.'"

The man in the cellar, who had kept his own appointment with death, was missing his hands. The stump of an arm stretched toward the stones of the cellar's eastern wall. Before death took him, he'd written in blood, with the amputated end of that arm, two Arabic words.

Danielle came from darkness, back to the body. She stood close to Shawn, holding him.

Tariq held his flashlight beam on the blood-daubed words.

"Meaning what?" Shawn asked.

"*La ilaha illallah.*" Danielle said. She spoke with difficulty. "There is no God but One. The man died before he finished the phrase."

Tariq turned his huge head toward her. "How would you know that, madame?"

Shawn was moving away. He had a bad feeling about this place, and a sudden crazy notion—which he knew to be impossible—that Danielle might have murdered this man.

"Never mind how she knows," he told Tariq. "This feels like a setup. We're out of here."

Shawn groped his way across the uneven floor, toward the door. He was shaking, stumbling a little. At the steps, he told Tariq, "The dead guy's Massood Omar Sheikh, but I think you knew that—you didn't need me to tell you."

"We do need to know if you listed him."

"We did. Number four on the most wanted, last time I looked." Shawn was back in the alley. "What we hear, he's been selling Qadir Khan's technology—this Islamic bomb you mentioned. I guess you know that, too."

At the far end of the alley, four car lights switched on to high beam. Heading away from them, Shawn grabbed Danielle's hand and broke into a half run. Moving easily, Tariq kept pace.

"Who opened the guy up?"

"We think it might have been your friend, Mr. McCord," Tariq said. "Or his colleague, Mr. Tarkani. You can see, it was a heavy weapon Mr. McCord used."

"If it was him."

"If, indeed. The range was close," Tariq said. "To make up, perhaps, for his tremor."

Danielle, ahead of them, turned. "Why the amputation?"

"Who knows? Fingerprints?"

"You have DNA," Shawn said.

"In this place? You think?"

Now they were back in the market.

"Tell me," Shawn asked Tariq, "whose side are you on? You bring me to a dead body—terrorist, al Qaeda operative, gut cut open, no hands. Why am I here? Where are the cops?"

"We believe they agreed not to discover the body until Mr. McCord and Mr. Tarkani are out of the country." Tariq pointed back the way they had come. "But you see them there—those lights—those are security police."

"Move," Shawn said, tightening his grip on Danielle's hand. "This is a setup." To Tariq, he said, "I'm telling you—stay back."

Danielle found a path through the crowd in the market, brushing past bearded men, apologizing in French.

"Shawn? What is happening here?"

"That guy in the cellar," Shawn said, "was maybe shot by an American agent. I'm an American agent, or I was. I don't want cops confusing us."

As Shawn spoke he divided his attention between Tariq and a young man watching from the side of the alley. Shawn wondered where the hell he'd seen this kid, then remembered. It was the biker who'd nearly killed him, coming at high speed down a crowded lane, driving right at him and Danielle. Now the boy was watching something, someone, behind Shawn—who, by reflex, moved, bending his body, shifting sideways, away from the white-robed figure who swung out a hand holding something short and black—and Danielle, a pace ahead, heard a blow, a sound both soft and dull. Moments later she turned to see Shawn go down, stumbling, crawling, on hands and knees—the attacker with a short, wide-bladed knife—Shawn feeling the close heat of the man—seeing in his mind the youth in the cellar, disemboweled—and then heard the robed man screaming—bending, kicking at Shawn's protective arms, seeking a home for his curve-bladed kris. As Danielle, too, screamed, fearing Shawn's death, the crowd parted: She saw the robed assassin stare upward, wide-eyed, at Tariq, who hauled the man high in the air, tossing him like a paper dart to the wall of the alley. Hitting stone, he slid to the ground and lay there, unmoving.

Bending again, the bodyguard gently lifted Shawn, bearing him through the crowd as lightly as a mother dandling her child.

23

RUE TALAA KEBIRA, FES, MOROCCO, 28 MAY 2004

In the hotel room on rue Talaa Kebira, Danielle sat on the edge of Shawn's bed, unbuttoning his ripped and bloody shirt. She set a hand behind his neck, lifted his upper body inches from the mattress, and eased the shirt from under him. The skin of his ribs was scarified: broken and bleeding, a crosshatch of dark and oozing cuts.

She soaked a sponge in a bowl of warm water, squeezed it, then cleaned the wounds, easing out dirt.

Shawn said, "What was it?" His mouth damaged, his voice was not his voice.

Looking down at him, she said, "Don't move. I'm putting you back together. Best I can."

He was surprised by the tenderness of her touch. "What the hell was it? What hit me?"

She unbuckled his belt.

"The boy on the bike—the one who nearly killed us. He found you again. Then a man in a white robe—a galibaya—I didn't see his face. He had something in his hand—you must have—I mean, you must have felt it coming—"

He was quiet awhile, thinking back to the scene on the street. Some of it he recalled. "What did I do?"

"You moved away from him. You were turning in his direction, then you—you sensed something, I guess. You went the other away, fast, and down"—she was thinking back—"that is maybe why he did not hit you as hard as he could have. Then, he had a knife—"

She put a hand under the small of his back. "Lift your hips?"

He tried. She slid his khakis down his bruised thighs.

He winced. "This is kind of intimate." She began disinfecting the cuts on his groin. "What then?"

"He hit you again." She fingered the side of his neck. He thought not even his mother in her best days had touched him as tenderly as this. "Hit you here. The knife—you know, that scared me. He would kill. I tried to hold him back. He kicked—" She touched a bruise with her sponge. "That's where this came. You maybe cracked a rib."

She eased down his shorts to clean the wound on his hip. Despite the pain, his sex swelled. Amused, she touched his cock, then covered him again. "Looks like you'll live."

"Doesn't feel like that, inside my head. Feels like I was sapped."

"Which is?"

He tried to think what it was. "A sap—you know, it's like a blackjack. Leather and metal. Soft and heavy. You hit the guy in the right place, it's a killer." He touched his neck. "Few inches more, around here, could've snapped my spine."

She touched his forehead. It might have been a caress. "I believe you'll survive."

"Wonder why they went for me—I mean, in this place. What the hell have I done?"

She covered his body with a blanket and went to work on his battered face. "Maybe it's what you're doing. Not what you've done." She sponged his check.

"Easy," he said. "Just take it easy."

Blood had dried on his forehead, and in the darkness of his brows. She tried sponging it out.

"You can't place the guy who hit me?"

She shook her head. "All I know is—I told you—he wore white robes. His skin wasn't so dark—more like mine—I'd guess he's not Maghrebi. I never saw his face."

He was speaking more to himself than to her. "Hassan Tarkani, maybe. Or the English guy—what's his name? Alfred." Though he couldn't imagine Alfred Burke in Arab dress. "Is it tomorrow we fly?"

She put a gentle hand on his forehead to hold him still. "I made a booking. It's okay. I know you're short of cash. You pay the hotel, I'll do the flight." She cleaned dirt from the wound on his jaw. "Can you get on a plane?"

"No idea. Doesn't feel like it right now. Not even sure I could stand."

"Don't try. Don't move."

He ran his tongue around his mouth, checking his teeth. They were there, all of them. One of the incisors was loose. "How did you get me back here?"

"Tariq carried you. What do you weigh?"

He thought about it. "Hundred ninety-six. Something like that."

"Looked like you weighed ten pounds, twenty maybe, the way he lifted you. Like a child. *Petit môme.* You are fortunate he was there."

"And you," he said. Then, after a pause, "It's always me, right? Don't you ever have bad things happen?"

"Of course. *Comme tous.* Like everyone."

"For instance?"

For a moment, she hesitated, then said, "A few months ago—I was on that train in Madrid—the one the terrorists—"

"Bombed."

"Exactly. I was not in that part of the train. I was only bruised. The worst was—police thought I was one of the bombers. Here I was—cut, and bleeding—they lock me up."

He wondered about that. "Locked up for long?"

She laughed. "Not so long. All the same—you have been in a bombing, an attack, and then—"

He tried turning on his side, and gave up the attempt.

She went around the bed to rearrange the pillows and the duvet, then began to shed her clothes. "I'm sleeping here tonight. Is that okay? Don't even consider sex."

He tried to make himself comfortable on his side of the bed. Scraps of a dream came back. "Please," he said. "Forget you said that word. Even thinking about it is painful."

Late in the night, Shawn lay with his back to Danielle, feeling her warmth, looking toward the window, seeing the city's glow in the night sky. The honking of horns was quieter now. Somewhere, a donkey brayed.

She held him loosely, one arm across his flank, across the side of him that wasn't bruised. "Are you awake?"

He didn't move, except his head. She felt him nod. "Can't sleep."

"Tell me something," she said. "Would you ever think of having another child?"

For a while he thought that through. Then he said, "With you?"

"Just answer the question."

"You're married," he said. "Why wouldn't you have a child with Darius?"

"He doesn't want children."

In the darkness he waited, then turned his head toward her. "If I had another child, I'd want to be involved, bringing her up. I wasn't there, you know—not for my daughter. Won't make that mistake again."

"One can work out such things."

He waited, listening to her even breathing; waited to see if she would say more. Drowsy, scarcely awake, he told her, "It's okay. I decided. If I can walk, I'll come with you."

"To where?" she asked, after a time.

He said, "To Cairo."

24

Eighteen hours after leaving Morocco, Shawn lay, still hurting, in another darkened hotel bedroom, this one in the Bulaq district of Cairo. Once again, sleepless in an airless night, he tried, and tried again, to catch his breath. Since his beating in Fes he could never seem to find the air to fill his lungs. He ran fingers over his body, checking the state of his wounds. Scattered and various pain; it was hard to breathe deeply. Maybe that was the kicking, maybe a lead-loaded sap—he'd never know. Danielle could be right—it might be, like Martha, he'd cracked a rib. Maybe it was the ambience of this vast city that made him breathless. He'd read somewhere that Cairo's population was touching eighteen million: an endless urban mass, stretching into darkness on either side of the Nile. Eighteen million mouths, gulping the city's polluted air.

They were going downmarket now, he and Danielle, following the prisoner's trail. Missing Abbasi's final payment, Shawn was short of money. This hotel, on Ar Rihani Street, was cheap, noisy, unclean. It was all he could afford. From Mohamed Farid—a throughway two blocks over—came cacophonies of sound. Shawn had once heard that Egyptian drivers believe in the magic of noise: Honk loud enough, long enough, traffic will vanish. Road space opens up; jams disappear. Not, Shawn guessed, something evidence could disprove.

At least the noise wasn't gunfire. The last time Shawn was on duty in Cairo, guarding men who made a treaty with Israel, armed men had tried to terminate him and Bobby Walters. It was just outside the Egyptian Museum in Tahrir Square. Bobby saw the men coming and pulled Shawn into the museum's entrance, saving his life. They lived. Not everyone did. Nine tourists died that day in crossfire between security police and bin Laden's companion, the Egyptian al-Zawahiri.

Shawn lit up his watch to check the time. It was late. He found it harder and harder these days getting to sleep without sex or drugs. He'd searched his travel bag for pills but nothing to make him sleep or relieve his pain. Across the room, he heard Danielle's calm and regular breathing. Almost two months, he figured, since she'd had sex. He kept waiting for the night when she'd no longer deny her need, the night she'd leave her bed and come to his. True, they'd briefly shared a bed in Morocco, but that, Shawn knew, was because he'd been hurt. Helpless and sexless.

Shocked and scared, if he were honest. It was hard for him to admit, but the street attack in Fes frightened him. The fact that he hadn't seen it coming, had no sense of danger. He was getting old, he thought: bad guys, young killers, catching up on him.

Now he lay awhile in a waking dream, trying to arouse himself with fantasy: trying to recall desire for the fleshless body of Ellen Reynolds. Her narrow ass; her wandering mouth.

When his watch told him it was two in the morning, and when sleep seemed no closer, Shawn left his bed and went to Danielle's. Pulling back the sheet that covered her, he stood for a moment, looking down. In sleep, her T-shirt rode up over the hinge of her thighs. She murmured something, some words he couldn't catch.

When Shawn shifted his gaze upward, he saw Danielle was awake now, motionless, her eyes wide—later, he thought he must have imagined this—like the red-eyed gaze of a night-roaming wolf he'd once caught in a spotlight, high in the Southern Rockies.

Filled with unreasoning fear—a crazy sense of panic—Shawn backed toward his bed.

Danielle spoke without raising her voice.

"If you ever try that," she said, "if you ever touch me when I don't want to be touched—if you ever try that, I will kill you. It's a promise. You're stronger, I know, but sometime you'll sleep. I swear, I will kill you."

She turned away then. Shawn saw her pull up the sheet, her face to the wall, hair spread promiscuously across a pillow. Again, her breathing was even. Hard as it was to believe, she seemed to be sliding back to sleep.

In his own bed, Shawn lay awake. His fears ebbed, exposing deep-seated disturbance. Once again, he thought of quitting the beautiful she-wolf across the room. Walking away. Then, in the heavy heat of the Cairo night, he remembered Danielle once more as he'd first seen her—first wanted her—as she stood watchful and beautiful in a Parisian apartment.

He was not yet ready, it seemed, to leave this city. Or the prisoner's wife.

25

At first light, Shawn slept. He woke when Danielle, in shirt and chinos, came again to sit on the edge of his bed, placing coffee on the table beside it. Lost in her own thoughts, she said nothing about the past night. She seemed calm, untroubled. Had Shawn not recalled the embers of her eyes, what passed between them in the darkness might have been a disturbing dream, dissolved by day.

Danielle drank a concoction the color of mango juice, with something pink—grapefruit?—added in. With fingertips she touched his bare chest. Her voice was gentle. "I'm curious," she said. "My guess, you've slept with many women. Am I right?"

This would not, Shawn thought, be an easy conversation. He went back through the years to his initiation: a first clumsy coupling with Miss Catfish, on the floor of a dog-trot shack, somewhere in the pinewoods of northern Alabama.

"Well," he said. "Women. There've been a few. We're talking thirty-some years."

"These women—the ones you had—where are they now?"

"Who knows?" he asked, thinking back.

"Someone knows," she told him, "but not you." She put her hand beneath his unshaven chin, tilting his aching head upward. "Do you ever wonder why I would wish to be one of them?"

"What do you want me to say, Danielle? What did I do?"

"You tried to rape me."

"Let me tell you about last night," he said. "I never touched you. I don't frighten easy, Dani, but for a minute there, you scared hell out of me. Your eyes, Jesus God. If it comes to forgetting, I doubt I'll forget you."

She was reflective. "Okay," she said, "okay. But there's a part of your life you'll have to deal with one day. If you live."

He was silent, suppressing what he might say.

"Now," she said, "tell me about this place."

"Cairo?"

"Cairo. Tell me how we reach the jail. How we get in. It is seven weeks now, they have Darius."

"Fifty-one days."

"He must think I forgot him." She put down her glass. "You have—what did you call him?—an asset here?"

Shawn turned his mind to the day ahead. "Samir Aziz."

"When do we see him?"

He tried his coffee. It was cool now, black and sweet and strong. He wondered where it came from.

"Samir? I tried him. His cell phone's dead. Or the network's down. This town, who knows?"

"You have an address?"

He nodded.

"Go shower, then." When he hesitated, she said, "Don't be shy. For what it's worth, I've seen you naked."

Shawn slid out of bed, hands covering his groin, and went to the bathroom. Behind him, he thought he heard her laugh. So far today, he'd found nothing amusing.

26

When Shawn last saw Samir Aziz, before 9/11, the man had lived off Muhammad Naguib Square, in a side street, an alley, behind a cloth market. He pictured it now: rack after rack of used clothes blowing in a warm breeze from the Nile. All the garments newly washed and ironed, all bargains. He'd bought a shirt there once—a good shirt, clean, blue denim, seventy-five U.S. cents.

Now, out in the street, in the heat, amid the hectic traffic of Mohamed Farid, Shawn stopped a black and white and red-brown taxicab. The red, he saw, was rust.

Getting in, Danielle paused. "How far away is your man? Your asset? Can we walk?"

He eased her into the aging Lada and gave directions to the souk. "You ever tried crossing a Cairo street?"

"They must do it."

"Sure they do. Watch." He pointed as the taxi turned right, passing Bab al-Futuh. "Look there—that guy—see what he's doing now? Walking through five goddamn lanes. Five lanes, solid traffic." He heard Danielle's intake of breath. "Like he doesn't see it. He's saying, 'Come on, hit me, I lived a good life, I believe in God, I believe in paradise, I'm ready to go.'" Again, he heard her breath catch. "Look at *this* guy. Just heads on out—cars coming right at him. Like they don't exist. Trucks touching him, three lanes to go. I'm not that brave. I didn't get to the age I am so I'd die crossing roads in this town."

Nine minutes later, the cabdriver nosed through a group of waiting bearded men to stop in Sharia al-Muski. The man pointed to the meter. "Sir, eight pounds, please, Egyptian. From now, you must walk. This place here, I cannot drive."

Out of the dying Lada, scanning the market, Shawn said, "You see what he means."

In the shadow of Ibn Tulun, the clothes market spread before them in rainbows of color. Scattered among the clothes sellers were aging shoeshine men, hunkered by their stands; robed youths pushing carts piled with strawberries and lemons; women seated on the sidewalk, guarding vast baskets of mint and parsley, and tubs piled with eggfruit, herbs, and garlic. There were onion stalls, coffee stalls, barrows of lettuce, casks of tomatoes, hanging bags of oranges, sweet and bitter, rolls of bright-patterned cloth. At the borders of the market, donkeys tied to lampposts drooped grizzled heads, ears flicking at flies.

Cages loud with singing birds hung high above the sidewalk.

Taking Danielle by the hand, Shawn led her through the square. Men preparing for a wedding used wind machines to air the kapok that poured from an old and unstitched mattress. Women watched, nodding, missing nothing. Grandmothers, hooded and patient, sat in plastic chairs; girls danced together, laughing, touching ringed hands in the carefree street. Permeating all, a smell of spice and sweat and sewage.

In the distance, minarets reached for heaven.

Danielle stared about her. "My God," she said, "I know Morocco, but this—this is chaos. Do you have any idea at all of where you're going?"

Shawn edged between a donkey-drawn tea wagon and a seller of used shoes. "I remember places. I've been here before. Once. Somewhere, there was an alley"—he turned into a dark declivity—"on the right, this, I think, could be . . . "

A six-story building, pink tiled, its windows glass bricked and metal framed. At random, Shawn pressed an unnamed bell.

Youths—one holding a baby like a rugby ball—rode through the alley on motor scooters, swerving around dancing women. In a gutter lay the body of a brindled cat. A boy bounced a balding tennis ball against a wall beside them. After a time, a nail-studded door was opened by a young man in cloth cap and galibaya. He spoke softly into a pink Nokia phone. Pointing to a spiral staircase, he held up four fingers.

"Fourth floor, I guess," Shawn told Danielle. "How does he know who we are? And why does he have a handgun?"

The young man still shouted into his phone. Shawn started to climb a marble-stepped staircase.

She said, "I heard. He was talking of an operation. Whatever that means. And he had no gun."

"Trust me," Shawn said, "he did. That's a thing I notice. Even with guys wearing sheets." He paused on the first landing, rubbing the small of his back, breathing hard. "Stairs," he said. "It'll get to you one day. Climbing these damn things. Remember where you heard it first." He started moving again, more slowly. "You'd never guess I used to be a quarterback."

"That's true," she said. "I never would."

On the third flight, Shawn paused again, holding the stair rail, looking down to the hall far below. "Something I read someplace— time you get to my age, your lung capacity's down to half what it was." He started climbing again. "Which I now believe."

She stopped, two stairs higher, looking back, laughing. "Should I give you a hand?"

"Get out of here."

He climbed a little faster then, trying not to show his age, stopping at a door that had been kicked in, then patched with unpainted plywood. He knocked and waited. There was a sound as if someone inside the apartment were moving furniture. Eventually, the door was opened by a middle-aged man wearing crumpled khakis and an Afghan cap. He stepped backward a pace, about to speak, then changed his mind.

"Samir," Shawn said. "Good morning. You don't remember me."

The man glanced behind him, then looked down the hall. He said, "I do. Who is this?"

"Danielle Baptiste. A friend. Not police, not FBI, not intel. French American. Can we come in?"

Samir hesitated, then stood aside. The room was small and filled with too much furniture. Wooden-latticed windows— *mashrabiya*—filtered subaqueous light.

"Ahmed," Samir said, introducing a black-bearded young man who sat alert on a torn leather couch, watching the visitors with interest. "Mr. Maguire, how can I help you?"

"D'you mind?" Shawn said. "I had some trouble recently." He backed out the still-open entrance door, looking up and down the empty corridor. He closed the door, crossed the overcrowded room, opened a door on the far side, and checked that the room beyond was empty. Then he sat on the unstuffed arm of the chair Danielle had taken.

Samir pushed a chair against the door.

Shawn said, "This lady's husband is Darius Osmani. Thirty-something Iranian, works in Europe."

Danielle said, "Did."

"Did work in Europe. We think now he's a frequent flyer, being held somewhere—somewhere in the city. Maybe by your people, Samir. Mukhabarat, I mean."

"There is more than one."

"Son, don't dick around. You know what I mean—Dairat al Mukhabarat. I'd guess, if we asked nicely, they'd say they were helping my people. Which, of course, they do."

The two Egyptians exchanged glances.

"Enhanced interrogation," Shawn said.

Someone tapped on the door. Samir opened it a crack. Shawn slipped the safety of his handgun, went to the door, and checked there was no one in sight. Samir returned to his seat. There was silence. Then Samir said, "I should tell you, sir, that I assisted you—your people, as you say—I assisted you in the past. But now, no more."

Shawn considered that. "Okay. Tell me. What went wrong? Didn't we pay you?"

"The way you treat men of our faith is what went wrong," said the young man on the couch, breaking in. "Here in Egypt. In Iraq. Afghanistan. Kashmir. Palestine. Chechnya. You expect that we should—we should simply accept this? We should stand by, we should help, while you"—he pointed at Samir—"and his people, you torture us? Kill us?"

Shawn was watching the young man. "Quite a speech," he said at last. "Ahmed al-Masri, right? I know who you are. You speak very good English."

"I was brought up in Manchester." Now the man smiled through a black beard peppered with gray. "Manchester, England."

"I've heard of it," Shawn said. "Like I've heard of you." He nodded at Danielle. "This lady's husband is Muslim. Maybe that's why you should help us."

Danielle said to Samir, "Please. I've not seen Darius for almost two months. I think about him just—I wonder how he is—"

"It's normal," said al-Masri.

"I worry that he's being hurt. Wherever he's held—"

Again, there was silence.

Finally, Samir said to Danielle, "It's true, your man is here. I believe he came by small plane. Gulfstream, I think. From Morocco."

"From Fes?"

"Indeed. I heard."

Danielle was writing fast on a page of her diary. "Has he been hurt?"

Samir considered her. He shrugged. "Why else do they send him to Egypt, if not for that? Did Mr. Maguire not tell you? It is what we do. It is, perhaps, our expertise."

"Can we see him?"

"I have no idea. You know what they say. It is not my department."

She tore out the diary page and passed it to Samir. "Could you please give that to Darius? Please?"

"I have no idea if I can do that," Samir said. "I do not have access to all parts of the prison. Where Americans are boss, I cannot go. Besides, I have heard your man will be moved again. You know—these people, these frequent flyers—they do not stay long in one place."

"If Darius is moved, where will he go?"

Samir shifted his attention from Danielle to Shawn. "You, sir, you will know where, more than I." He hesitated, glanced at his companion, then said, "Peshawar. Often, for them, Peshawar is next stop."

Al-Masri, checking the time, stood suddenly. "Till tomorrow," he told Samir. "The same time." To Shawn he said, "One day, you must tell how you know me—and what you know."

"I can tell you the last bit part," Shawn said. "Embassy bombing in Dar."

Al-Masri smiled. "A rumor," he said. "There was not ever proof." As he spoke, there were two echoing shots, in rapid succession, shockingly loud in the building's enclosed space.

Before Shawn could move, Samir disappeared. Al-Masri went the other way. Shawn followed Samir out the door, extending an arm to keep Danielle inside the room. She ducked under it and came into the corridor, running toward the stairwell. Looking over the metal balustrade Shawn saw, three floors below, that the robed man who first opened the street door had pocketed his pink phone. Fitting a silencer to what Shawn thought was a Baikal semiautomatic, the man moved into a position from which he could target al-Masri as the running man came toward him down the winding stairs. Seeing the marksman below, al-Masri bent double, made for the building's outer wall, opened a long window, hesitated a long moment looking down, then jumped. Danielle, coming fast down the stairs behind him, paused at the open window, looking out. From behind Shawn came the sound of booted feet. Turning, Shawn saw a tall man running, holding a familiar weapon. A reflex action, Shawn stretched out a leg, forgetting the knife wound from Fes. Pain shot through him, thigh to spine. The tall man, moving fast, tripped. Unable to break his fall, he went down like a falling tree. A crack of bone as his shoulder hit concrete. The handgun, a 1911, skidded across the floor.

Shawn, too, found himself lying flat, nursing his injured leg. Grabbing the pistol, face to the fallen man, he saw this was an operative he knew: Gordie Slade, a onetime Langley colleague. There was history here, too. Gordie had started off disliking Shawn until Shawn briefly dated Gordie's twenty-year-old daughter. Then dislike turned to hatred.

CIA assassination squad in Egypt, Shawn thought. They sure as hell kept that quiet.

"Gordie," he said, trying to stand, "what the fuck are you doing?"

Slade eased himself from the floor, gently flexing his injured arm.

"Give me back my gun." Shawn held the weapon out of reach.

"Double tap, if you want to know." Slade touched his temple. "Boom, boom."

Shawn passed back the weapon. "Double tap on who?"

Slade moved to the iron balustrade. Looking down to the lobby, three floors below, he cocked the Springfield. "He's a terrorist. Name classified."

"If it's Ahmed al-Masri," Shawn said, "he's not down there." He pointed back toward Samir's apartment. "Al-Masri went out a window. Onto the roof, I'd guess."

Gordie headed down the stairs. Over his shoulder he said, "I could arrest you, Maguire."

Shawn stood, massaging his leg. "For what?"

"Obstructing me."

Shawn followed down the stairs, limping a little. "Slade," he said, "if you want to try that, you need to be a lot smarter than you were when I knew you."

Outside the apartment building, Shawn looked for Danielle. There was no sign of her. Or of Ahmed al-Masri.

Which, Shawn thought, was not in any way a good thing.

27

Somewhere in Cairo, Shawn believed—somewhere in this multi-farious city—Ahmed al-Masri held Danielle hostage. That was how he figured it as he stood undecided, at a loss, in the narrow alley of Qasr Badawi. The thought of kidnap made him momentarily nauseous. Memories came floating up: memories he'd tried to forget. A missing friend, a hostage, death by decapitation.

A severed head, startle-eyed and staring.

He stood for a moment on the sidewalk outside Samir's apartment building, shaken, fearing for Danielle, helpless amid the noise and color and jostle of the market.

In another town, he might have called the police, but here? Samir was a cop, and what could he do? Shawn had no faith in Samir's ability to rescue Danielle, or anyone else.

The police sharpshooters—if they were police—had vanished.

As had al-Masri and Danielle. Shawn had no idea which way they'd gone.

Behind him, Samir came around the corner of the building, looking to left and right: an animal emerging, fearful, from its burrow. "Mr. Maguire," he said. He came close, his voice low. "You know, sir, what this means? Americans know I had Ahmed in my apartment? If my people learn of it—"

"What?"

"I will lose my job," said Samir. "Why?" He answered his own question. "Because he is on the list, Ahmed. Your list, our list. Terrorist."

Shawn grabbed Samir's arm and pulled him from the alley, through the teeming square. "Tomorrow, son, you worry about your job. Right now, we're keeping Danielle alive." He looked around him. No traffic came this way. "We get to some road, we catch a cab."

"Sir? Cab to where?"

"Where al-Masri lives."

"I don't know where he lives."

"Hundred bucks says you'll remember. Which way? Where's a cab?"

Samir, pointing, headed down a muddy track beside a litter-filled canal. Shawn followed, his heart beating faster than it should. Ignoring his injured leg, he ran, overtaking his guide. Coming around a bend, he found the narrow path blocked by a slate-topped billiard table—God knows how it got there. Four city kids were in midgame: one now lining up a shot on the tilting, still-perfect baize. Between a clay-brick wall to the left and the canal to the right, there was no way around. Shawn leaped onto the table, scrabbling for a foothold, hurting his leg, as the baseball-capped boy shot for a pocket. The table rocked. Shawn spread his arms, trying to balance. The table slid, smooth and sidelong, to the mud-brown water.

As it sank, Shawn hauled himself from the canal, fending off skinny boys. Shouting and laughing, they attacked him with their cues. Back on his feet, wet and stinking, Shawn ran east. When he looked back toward Samir, he saw the boys weren't following: Knee-deep in mud, they tried to lift the massive table. Beyond them, another figure. Even at this distance, Shawn recognized the fallible marksman with the pink phone. In one swift movement, the boy nearest the bank angled his cue between the gunman's legs. Shawn saw the man spread his arms as he dived, yelling, toward the canal. There was a single shot, then a second.

Someone screamed, a high wailing yell.

Shawn turned a bend in the track and ducked beneath a bridge. Boys, sniper, and table were lost to sight. "The way that guy shoots," he called to Samir, "the boy should live."

Samir said nothing. He had no breath left for speech. He pointed ahead as they reached El Gamaliya. The street here was filled with yelling men, carrying signs. Though he read no Arabic, Shawn understood, from crude images, they were protesting the price of bread on which, he guessed, they lived. Toward the edges of the crowd, uniformed police clubbed any head they could reach.

Shawn waved to the driver of a black-and-white taxi brought to a stop by the riot. When Samir caught up, shielding his face from fellow policemen, Shawn pushed him into the car.

To the taxi driver, he called, "Wait." To Samir he said, "Brother, if you don't remember al-Masri's address, believe me, I'll tell your boss what you were planning with that guy. Don't say you were shooting the breeze. I know who he is. We both know. Like you said, al-Masri's on your list, he's on our list. He's roadkill. He organized the fucking embassy hits. Our guys died."

To the driver, Samir said, "El Sagha." Then something else, in Arabic.

The man drove, draping his wrists over the wheel, the way a wolf might, if a wolf were driving a cab. As the car turned right, passing Salah ad-Din, Samir said to Shawn, "Ahmed denies he was involved in those bombings."

"Tell the cops, not me."

"I am a cop."

"Okay. Tell your boss. Tell Mukhabarat. See what your job's worth. See what your life's worth. My guess, al-Masri's holding Danielle as a hostage. What do you think?"

Samir shrugged. "Maybe. Try her mobile phone."

Shawn stared. "Say what? This guy's al Qaeda. Works with Zawahiri. He's not going to leave her with a phone." He flicked through speed-dial numbers on his own phone and pressed the call key.

He listened, then said, "Jesus, Dani, talk quiet, okay? You're in his apartment? Listen, we know where you are. He's doing what with a laptop?" He listened, then said, "Crushing it? Okay, forget that. Not our problem. We're on our way to pull you out. Cops may get there first. If there's shooting, don't do any brave shit. Stay down. Run, if you get a break. Keep cool. Love you."

It was the second time he'd said that.

Breaking the connection, he told Samir, "Get the driver to go faster." Then he said, "You're right. He's careless, al-Masri. He's destroying his laptop. Tough work. Dani's still got her phone."

"Not careless," Samir said. "Frightened for his life. Those men in my building have nearly killed him. Maybe they will follow. It could be they know where he lives. Today, the man might die."

"Who gives a damn?"

"Your girl might die."

"If she does," Shawn said, "someone else will, too. Maybe him. Maybe you."

The taxi stopped. Samir pointed. "Here is the place."

Shawn looked out at a tall gray concrete-block building, each balcony hung with white garments and bright-colored cloth, stirred by a breeze from the Nile.

"Which floor?"

"Second."

"What vehicles do you guys use when you're not in patrol cars?"

"Police? Ford Transit."

"Like that one, parked there? Okay. Tell the driver, make a U-turn. Tell him, stop real close to that door. Then tell him, wait. He doesn't move. Got it?"

Somewhere, a muezzin called for midday prayers.

On the far side of the road was a makeshift mosque, hardly more than an alcove set back from the street. The building, once a warehouse, was now in ruins: a mess of rusting steel. Off the street, someone had used mud bricks to build a low barrier, four feet high, closing off part of the industrial ruin. Men ran to enter this place of prayer. Shedding boots and shoes in the street, they knelt behind the wall. All were barefoot, foreheads touching ragged prayer mats.

Samir spoke to the driver in Arabic. The man obeyed, turning his taxi, parking close to the curb. Leaving him with sheaves of worthless pounds, Shawn left the car, keeping low. Moving as fast as his limp allowed, he approached the street door of al-Masri's building. Inside, the ground floor hall was white tiled, blank and empty, the only decoration an urn filled with fading strelitzia flowers. A black-clad figure—a woman—sat unmoving on the lowest step of a concrete stair. Under a hood, in shadow, her face had the shape of a man's. Expressionless, she watched Shawn as he passed her, running up the stairs. On the second floor he stopped a headscarfed maid carrying a bundle of towels.

"You speak English?"

With her free hand, the woman held up a close-spaced thumb and forefinger. "Little."

"I want a man with'—Shawn gestured—"long hair. Beard, like this—black, with gray."

The maid pointed behind her, to the corridor's second door. Shawn took a breath. He hit the woodwork with his good shoulder and bounced off, bruised.

When they do that in movies, he thought, the goddamn door breaks.

He hit the door again. This time, the jamb did give: The door swung wide. Danielle lay prone on the uncarpeted floor—her feet bound, mouth gagged. As far as Shawn could see, she was un-injured. When he released her, she took deep breaths, sat up, and pointed to a blue-painted inner door. "He's in there."

"Alone?" She nodded. "He's got the laptop?"

Cocking his Makarov, Shawn approached the blue door. Danielle spoke with sudden urgency. "God, Shawn—get down. He's got—"

The upper half of the blue door splintered, shattered by a spreading hail of shells. A window fractured; glass, like a sheet of ice, slid to the floor and cracked in two. Standing lamps blew to pieces; on a mantelpiece, a liter of vodka vaporized in a mist of spirits. Shawn crawled back across the floor, away from the shattered door. Grabbing Danielle's wrist, he dragged her to the corridor outside. He was trying to catch his breath. "I guess," he said, more to himself than to her, "the end of that sentence was a 'Kalashnikov.'" At a limping run, he went for the exit stairs, looking back to check that Danielle kept pace. "Something I never got used to," he told her, "is being shot at with submachine guns." Forgetting his injured leg, he went down the concrete steps three at a time. "Move," he said. "We need to get out of here."

Danielle followed more slowly. "You're leaving al-Masri?"

"Believe me," Shawn said, "I wanted his laptop more than him. Could have done a deal with the Company, if I'd got it. But—" They were in the building's lobby. The black-clad woman, who was now a man, was heading outside. From his robe he drew what Shawn saw was an American .38 Magnum.

"But—what?" asked Danielle, watching the robed man.

"But I know when I'm outgunned," Shawn said. "An AK's not that accurate. If it's on automatic, that doesn't matter too much. Ten rounds a second, you're going to hit some damn thing. Which could be me." He held open the building's steel-lined entrance door. "I want to see what's happening here."

Outside the apartment building Samir stood by the taxi, looking upward. The gray structure loomed over them, its eastern wall blank and rough, unfinished. From the top story, wide joists— balks of darkened wood—projected outward, like cannons from a warship.

On one of the joists stood Ahmed al-Masri, a puppet, a dwarf, black against a cloudless sky. Balancing; swaying; edging outward.

Samir backed away from the building. "I believe Ahmed will— he will—I believe he is about to jump."

"To the next building?" Shawn asked. "From there? No way. No chance." In his mind he measured the angle for a shot. He wasn't sure he could do it. With a rifle, perhaps. Not with a handgun.

Danielle's lips were moving. No words came.

Now there were other black-clad men kneeling on the building's roof. CIA hit squad, Shawn thought, awaiting an order to shoot.

Al-Masri, arms wide, balancing like a man on a tightrope, came to the end of the beam. He stood there a moment assessing the gap, poised in space. Even from where he stood, Shawn could see the man was shaking.

"No," he said again to Samir. "No. Never make it."

Afterward, Shawn was unsure whether he heard a shot before or after the young man jumped, in a high parabola that did take him to the next building, but not to its roof. Shawn saw al-Masri grab at a balcony rail, startling the old woman who stood there gathering armfuls of washing. As she backed away, into her apartment, the rail tore from its mooring, sending the Egyptian downward—a tiny flailing figure, black against an Egyptian sky, falling, and falling, and falling.

Shawn bundled Danielle into the back of the still-waiting taxi. He said, "I have your passport."

Samir climbed into the shotgun seat. Shawn looked back to see what was happening behind them. A curious crowd had gathered, gazing down at the terrorist's shattered body. The cop with the pink Nokia stepped forward to put a single shot in the head of the corpse.

"That range," Shawn said, "he can handle." To Samir, he said, "Tell the cab guy to turn. Tell him, don't go past the Transit. Don't drive fast. Then tell him, take us out to the airport."

The taxi was driving along the banks of the Nile when Danielle asked, why the airport? Where were they heading? To Peshawar?

Shawn shook his head. "I really don't want to do that."

She asked why.

"Memories," he said. "Peshawar, I have memories. Guy called Raphael Ramirez. He died there." He paused, then said, "I helped to kill him."

28

Shawn had had some bad weeks, but the week Rafe Ramirez died in Peshawar was the worst he could recall; the worst in a bad twelve months.

The year started well—Shawn was settled in the Agency, promised promotion—but now Lala was demanding a divorce, for reasons she was prepared to list, and did list, with the help of a hungry female lawyer. Alcohol and pills and assorted flirtations all figured in Lala's accounting. She moved out of the family home in Brandywine; by court order, it had to be sold. When Shawn found a buyer, Lala refused to sign. The house wasn't in great shape, due to fights at the messy end of the marriage, but she thought it was worth way more than what was on the table.

Shawn called his soon-to-be-ex-wife where she was living with her new boyfriend, an unemployed actor called Chet. When Chet worked—not often—he specialized in action movies. His acting ability lay in his arms: a great set of delts and pecs. Without irony, he called himself an action hero. Shawn asked to speak with Lala, not the hero. He tried to stay polite. He told his wife the house would go to the bank if not sold by the end of the week.

Keeping his voice down, he said, "You know what repossession means? Should I spell it for you, you dumb bitch?" At which point Lala hung up the phone. It was Rafe Ramirez, the good buddy, who got her talking again. Rafe who organized the house sale. Rafe who sat in sad bars, hearing Shawn rehearse his troubles with marriage, and with women.

Late in '98, the two men went separate ways. Rafe was dropped into Iraq to check on what might be a nuclear weapons program. Shawn was posted to Sudan to keep an eye on assorted bad guys. Among them were bin Laden and al-Zawahiri, camping there, though not yet seen as a serious threat.

When the Agency closed down its Sudanese operation, al Qaeda dropped off the map for a time. Shawn was sent to Afghanistan, crossing the Pakistani border from Peshawar, delivering lethal weaponry—Stingers—to what became the nucleus of the Taliban. He was there, in Pakistan, at the end of the year when terrorists blew up American embassies in Nairobi and Dar es Salaam. Langley brass were, as ever, blindsided. After Sudan, they'd lost touch with al Qaeda, but now they made a guess that Afghanistan—bin Laden's new base—figured in the mix.

Rafe was pulled out of Iraq and sent to meet with Shawn in Peshawar, on the Afghan-Pakistani border. Conventional wisdom held that if there was any one place to gather intelligence on religious terrorism, that place was Peshawar. Unlike most conventional wisdom, this was, in fact, the case.

Shawn and Rafe took rooms at the Rose Hotel, in Khyber

Bazaar, on Shoba Chowk. Rafe had a young sidekick learning the trade: a southern kid from outside Little Rock called Dodie Sale. He had some proper Arkansas-type name, but Shawn never remembered what it was. Most of the time Rafe just called the kid "fuckwit." Dodie called his boss Chief or—if he was feeling lucky—Jefe. Between the three of them, they picked the Rose Hotel partly because there was not a lot of choice in Peshawar among places that had not been bombed, and partly because the hotel had a restaurant where all sorts of people came to eat, and some of those people likely had information about the embassy bombings. Getting it was a whole other issue. Shawn didn't wish to criticize his friend, but Rafe spoke no Arabic. Not even basic. Even if he had, extracting information from foreigners was not one of Rafe's skills.

In Peshawar that scorching summer, in the restaurant of the Rose, Rafe raked over the problems he had with his various bosses. Dodie sat silent and listened, as he commonly did when Rafe spoke. Shawn and Rafe tried to understand what was happening in the Agency, then seemingly confused as to mission. *Did Langley ever read field reports?* Rafe asked aloud. *Had those assholes ever heard the words "al Qaeda?" Did they not know ISI was sending American cash to the Taliban?* He stopped midsentence to point out an Arab-looking man sitting alone in a shadowed corner of the restaurant.

"Bilal Sayed Salaah," he said. "Am I wrong?"

Shawn had an eidetic memory for the photographs the Agency held on its Terminate file. After a cautious glance he said, "If I had to guess, I'd say that's him."

"Well, then," Rafe said, standing, "he speaks English, right? Let's go chat."

"Believe me," Shawn said, "not a good idea. Not here, not now." But Rafe was already crossing the room, carrying his magnum glass of gin and juice, which looked, from the outside, like straight OJ. He sat himself at Salaah's table and, though he knew the answer, asked if the man spoke English.

Salaah glanced at Shawn and Dodie, who took seats at the same table. He said that he did indeed speak English.

"Then," Rafe said, "help me. Tell me what's happening across the border. Tell me what's happening in the south. Start with Kandahar. Then tell me what goes down with ISI. With Mullah Omar. With the Taliban."

Salaah asked why Rafe imagined he would know.

"Because," Rafe said, "according to my information, you are an adviser to the mullah. You are his liaison with groups outside the country, since he's never been out of Afghanistan. Isn't that right?

"No," Salaah said, "that is not right. None of it."

Rafe brought his heavy glass down hard on Salaah's right hand. Shawn thought he heard some small bone crack. Rafe took the man's hand in his own and gripped. Salaah yelled and half-stood, tipping the table, trying to get away, trying to break the agent's hold. With his free hand, Rafe reached out to squeeze the man's balls.

Across the restaurant, armed men also stood, to see what was happening.

"We should leave," Shawn said. "Now."

Rafe let go of Salaah's hand. The man's eyes were bright with tears.

"Next time, brother," Rafe said to Salaah, "don't lie to me, or I'll hurt you. Truly. I don't like being lied to. Ask my buddy here.

Makes me act mean—do things I might regret. Things you might regret."

Shawn took Rafe's arm and eased him out of the restaurant. When they glanced back, Salaah was still in his seat, nursing his hand and, it seemed, watching which road they took.

After that, things went steeply downhill. Shawn had only one reliable informant in Peshawar: a hotel waiter who called himself Jamal, though that was not his given name. The self-styled Jamal had brothers in a Taliban training camp in the mountainous regions of Wana and Miranshah.

Jamal was edgy. He would speak to Shawn only when he was doing his job, serving food. After the incident with Salaah, he doubled his price for information. His most urgent message was that Rafe and Shawn and Dodie should leave town.

"Why would I leave?" Shawn asked. "I'll have the chicken tikka."

"Sir," said Jamal, low-voiced, "I tell you again, you and your friends should leave. Do you know where they are?"

"Right this moment," Shawn said, "no."

Jamal turned away. "I will bring you bottled water."

As things turned out, it was already too late to leave. Before Shawn finished eating, Jamal came back. Speaking quietly, he said, "Sir, I told you."

"Told me what?"

"You should leave. Now, they have your friends."

Shawn felt his heart miss a beat. He stood. "What do you mean—they have Mr. Ramirez?"

"And the other man. Young man."

"Who has him? Where? Tell me."

Jamal, who was already whispering, lowered his voice further. "Men put them in a car. A blue Lada."

Shawn held Jamal's wrist in an unbreakable grip. "What men? They took them where?"

"Sir, please let me go. You are hurting. I don't know where they have your friends."

"Then," Shawn said quietly, "fucking find out, Jamal. Do it fast."

In those days, Shawn still talked by satellite phone to Langley. Langley called in a group of special forces based outside Quetta, to search for Mullah Omar. These men had CIA links, though they were said not to be paid by the Company, or officially part of it. Langley told Shawn there would be a time gap. He guessed the crew would be driving into Peshawar in their usual style, in Humvees, firing at motorcyclists who might be suicide bombers, edging other traffic—cars, mules, auto-rickshaws, and people—off the narrow road. Even so, the squad might take time.

By then, Jamal knew where Rafe and Dodie were. Once again, the waiter doubled his price for the information because, he said, he, too, would need to leave town, would have to cross the border, in case he had been seen talking with the American agents more often than serving food would merit. Mr. Ramirez and Mr. Sale were held, he said, under a dried-fruit warehouse out on the Warsak Road. If not there, in a gas station beside the warehouse.

"Under? You said *under* a warehouse?"

The waiter nodded, lowering his voice further. "Beneath, sir. Tunnels have been made. Now, your friends are there. Or in the place next door."

Shawn passed Rafe's location to the captain of the unit he'd called in. The captain said he was three miles out of Peshawar. He gave an ETA and advised Shawn not to go near the target location. Shawn omitted to say that he was already on his way there. As unobtrusive transport, he'd hired a local taxi, a Morris Oxford. If the driver wondered why an American would go to such an isolated and dangerous location, he said nothing about it. He hoped for—and finally got—an unusually large tip, which might, Shawn hoped, persuade him not to talk with the local men of al Qaeda. He was asked to wait a quarter mile down the street.

The fruit warehouse on Warsak Road was a three-story gray concrete monolith seemingly devoid of life. Shawn waited in the shelter of a parked truck, a Russian KAMAZ. From behind the cab, he watched a shalwar-clad Pakistani exit from the building's rear entrance. The guard was young and restless: a kid, really. He propped his rifle against a graffiti-covered wall and moved from foot to foot, scratching himself. Back home, Shawn would have assumed this was a man in need of a drink. In Muslim Pakistan, it must be something else: a smoke, Shawn guessed, as the man made a cigarette sign to a passing seller of khat and was briefly rebuffed. Moments later, the guard retrieved his rifle and disappeared around the corner of the building in search of more generous smokers.

Shawn cocked the Beretta he carried and went fast into the warehouse. Quietly closing the street door, he was confronted by a passage on ground level and steps leading down in half-darkness to a level below. On this lower level, Shawn surveyed a network of tunnels—by the look of them, recently dug from subterranean clay.

The central burrow, airless, was lit by a single electric bulb. A goddamn grave, Shawn thought. I could die down here.

You think like that, he told himself, you *will* die. Concentrating, he considered his surroundings, working out the way forward and—when he'd need it—the way back.

Taking shallow breaths, he followed the central tunnel deeper into damp earth, guessing he was now amid the foundations of the warehouse, or some earlier structure. Around him rose smells of rot, of corruption. Dead flesh. The walls here were shored with metal sheeting, which, farther on, gave way to stone. This section, Shawn thought, must have been a cellar, maybe before the warehouse was built above. He stopped short, taking in a dimly lit shape ahead; seeing then that this was the ass end of a kneeling man on a straw mat, praying to where he thought Mecca might be. Beside him on the mat lay a machine pistol—a Steyr, Shawn guessed, though in this light, it was hard to tell. Moving quietly, he knelt beside the man, picked up the pistol—it was indeed a Steyr—and touched his own Beretta to the side of the supplicant's head. Shawn had always found that a gun barrel in an earhole would reliably get a man's attention.

It worked. Moving gently, the praying man sat up, glancing at the place where his pistol had been. Not seeing it, he raised his hands in the air and murmured words under his breath.

In basic Arabic, Shawn told him, "You make a noise, my friend, I will kill you. Kill you quietly. Now, show me where the Americans are."

Moving carefully, the man raised a single finger. One American.

"Stand up," said Shawn. "Show me."

The man stood. Like the guard on the street, he wore a blue shalwar kameez. Leaning his head a little away from the Beretta—which, Shawn thought, was understandable—the Pakistani walked down the tunnel at a slow, somnambulant pace. From somewhere, Shawn heard the sound of voices raised in argument. If he could hear these guys, they would certainly hear him, if he had to fire a shot. For several reasons, he hoped that would not be necessary. Apart from the noise, he would have to kill the small man beside him, who now paused before a metal-braced door, set in a wall of stone.

"Open it," Shawn told the Pakistani, who was shaking slightly. Not cut out for this business, Shawn thought. The man pointed to a pocket in his shalwar kameez. Without shifting aim, Shawn took a key from the pocket, passing it to his prisoner.

Still shaking, fumbling the key, the man unlocked the metal-braced door.

"Okay. Go in." The man didn't move. "I said, go in."

Still moving slowly, glancing at the object in the shadows, the man did as he was ordered. Within the cell sat Dodie Sale, tearful, snuffling, but apparently unharmed. His back was against a wall, his head bent to upraised knees. Farther into the cell, in shadow, was the object that Shawn knew, instinctively, that he should not see.

To Dodie, he said, "Where's Rafe?"

Dodie looked up, wiping his eyes. He seemed unsurprised by Shawn's appearance. He pointed upward. "They've killed him."

The Arab understood. "No," he said, slowly turning his head until he could see Shawn. In Arabic, he said, "No, no. Not true. Not yet." He pointed westward. "He is moved there. To the place of gas."

Shawn passed the man's machine pistol to Dodie. "Stand up," he said. "Move. We're getting the hell out of here." He pointed to the end of the cell, averting his gaze from the thing he would rather not see. In Arabic, he told the Pakistani, "Get over there."

Moving slowly, looking back, the man stood against the far wall.

"Please," he said to Shawn. "Please do not shoot."

"I won't, if I don't have to," Shawn told him. "I don't want to kill you." Pushing Dodie out the door, he locked it behind him. In the tunnel, the sound of voices was louder. Moving fast now, Shawn led the way toward the steps he'd come down from the street. Over the prevailing odor of rot, he smelled something else. Keeping his voice low, he asked, "Did you shit yourself in there?"

"No, sir," Dodie whispered. "Pissed my pants is all. That thing—what was on the floor there—"

"Shut it," Shawn told him. "Shut your mouth."

"A head, a cutoff head," Dodie said, still in a whisper. "You know whose head it was?"

There were close to the steps now. "I told you—shut the fuck up."

Dodie wiped snot from his nose. "Lieutenant Bartosik, sir. I played cards with him one time. Before he was dead, I mean."

"If you don't shut up," Shawn said, "I swear I'll shoot you myself."

Dodie was weeping again. "His head, sir—his head, on the floor back there. I thought they—" Behind him, deeper in the tunnel, Shawn heard shouting—voices raised in a torrent of abusive Arabic. "Sir," Dodie whispered, "that's them. They cut off his head. They're coming after me."

Shawn grabbed Dodie's collar and pushed him up the cellar steps. At the top, they paused. The street door was ajar. Shawn saw the guard was at the end of the alley, leaning on the warehouse wall. Somewhere, the man had found cigarettes; he was relaxed, smoking.

To Dodie, Shawn said, "Move fast. Go left, onto the street, then slow down, walk toward town. Should be a taxi there—shit-colored Morris. I paid him. Call Langley, tell them we'll have Ramirez out."

"Sir? What are you doing?"

"Covering your back, right now. Then getting Rafe. Move."

"I really want to thank you," Dodie said, wiping his nose with his hand. "I thought, sir, thought, like I'm too young to die. They'll cut my head off—"

Dodie and Shawn exited the street door at the same moment. Shawn shoved Dodie out and to the left. He dropped to a crouch, facing right; saw the guard, at the end of the alley, spit out his smoke, go for his Kalashnikov. Shawn took a moment to aim—left hand steadying right wrist—then shot the man's legs out from under him.

"Sorry about that," Shawn said, more to himself than to the Pakistani, who was now on the ground, doubled up, yelling. Shawn *was* sorry, too. The guard's need for a smoke somehow made him human—a fellow being, a fellow addict, not a man to be killed without thought, or casually condemned to a life of pain. This was not a country, Shawn guessed, where you'd check in to order new knees. Nevertheless, American lives were at stake, and between his countrymen and the Taliban, Shawn saw no contest.

Hearing the throaty growl of a Humvee convoy, Shawn saw that the guard was still on the ground, still struggling. He checked the road, then emerged from the alley, waving down the lead vehicle of the strike squad.

"Shawn Maguire," he told the captain who opened the forward door. "Special Ops, sir. I just got one of our boys out." He pointed to the warehouse. "Out of there. They're still holding my partner, Ramirez. I'll show you where we'll find him—above a gas station, next to this place. What we need to do—"

"Stop right there, son," the captain said, without raising his voice. "We don't work for Ops. We're here helping get you out of the ratfuck you got yourself in—you and your buddy. We decide what we do."

What the captain decided was a simultaneous hit on the warehouse and the gas station. The squad used Humvees to clear the street. The garage—a three-story cinder-block building—had only two gas pumps, both rusted, but working. Behind them were a car, another shit-colored Morris, and a Dodge truck. Both on chocks, both without wheels.

Bearded men appeared from stores and apartment buildings. Some carried weapons but backed away when they saw the Americans' armament. One thing we do real well, Shawn thought, is weaponry. Sure as shit have the rest of the world outgunned.

The captain ordered his men to blow the doors of the garage building, follow up with gas grenades, and then, gas-masked, rush the upper floors.

Shawn said, "You do that, sir, you're going to get my man killed. He's in there someplace, with a bunch of hajjis. If I talk to them, these guys might bargain. You rush them, sir, no one gets out alive."

"Correction," said the captain. "Your man's not going to get hurt. We'll get him out. Surprise assault. Anyone terminated, it's going to be a fucking hajji." He pointed to the body of a frail bystander, now sprawled in blood near the gas pumps. "We got one already. Armed insurgent."

Shawn didn't argue. There was no time. He went at a run around the back of the building. All of its metal doors were padlocked. A lightweight aluminum extension ladder leaned against a wall. Stumbling, rushing, Shawn doubled the length of the ladder then shifted it along the wall until its top touched a wide window on the second floor. Moments later, he was on a level with the glass, except, he now saw, it was not glass but some kind of reinforced and semiclear plastic.

From where he stood on the ladder, Shawn looked directly into a large unpartitioned space. Rafe Ramirez was near the window, staring toward it. He was bound by duct tape to a swiveling office chair. The strips of insulation wrapped tight around his body made him look like one of the mummified bodies Shawn had once seen in coffins in the Cairo Museum, where al-Zawahari's men came close to killing him.

Rafe's mouth was taped, only his startled eyes uncovered. Beside him was a white-robed man, exceptionally tall, his face fully masked. He wore a flat Afghan cap and held a skinning knife. His head cocked, he seemed to be listening. As the second round of explosives smashed through a door on the far side of the building, the masked man drew his knife around the skin of Rafe's neck, leaving a fine and bloody line. When Rafe jerked his head away from the blade, the executioner took a handful of the prisoner's hair to adjust his position, as a barber adjusts the set of a customer's head.

Now the big room's floor filled with rolling mists of gas. Somewhere below, men beat at metal barriers. Shawn heard a muffled explosion—dynamiting a door, he guessed. Rafe's disbelieving eyes swiveled rightward, then downward to where the blade caressed his neck. Shawn smashed a fist vainly against the window's double plastic. Then, gripping the ladder, he lifted the Berretta and fired two shots. Both punched neat holes in the plastic, which, diverting them, left the executioner to complete his work. Concentrating now, he hacked and sawed: Muscular, he severed sinew, cartilage, and bone, struggling to separate Rafe's bloodied head from the column of his neck.

The prisoner's beating heart pumped fresh blood over the fingers of the man beheading him. The robed man at times glanced behind him, then went back to the work at hand, like one who rushes to finish a given task in a too-short space of time.

Rafe, still conscious, glanced first sideways and down, disbelieving his own dismemberment. He turned wide, weeping eyes to Shawn at the window.

Helpless, Shawn saw his buddy pull and strain against the ties that bound him. Under the tape, Rafe's mouth seemed to form some final words, or a shout, it might have been. There was a howl then, a bawling scream, and Shawn knew it was he who had screamed. Drawing back on the ladder, he punched at the window, using all the strength he had. Though the plastic did not break, the blow sent the ladder arcing away from the building. For a moment, it stood perpendicular, hesitant—it could have gone either way—and then, as Shawn gripped its sides, the ladder tipped backward and fell, taking him down to the metal-strewn ground, stunning him. At that same moment, or moments later, the filling station exploded, triggering fuel-fed fires. For an instant, Shawn lay still, the ladder sprawled across him. Something heavy fell from the building. Turning, he saw Rafe's head askew on the concrete slab; startled eyes still open, mouth still taped, blood clotted on the severed neck.

Another of the station's tanks exploded. In waves of heat and fume, the head blew, rolling like a tumbleweed toward a burning gas pump, and Shawn was on his feet, running for his life, running from the severed head, from the flaming tanks, racing out, bent double, before the next explosion hit.

When he collapsed finally on the far side of the pavement, Shawn lost consciousness. He remembered nothing until he woke in a helicopter as it landed in a strange town, which, he learned, was Rawalpindi. There he was treated for shock and burns and later, in D.C., for post-traumatic stress.

It was, he told Bobby Walters, a while before he could sleep through a night.

Since then, when Shawn heard of hostage taking, he had moments of nausea, recalling the time he lay on concrete, beside Rafe's head, staring into its wide bewildered eyes.

"You did good, son," the captain told Shawn when they met again. "Got a live one out." He put a hand on Shawn's shoulder. "More'n what we did. That's something stays private—just the two of us. We clear about that?"

By then Shawn had seen the captain's written account of a successful antiterrorist action in Peshawar, with one American agent saved and another unfortunately beheaded before the rescue force arrived. All other casualties were enemy aliens from across the Afghan border. "Armed antiliberation forces" was the term used.

At that moment, speaking with the officer, Shawn, still traumatized, made no reply. Later, though, recalling the startled gaze of his buddy's eyes, he did think of things he might have said.

29

Four years after Rafe's death, traveling back to Peshawar—this time with Danielle—Shawn was restless. The flight across the Gulf seemed not just long but endless. Until they changed planes there were two hijab-shrouded women in the row ahead. They huddled, unspeaking, among a hundred white-clad males: pilgrims returning from the hajj. The women occupied a full row of seats on that crowded plane; no man would sit beside them.

After Karachi, there were only men aboard. Some carried long-barreled handguns beneath their loose robes. That was the kind of thing Shawn noticed. These days, he thought, weapons weren't generally approved on planes, even in his own gun-loving country.

An hour into this last leg of the flight, when Danielle's hand brushed his arm, Shawn felt that slight shock her touch evoked. Turning, he saw that she was close, her gaze reflective.

"As a woman," she said, "it's hard for me to understand. The way you are, as a man. But, now—"

As she leaned in, the way she did, he inhaled her soft and musky scent.

"Tell me," he said. "Tell me what you understand."

"When things go wrong for you," she said, "in your life, in your work, you look for a new woman—am I right? You take her, you forget where you failed—" She hesitated. "At least, when I think about you, that is how it seems."

"You make me forget I'm a failure?"

She laughed and leaned closer, her hair loose, brushing his cheek. "No. I think it's more. It must be—you follow, you let me lead you round the world. But also I think, for you, women—we are, I don't know, like a drug? Is that a hard a thing to say?"

"I know people," he said, "who've gone straight. Kicked the habit. I'm giving it a shot."

"Tell me," she said. "Tell me how you kick the habit."

"You go to meetings. Admit you're addicted—"

"To sex?"

"Sex. Or whatever it is eases the pain. Admit you can't control the addiction. You make amends to the women you've wronged. You abstain from sex."

She turned fully toward him. "You? You abstain? For how long?"

"A year."

"Which ends?"

"In a while," Shawn said. "This is embarrassing. Can we talk about something else?" He waited a moment, deciding whether to say what he had in mind. "If you weren't married," he said, after a time, "I'd have a question for you."

In that pilgrim-filled plane, he leaned close, to kiss her. Danielle, quite gently, turned his mouth away. She watched cloud patterns shift and reshape, then, as they flew lower, saw the desert spread below. Leaning across her, seeing the mountains of Waziristan, Shawn felt a frisson of fear. Something he felt more, as years passed: knowing he was not immortal.

Here he was, God help him, flying back to a place he'd hoped never to see again, a place where he'd seen his buddy's head hacked off, a town where he himself came near to death by fire. He badly needed alcohol; on this Arabic airline, of course, there was none. The pilot—who sounded Australian—announced they'd be landing at Peshawar in seven minutes. A modestly dressed woman, a stewardess, repeated the announcement in rapid Urdu. At least Shawn guessed that's what she was doing.

He saw the desert below them ridged with lines of gray-white tents.

Danielle leaned forward, staring downward. "Those," she said. "What are they?"

"What do they look like? Refugee camps, right?" He pointed downward and westward. "Out that way, far as you can see."

"The people are?"

"Afghani. Getting away from the war." He thought back. "You know, first time I came here, they were running from the Russians. Now, poor bastards, they run from us." He thought for a minute. "Back in the day, I had to question a guy in that camp"—he pointed—"back there. Saw him and his family. Eight kids—ten of them, total, in two little rooms, in a mud hut he built. I said, must be crowded. He said, no, sir, it's fine. Thank you, sir."

"He was al Qaeda?"

Shawn shook his head. "Uh-uh. Got the wrong guy. My boss

said, what the fuck, take him out anyway." He shrugged. "I wasn't up for that. But someone did."

"Tell me," she said, "do you ever doubt what you've done? The way you spent your life? The things you do to others—to people less powerful—"

"War on terror. Covers any damn thing."

She pointed downward, interrupting. "Yet you are killers, are you not? Of the innocent. From a plane, not a suicide bomb, that seems cleaner, no? More civilized. A plane, a guided bomb, way below, some are guilty, some are innocent, who knows which? Still, people die—they are dead, as much as in a suicide bomb."

He knew there must be smart answers to that. While he was thinking, she spoke again.

"Fighting these wars—which in the end you lose—don't you play al Qaeda's game? Do you people ever ask what gives you the right to bomb other countries? To fly drones? To assassinate their people? Do others have that right? Is Iraq allowed to attack Kentucky? To bomb Connecticut?" She turned toward him. "To ask that question, surely, is to answer it."

He looked at her, thoughtful. "I never heard you talk this way."

"Because you never listen. I know this—I said before—you don't listen to women."

"Spent a lot of my life listening to women."

"*With* women," she said. "You listen, of course, until you get us in bed. I spoke of something more." As the plane descended, she pointed to the desert below. "Those people down there—if they are liberated, why don't they leave?"

It made him uneasy when she talked like this.

"Babe," he said, "we do our best. I believe we do. We don't plan on hitting women and kids. You know how it is."

"I don't," she said.

"Some kid in Nevada, flying a Predator"—Shawn pointed—
"over those hills . . ."

"Predator?"

"Drone. Pilotless plane. That's what we use. They fly here,
driver's in Nevada someplace. Another country. Another conti-
nent." He was watching her face. "How's this kid over there—
never been further than Vegas—how's he pick out a bad guy in a
turban? How's he tell who's not a bad guy? Think about it. Kid's in
a big chair, aircon room, he's on camera, drinking Coke, looking
down at this place—little hajji guys running round, wearing robes,
beards, damn, they all look the same. It's a video game. Pick the
guy who gets it. Kid makes his guess who he'll kill, then—zap.
Maybe right, maybe wrong. Moral of that—don't live in the wrong
damn place. Don't live in places we want to turn into bases." He
peered at her. "Are you okay?"

She pressed a hand between her breasts. "Maybe not. I don't
feel good. Not serious, perhaps. I feel it here."

"It's what you had in Fes?"

She shook her head and was about to speak when the plane
flew low across the airport's unlikely railway line to touch down.

Some of the passengers clapped hands. Others rushed at the
still-locked exit door.

The pilot announced that there had been an error: Some passengers' baggage was not on the plane. Missing pieces would—he
gave his word—be on the next flight to Peshawar.

Shawn reached down to his valise. "Whenever the hell that is.
How much you want to bet our bags got lost?"

"I couldn't care less," she said. She was sweating. "They can have
my bag. Have everything. I just want out of here. I want a bed."

Forty minutes later, knowing now that both their bags were missing, having left at the airport the address of the Indus Grand Comfort Hotel, Shawn stood in Peshawar's shimmering heat, ignoring flocks of thin porters and the fatter drivers of auto-rickshaws. Hungry men, clutching at him. He was their evening meal.

He waved down an ancient taxi and helped Danielle into the backseat. It was like helping an old woman.

Settling on the ripped fabric, she said, "God, I so need a bed. What is—I mean, what is the hotel? What is it like?"

He shrugged. "No idea. Could be a flophouse." She turned suddenly, to look at him. "No choice. Every place I called was full. Who knows why? Maybe something's happening here. I guess we got the last room in town."

Covering her face with her hands, she began, without a sound, to cry.

"If the car goes the right way," he said, trying to distract her, "I'll show you one of my memories. USAID building. There was a local mob, burned the place."

She looked up, wiped a hand across her eyes. "You remember it, why?"

"When they burned it," Shawn said, "I was inside."

30

After Rafe Ramirez lost his head in Peshawar, Langley made changes to the regional structure on the AfPak border. Shawn's old CIA buddy Robert Hamilton Walters came into Peshawar as chief of station: a last-choice posting if ever there was one. Bobby was given a temporary building, a former USAID two-story office modified with a newly built steel-lined safe room in what had been the office basement. As with all Agency outposts, the safe room was filled with secure-communication gear. Though the building was still officially USAID—so its signboard said—the former tenants pulled out when two workers, both women, were shot through the head while opening a school for local girls. Though markings had been scrubbed off the bullets, ballistics determined that the murder weapons were part of an American shipment delivered—by way of a Polish middleman called Kowalka—to the anti-Russian revolt in Afghanistan. To the Taliban.

One of Bobby Walters's unofficial tasks in Peshawar was sorting out Shawn's troubled life. As Bobby saw it, Rafe's execution took his friend to some dark chamber of the soul from which there was no easy return. Shawn became obsessive. There were physical symptoms, too: He found his vision blurring, could no longer see clearly the snow-peaks of the Hindu Kush. Not good for a man trained as a sniper. He concentrated on what was close at hand, spending his days hunting leads to Rafe's killers; his dream-haunted nights in bed with a unit secretary, an educated Shia Muslim girl, Khalida Gul.

On his second week in Peshawar, Bobby told Shawn he had a new assignment for him: He was being reassigned from the hunt for the men who kidnapped and killed Rafe Ramirez.

Shawn said, "Bobby, butt out. You can't do that."

"Peshawar may be a dead-end assignment," Bobby said, "which, no question, it is, but it's what I've got. Sorry to tell you this, my friend, but while I'm chief, you do what I say."

"What do you say?"

"I'm saying, Shawn, this thing's driving you crazy. Check the mirror—you look ten years older than you did last month, and you didn't look so young back then. I want you off of this thing. Langley's sending a special squad to get those guys."

"The ones who killed Rafe?"

"The ones who killed Rafe."

"That's it?" Shawn asked. "End of story?"

Bobby shook his head. "There's more. I want the girl out of your bed."

Shawn looked at him.

"You're going to tell me it's none of my goddamn business who you sleep with," Bobby said. "I'm here to tell you, it is. The woman's on my staff. She's Pakistani. Okay, she's been in Islamabad, she's trained, but she comes from this town. She speaks Urdu. She has no security clearance. How do we know she's not taking every damn thing you tell her in bed back to the bad guys?" He watched Shawn react. "This burg has more fucking bad guys than any place I know."

When Shawn said nothing, Bobby tried another tack. "Plus," he said, "there's Martha."

"What about Martha?"

"Don't be that way," Bobby said. "I'm here to help you. You been chasing Martha half your life. The minute she says she's free to marry, you get in bed with a girl who is what? Twenty-one?"

Shawn said, "Bobby, what's happening?"

"Happening to you?"

"To me. Us. The world. The world we're running. We started, it was clear, right? Good guys here, bad guys there. Now, who the fuck knows the difference?"

After thinking it through, Bobby said, "Shawn, listen. Here's the deal. I forget about the girl, you take a new op."

"Which is what?"

"Polish guy, American passport. Henryk Kowalka."

Shawn searched his memory. "Pentagon weapons contract?"

"That's him. Contract to supply weaponry to various friendly guys around the globe. Ones we want to help. Mujahid next door, for instance."

"I'm interested because?"

"Because Kowalka's in town. Our friends over the border say he's been selling them crap gear. They complain, which I understand. Kowalka holds up hands. Tells them, not me, buddy, stuff comes from Langley, through him—but do we ever see it? Do we hell. Polish son of a bitch buys from some damn bazaar. He delivers. Never comes near us." Bobby consulted a typed list. "He's selling the muj Lee-Enfields—you believe this, Lee-fucking-Enfields, fifty years old?"

"Good gun," said Shawn. "I trained on them."

"AK-47s," said Bobby. "Chinese make—plus RPG-7s, 60 mil mortars, 12.7 mil machine guns. Most of it not right, is what I hear. Shit stuff. God knows where he gets it."

"I guess God would. So I should do what?"

"Check on the gear. You're a shooter, you'd know. See if it really is crap. If it is, go meet Kowalka. Squeeze his balls. Remind him he's Polish. Tell him we'll take away his passport. Cancel the damn contract."

"When do I do this?"

Bobby looked at his watch. "Now. You head on out. You get a ride with a guy called Akmal Something-something. Pashtun hajji. Don't know his last name—it's on file. He's a mujahid. Used to be with Shah Massoud, before he was terminated. Massoud, that is."

"Do we trust this Akmal guy?"

"We should. We trained him."

"On the Farm?"

"On the Farm." Bobby pointed. "He's outside. He'll take you over the border. Okay?"

Though late in the day, it was still hot when Shawn left the Agency's office.

We could have worse people running the country, he thought, though he could not, for the moment, imagine who that might be. He crossed Sahibzada Road to where a green-painted jeep was parked in the shade of a white mulberry tree.

The driver was a young man whose beard and shades made him look older than he was. He said, "Mr. Maguire? I am Akmal. Please get in."

In the jeep, Shawn said, "Here's the deal. You show me the weapons you've been sent—you and your buddies. If I don't think they're right, we go talk with Mr. Kowalka. He's the guy who bought the stuff. Sound right to you?"

Akmal made no attempt to start the machine.

"That was the plan, Mr. Maguire. Indeed. However, something happened. You may not know this, but yesterday your people bombed a village in the hills." He pointed toward the mountains: toward the Afghan border. "Fragmentation bombs. It was, at that time, a wedding. Men had come from many miles around, across mountains. Almost every person who came is dead now. Those not killed are injured. Women and children, both. Many children. A whole village, almost, is gone."

Shawn had once been in a Pashtun village at the time of an intertribal wedding. Months of preparation culminated in the offer of bride dowry—silks, perfumes, mules, and jewelry—displayed for all the village to see and assess. The groom, bearing gifts, made a secret, heavily chaperoned, visit to his bride-to-be, before the village filled with visiting families—men staying in one mud-walled *qala,* sleeping on floors, women lodged in another compound.

On the day Shawn arrived in the village, men were practising complex, dervishlike dances—until enforcement squads of students swept down from the hills, and the music stopped.

Turning to Akmal in the jeep, Shawn said. "I've seen one of your weddings. But we, down here, we're not military. We don't control air attacks. What can I say? I'm sorry?"

"I don't know what you can say," Akmal replied. "Or what would make a difference. My people believe Americans are all the same. You will tell us it was okay to kill these families. You will say it is insurgents who died."

Shawn nodded; he did know that. "You're telling me this because?"

"Because we Pashtun, we live on both sides of the border. Pakistan, Afghanistan. Many relatives of those killed live here." He pointed up the dusty street. "Here, in Peshawar. You will understand, they are angry." He nodded across the road, in the direction Shawn had come. "They are planning to burn your office."

Shawn was quiet a moment. Then he said, "Say again? There's people planning to burn it?" He pointed across the road. "Burn that building?"

Akmal nodded.

"When?"

Akmal said, "The time I left, they were gathering up there. Praying to God for guidance. I think perhaps they are here soon."

"Believe me, Akmal, the White House won't like it. Not one little bit. There will be a shitstorm. More than one village will be taken out."

Shawn swung himself out of the jeep and hustled off to the Agency building.

In the Agency building, Shawn spoke with his lover. "Khalida," he said, "tell the women in the office, go home now. You, too."

"I have told them," Khalida said. "They are gone. For me, I am not going. Mr. Walters asked me to burn the papers—do you say documents?—in the room below."

Shawn followed Khalida down to the metal-lined cellar. He said, "You don't understand what's happening."

She was collecting documents in piles. She said, "I live here. These are my people. I understand better than you."

"What do you understand?"

Khalida pointed north. "They are on their way. Now, I think, nothing will stop them."

In the basement, Bobby called Langley. Waiting for a connection, he said to Shawn, "Give us a hand here. Khalida, you, too. Stuff we need to burn."

"Like what?"

"Like confidential papers. Code books. Remember what happened with the Iranian Embassy? Reassembled all the shit from the shredder? I'm not about to go down as the chief who lost the Company records."

In the basement safe room, an incinerator was already lit. Documents were fed into it, one page at a time. The heat, on that hundred-degree day, was intense. The air conditioner died. One file cabinet had been cleared by the time Lewis Jeffers beat on the metal-lined door of the safe room.

Bobby used the door's spyhole, then let the man in. His size made the small room feel smaller. Even out of uniform, Jeffers looked like the marine sergeant he was.

"Lewis," Bobby said, "what the hell are you doing here?"

"Sir, I could ask you the same question. Big crowd of men outside. Some preacher—I think the guy's a preacher—he's standing there, telling them we planned to kill their families." He pointed west. "Up in the hills. Which is where I was this week. Excuse my language, sir, it's a ratfuck outside. Can I ask, sir, what you're planning to do?"

"Stay here," Bobby said, "is what I'm planning to do. This room's designed to resist attack."

"For how long?"

"God willing," Bobby said, "long enough for Langley to get some more guys in here."

Khalida, forgetting modesty, took off the scarf that covered her head. "It is so hot."

"Incinerator in a metal-lined room," Shawn said, "that's what you get."

"No," she told him, "no. It's more. Can't you smell? Can't you hear?" She pointed. "Up there, I think the building is on fire."

The heat. When it was over, it was the heat, the unendurable heat, that Shawn remembered. There were other things, too—Pashtun men beating with hammers at the door of the safe room; men trying to pry open the security-locked ceiling hatch—but the heat was the worst. Inside the metal basement room, it was like being slowly cooked in a high oven.

Khalida—in daylight, usually modest—shed her burka and took off her shoes. Lewis and Shawn were down to shirtsleeves, their shirts unbuttoned. Bobby—already struggling with the weight problem that would, in coming years, blight his life—had the worst of it. Stripped to his undershirt, his soft white flesh ran with sweat.

He took one call from Rawalpindi—the Pakistan army base—before the phones went dead.

The room grew hotter. Lewis was the first to break. He said to Bobby, "Sir, if I'm going to die, I don't want to do it down here."

He collected a submachine gun. "I'm heading on out. That okay with you, sir?"

Bobby had trouble speaking. He nodded his head.

"Secure the door behind me, sir." Moments later, Lewis went, firing ahead of him. That was the last time they saw him alive.

Shawn, too, was preparing to take his chances outside the safe room. He said his farewells to Khalida. She murmured something he couldn't hear.

"Say again?"

She said, "I wish you could marry, before we die."

"Me, too," Shawn said, thinking of Martha, not Khalida.

Moments later, they heard the sound of helicopters.

"You think that's the Pakistan army?" Bobby asked.

"If it's not," Shawn said, "we have a problem."

Khalida brushed sweat-drenched hair from her face. Still in Shawn's arms, facing death, dreaming of weddings, she murmured, "Inshallah."

31

It was late in the day when Shawn and Danielle arrived at Peshawar's Indus Grand Comfort Hotel, a tall and narrow unpainted building in the poorest section of the town. In the lobby, Danielle collapsed into a faded purple fake-leather chair. Shawn approached a portly middle-aged man behind the hotel's faux-marble desk. The receptionist wore thick and misted glasses and a tightly fitting greenish-black suit that shone where it caught the light. His face, lacking expression, was smooth-skinned: younger than the rest of his body. His hair—so black it might have been dyed—parted in a straight white furrow along the center of his skull.

He coughed behind a manicured hand. "I wish you good morning, sir."

Shawn checked the time.

"I should correct this statement," the receptionist said. "I see it is afternoon. Your documents, please?"

Shawn laid two passports on the desk. The man inspected them closely, holding them in the air above his head, looking upward, as if secret writing might reveal itself. "You are married to the woman?"

"He is," Danielle said from her chair, before Shawn could deny it. She was standing now, holding the counter to support herself. "I am his new wife. In our country, the woman keeps her own name."

The receptionist surveyed her. "Not good," he said, unmoved. "I think," he added, "you are not really well, madam." He pointed at the newspaper she was holding. "That is Urdu. You will not read it. Tomorrow, maybe, we have English news." He turned to take down a key. "Maybe not. Room six hundred and twenty-seven. Very nice room. Fourth floor."

Shawn asked why, if it was the fourth floor, the room number did not start with a four. The receptionist looked past him, as if he had not spoken.

"Is there an elevator? A lift?"

"There is a lift indeed," the receptionist told Danielle. "It is broken." He pointed. "Stairs are there."

"Dear God." She was shouting. "You drag me around these shitty places, Shawn, you make me ill, you say you're helping, all you want to do is get in my bed. You don't care about Darius—you don't care about anyone. Not anyone. You make this big deal about your wife—the way she died—and you were cheating on her. You didn't give a damn." She was weeping now—"you don't give a damn about me . . . you just . . . you don't give a damn—"

The receptionist coughed twice and shuffled papers, announcing his continued presence. Ignoring him, Shawn took Danielle in his arms, holding her until the sobs subsided.

"Shawn, I'm sorry. I shouldn't have said—I mean, about your wife—"

"Stairs," said the receptionist, raising his voice. "They are there."

"Bellboy?" asked Shawn.

The receptionist merely smiled.

Danielle was calmer now. "You're not good on stairs," she told Shawn. She struggled for breath. "Today—today, I'm not good on stairs. We have to help each other."

As Shawn turned Danielle toward the stairs, the receptionist called him back. Considering Danielle, he shook his head. He passed over a folded yellow note.

"A message," he said to Shawn. "From Mr. Walters." His expression changed to what might have been a smile. "A man we believe is an American spy. He will urgently wish to see you."

"How does he know I'm here?"

The receptionist shrugged. "Is it not a spy's business to know such things?"

The hotel room was small, hot, and crowded with five items of furniture. An iron-framed double bed occupied most of the room. Hung on the wall above the bed was a gilt-framed mirror and a vast, rusty air conditioner, which carried a notice saying that it was out of order. Cold flickering light fell from ceiling-mounted neon tubes. On lime-green-painted walls hung framed portraits of Pakistan's president, each showing a different aspect of the general's unsmiling and vigorous youth.

On one wall, a sign said that an operator would, for a fee, make international telephone calls before nine at night. Beyond the beds, a closet had been turned into what passed for a shower room.

"This whole room is a closet, no?" Danielle asked. "If I was not feeling like this, I would say we should look for something else. Right now, no. I have started my period. I can take a T-shirt from your carry bag, okay?" She opened the door of the shower room, then hesitated. "God. Don't look. I'm getting undressed. I need bed."

The room had a single window, looking out onto the street below. While Danielle changed, Shawn stood staring down at the crowd in the square below. "I spent months in this town," he said. "Never seen so many people."

From the shower room, she called, "The paper says it's an election. Prime minister comes."

Shawn thought back to their time in Fes: to when he learned that Danielle spoke Arabic. Now, it seemed, she knew Urdu.

"The guy downstairs was wrong? You could read the paper?"

She was calmer now. "Of course. You know Nashida Noon won? Apparently a landslide. Power to women, one might say. They say she takes office next week. Now, she crosses the country—what do you call it? Meet-the-people tour?"

Shawn turned away from the window to watch her get into the bed. He was trying to make sense of what she'd said. "You never told me where you learned your languages. What else did the paper say?"

She turned on her side, away from him. "About Nashida? You know this. She promises to fire the president."

"Because he hanged her father?"

"Because he is an American puppet."

Shawn stood for a moment, wondering whether he could articulate what was in his mind. "Dani? Can I tell you something? Will you listen to me, please?"

The wings of her shoulder blades moved in the slightest of shrugs.

"What I'm trying to tell you," Shawn said, "you think I'm ad-dicted to—to sex—"

"It is what you said."

"Maybe I was like that," Shawn said, "back in the day." He paused, then said, "Even men like me—it's not impossible. We can straighten up and fly right."

Without turning toward him, she murmured something he couldn't hear.

"I'm just saying, give me a break. I didn't play around, not after Ellen. Are you hearing this? I changed. I go to meetings—"

The phone rang—an old-time ringtone, reminding Shawn of childhood.

Danielle, her face still to the wall, said, "You get it."

Calling from the lobby, the receptionist told Shawn that Mr. Walters, the American spy, was arriving in five minutes. He would be waiting in the lobby.

"Someone told Bobby we're here. I wonder who that was."

"Does it matter?" she asked. "Go. Look after yourself, my love."

Shawn pulled on a jacket. "Could you say that again?"

"Look after yourself, my love," she said, without turning her head. So soft he could hardly hear.

Leaving the room, Shawn closed the bedroom door behind him. He paused a moment outside, thinking it was the first time he'd heard her put those two words together, at least for him; thinking, too, that Danielle had started her period in Fes.

Which was nearly a week ago.

32

In a newly built boutique jail on the edge of Peshawar's market, Darius Osmani sat shackled to a shiny metal chair manufactured in Rome, Georgia. Otherwise naked, he was head-bagged and wore two conjoined baby's diapers from which twin electric cables ran to a small portable console some feet away. From overuse, the cable insulation was in places worn down to copper wire.

The room, belowground and damp, was lit by a single high-white fluorescent strip light. At the door, Hassan Tarkani spoke to a very young pink-skinned man in a white coat sprayed delicately with blood.

Looking around the room, the man in the white coat said, "Video off?"

Hassan nodded.

The intern said, "No terp?"

"Hey," said Hassan, "this hajji talks better English than you do." He glanced back at the detainee. "Speak to me. I'm interested. Tell me why you think he needs a doctor?"

Both men turned to look at the prisoner.

The intern—who had trained as a psychiatrist in Atlanta—shrugged. "It's not what I think. It's what the Company thinks. You know the procedure. Detainee dies, they don't like it. They say you're doing it wrong."

Hassan said, "I see that. Tough getting intel off a body bag. But take a look there. Just look at him. Is this guy fit, or is he not?"

"Well," the doctor said, "I don't know. I mean, he's bleeding. Mouth, ear—broken cheekbone—that's something, you know—Red Cross might notice."

Hassan shook his head. "No way, José. Red Cross, forget. They go to the main jail. Not aware that we exist."

"Please," said the doctor. "This is Peshawar. There are no secrets." He moved to the prisoner's side and took his wrist to check a pulse. The prisoner struck out blindly, although—his wrist being shackled—he did no harm.

"At least," the intern said to Hassan, "he has a pulse."

The trainee spent moments checking the prisoner's heartbeat. Beneath his head bag, the man made a sound that might have been rage or might have been distress.

The doctor said to Hassan, "Try and keep him that way, will you? I mean, breathing."

"Why is it," Hassan asked, smiling, "I keep hearing that line?"

An hour later, Darius sat in another, slightly larger, room. Here, the floor was tiled, the chair unpainted and wooden. He was now completely naked except that he wore a brassiere made for a very large woman, had panties with hearts on his head, and was blind-folded. Except for his ankles, the prisoner was now unshackled. He bled a little from one ear. As the intern had noted, it did seem as if one cheekbone might be broken.

This room had a small barred window, shaded with a torn blind, which had once been cream. In another chair—this one lined with plastic leather—sat Calvin McCord. He reached out a hand to touch the prisoner's arm. Darius jumped as far back as the chair allowed.

"It's okay," Calvin said. He spoke gently. "It's okay. Relax. No one's going to hurt you."

Though he disliked the whole process of interrogation, it was, he believed, a necessary evil. For his country, to save American lives, Calvin would do worse things than this.

Darius, feeling the agent's touch, turned blindly to his left. His fingers clenched and loosened. He tried, behind his back, to un-snap the bra but could not manage the clasp. He said nothing.

"Two things you should understand," Calvin said. "You love your country. I love my country. Difference is, my country's win-ning. Yours is losing. You follow me? Maybe you should think about what side you're on."

Calvin waited. The prisoner shifted in his chair, said nothing.

"Tell me, Darius. Tell me, is there something I can do for you? Talk to me. Is there some way I can help?"

Darius turned his blind head, seeking the voice. "Do you," he asked, "do you really, sir—do you mean that? Can you stop the electricity? The drowning?"

"Sure," Calvin said. "I can do that. I can do both those things. You just have to ask."

Wincing, the prisoner touched his face. "I need medical treat-ment."

"Come on," Calvin said. "Don't give me that. We have a doc. He's seen you."

"The doctor looks at me. He takes my pulse. He checks that the other man has not killed me. This is not treatment."

"Now, now," Calvin said. "Be fair. We're not expecting gratitude, but a thank-you would be nice."

There was silence for a moment. Darius cupped his hands over his genitals, hiding them. Calvin noted that this was the first time the prisoner had registered his nakedness.

"What do you want from me?"

"I want to help you," Calvin said. He went behind the prisoner to unfasten his brassiere. He said, more to himself than to the detainee, "I really wish they wouldn't do this shit. Such kid stuff." He took the panties with hearts from the prisoner's head. "It's, like, give and take, Darius—we can help each other. I understand you, brother. Those guys back there, giving you a hard time, they have no spiritual dimension. The bad dude downstairs—the one who hurts you—what can I tell you? He's a Paki. Uncivilized. Myself, you might not think so, but I'm a Catholic. You may be a Muslim—"

"I am Muslim."

"Okay. You are a Muslim. Okay, right. Like I say, we have religion in common, you and me. We both believe in a transcendent God. A force for good. I understand your anger. I feel your pain. You believe that we—I mean, people like me, Americans—we're killing Muslims. You think we're doing it in Iraq, in Afghanistan, in Lebanon, Palestine—we're helping do it in Chechnya—we did it in Iran, a little help-out from our friends in Iraq, and you think, what can I, Darius, what can I do to stop it? Of course you do. I understand. Hell, if I was a Muslim, I might feel that way. You have no tanks, you have no bombers, you have no fighter planes.

You think all you can do is kill Americans. You turn our airplanes into weapons."

The prisoner said, "No, sir. Not me. No. I condemn that."

"It's okay, Darius," Calvin said. "Don't be defensive. I mean, what choice do you have?"

"But that is not how I feel," the prisoner said. The wounds to his face made speaking difficult. "I have—I had, before you took me—I had many choices. I am an academic. I spoke out. I never wished to kill."

"Don't get me wrong," Calvin said. Again, he touched the prisoner's arm, lightly, confidingly. "Not all Muslims are terrorists. I appreciate that. You have children?"

The prisoner was having trouble breathing. "You know the answer, sir. I do not."

"But you have a girlfriend—"

"—a wife."

"Ah," said Calvin, "no. Not a wife. You see, we check on things like this, Darius. Let's call her a girlfriend. I met her in England. And Morocco, come to think of it. Damn, I thought, this puss looks good enough to eat with a spoon. I'll bet ten bucks she comes on like the Easter bunny. Sooner or later, what do you know, she's forgotten to take her pill—bang, you got a pickaninny in the oven. Now, Darius, believe me, when you guys have this rugrat—"

The prisoner nursed his damaged cheek. He said, "Rugrat?"

"Kiddie. Small person. You have this kid, you're going to see things differently. Happened to me. I get to be a father, all of sudden I think, hey, I love this boy. Makes you value human life, Darius, having family. You won't want crazy hajjis wandering around with nukes." His voice changed. "Who *were* those guys, going to pick up the warheads?"

"I told you," the prisoner said, "I told you, sir, I do not know.

And let me say, sir, I don't have to wait for children to value human life. Sir, I have always valued human life."

Calvin's tone was reproachful now. "Don't do this to me, Darius. We know you found those papers in Kandahar. In Abbasi's office." He paused. "You do know he's dead, right?"

Darius shook his head.

"Killed himself. Jumped off of a roof, poor bastard. Now, what I'm saying, I know how you felt, you found those Abbasi papers. You read them, all of a sudden, you know where the nukes are— you think, thank God, thank Allah, here's a chance for the perfect storm. Revenge on those infidel Christians killing my fellow Muslims. Of course you'd think that. You'd use the knowledge you had. You were the only one who could read those papers. You could understand them. Here's your big break. Chance to grab a nuke. Small device, sure, but big enough for what you wanted. Big enough for New York, say. You took the chance. I understand that. I see where you're coming from. In your place, maybe—maybe I would've done the same."

He stood close beside the prisoner. Sensing his presence, Darius cringed. Calvin removed the man's blindfold. Sighted, the prisoner seemed more acutely aware of his nakedness.

"How do you know what I found in Kandahar?"

"We know most things about you," said Calvin. "We know what makes you tick. What we don't know is what you told Dr. Khan. We don't know where the nukes went. We don't know how they got to where they went. That's how you can help us."

The prisoner's hands tightened over his scrotum. He shook his head no.

"Now, Darius," Calvin said, "do yourself a favor. You talk to me—a man with sympathy for Muslim folk—or you go back to the bad boys downstairs. Knuckledraggers, we call them. Unkind, but true. I tell you this, my friend. They're likely to get grouchy, those boys, when they hear you're being difficult. When they get grouchy, you know, they're likely to smack you around—and they shouldn't do it, but you likely got that old electric wire up your ass, plus one of those pit bull dogs with all the teeth—dog's just waiting to get his mouth around that big old dick you got there. I tell you this, Darius—once they get a good bite, those dogs, damn hard to make 'em let go. Might have to put off those kids." Calvin shuddered. "Myself, I'd hate that. I'm truly allergic to dogs. Always have been. Specially anyplace close to my cock." He sighed. "It's a real question, my friend. Are you going to do yourself a favor and talk to me? Or do you want to go back there—talk to the boys downstairs?"

The prisoner wept. Calvin saw that he was shaking now, and urinating in small spasmodic spurts. The urine smelled rank. For some reason, Calvin found, it often did, after a long interrogation. He'd need to have the whole damn place disinfected. Just as well the floor was tiled. In itself, though, pissing was a good sign. If Calvin was any judge of character, the wretched business was nearly done. This sorry-ass hajji needed no more pressure. He was about to talk.

"I know," Calvin told the prisoner. "It's a bitch. If I could stop those thugs doing what they do, believe me, I would, but I don't run this place. I'm just a cog in the wheel. They're out of control, those guys downstairs. They think up things—they do things—I truly do not wish to know about."

"Tell me what you want," the prisoner said. "Just tell me. Whatever it is, I will do it."

"Well, my friend," Calvin said, "first thing I want you to do is read this bit of paper. Read it out loud. Here's what it says. 'My name is Darius Osmani. I am thirty-nine years old and a Muslim fundamentalist, working with al Qaeda. During the months of April through June of 2004, I was well treated in the jails where I was held. I was not questioned by Americans. I was not subject to any kind of ill treatment.'"

"You want me to read that?"

"You bet your life," Calvin said. "We have your voiceprint. If we keep you a little longer, another year or so, say, you'll maybe need to read it again." He was setting up a tape recorder. "Give me a minute, get this damn thing running. After that, you read the boilerplate, nice loud voice. You identify yourself. Then we help each other, you and me. Starting with you telling me everything, and I mean everything, I want to know about Dr. Khan and the nukes."

33

In the lobby of the Grand Comfort Hotel, Shawn searched his pockets for his satellite phone, wondering if it could be packed with his still-missing baggage. Then he recalled the porter who had, for a moment, grabbed him at the airport, a hand inside his jacket. Thinking back, that must have been when the damn thing went south. What use was training, if you fell for a move like that?

He wasted time speaking to the plump receptionist, reporting the phone missing, then fought his way into the street, through moving crowds of robed and bearded men. He was searching for a back-alley gun shop he'd used a few years ago, at a time when he wanted an untraceable weapon to kill the man who murdered Rafe Ramirez.

Wading through this human sea took Shawn back to childhood outings to the coast of Alabama, struggling neck-deep through the sea-wrack of an incoming tide. Here, in the back streets of Peshawar, he made slow progress, turning eventually down a narrow half-remembered passage, where the crowd thinned. Toward the end of the alley, two Pakistani men perched on three-legged stools, close to a wall hung with patterned rugs. They watched him. These men were ageless: They could have been in their dotage, but Shawn knew, from earlier dealings, they were shrewd in business and perhaps no older than he. Though for them, he thought, in this town, and this trade, reaching the age of fifty might be a real achievement.

It was, Martha would have said, no country for old men.

Above the businessmen hung a weathered sign, painted in green and purple. It read PESHAWAR ARMY SUPPLIES (PVT). Shawn made a pistol gesture with thumb and forefinger. One of the old men rose stiffly from his stool. He held aside a beaded curtain hung over an open doorway, then followed Shawn down two steps and into a shadowed and suddenly cool weapon store. The walls were hung with weapons. A single blowfly circled the room.

Shawn's notion of these places was formed by the gun shops of Alabama: little roadside stores selling handguns and hunting rifles, bait worms, and NRA decals (KEEP HONKING, I'M RELOADING), along with eye-catching jackets, so your buddies don't take you for deer.

Peshawar Army Supplies was different. It offered rocket-propelled grenades, missiles, land mines, machine guns, cannon, fragmentation bombs, rocket launchers, Kalashnikovs, and artillery shells. A young man in a skullcap brought Shawn a cup of cardamom-spiced tea. A notice on a wall announced the availability, to order, of American-made Stingers—maybe the same heat-seeking missiles Shawn once shipped across the border into Afghanistan. He pointed at a short-barreled, nine-mil double-action Russian-made Makarov in a dusty glass case. He was giving up on Glocks. Disappointed that this was all his customer needed, the old man briefly checked the weapon, found a brick of shells, and passed the pistol over the counter. Calculating what money remained, Shawn paid cash.

The storekeeper indicated a battered RPG launcher. "You are wanting nothing else?"

"The minute I need missiles," Shawn said, "I will let you know."

The old man laughed politely and ushered his customer from the shop. "Sir," he said, "go carefully. This is not a safe town for American spies."

"I'm not a spy," Shawn said. He turned right out of the store. "If I was, I'm not now."

Walking toward Khyber Bazaar, Shawn had the feeling, the sense, that he was being followed. He stopped suddenly, backed into a café doorway, put a hand on his new purchase—he hoped to hell the pistol worked—and faced the way he'd come. Avoiding a group of young Pashtuns, along came a thickset man last seen in Fes: the lethal handyman, Alfred Burke.

His right hand in his windbreaker pocket, Shawn leveled the Makarov. "Alfred," he said.

Without changing pace, Alfred came toward him.

"Not too close," Shawn said.

Alfred pulled out one of the café's plastic chairs, seated himself, and waved Shawn to another. "Don't be that way, matey," said Alfred. "I want to talk with you. Take your hand out your damn pocket. If I was on a hit, you think you would've seen me?"

Shawn, seating himself, shook his head.

"Well, then," Alfred said. He sat a while in silence, staring into space. "You know I been working for Mr. Abbasi," he said finally. "You remember that."

"You told me in Fes. When you took me to the cellar."

"Jesus," said Alfred, "don't you hate them underground places? Give me the creeps, personally speaking. Mr. Abbasi used to say they make him feel safe. Not me, they don't. Make me feel like I been buried. Before I was dead, know what I mean?"

"Which reminds me," Shawn said. "Something I want to ask you."

Alfred waited.

"A man in Fes tried to kill me."

Alfred clicked his tongue. "Weren't me, squire. Principle I work on, someone's trying to take you out, they don't appreciate what you're doing. Which, in your case, it's chasing that schwartzer they keep shifting around." He paused, then said, "Same with Mr. Abbasi, Lord love him."

"Are you telling me," Shawn said, "Abbasi's dead?"

"Dead as they get," Alfred said. "Garroted. Pity. He was Paki, okay, but I liked him."

"Me, too."

"They banged him up in jail, some bullshit charge." Alfred pointed northward. "One of them hajjis had a wire, got to him. Or, another story, hajjis blow up the jail wall, they go in, find our guy"— Alfred made a pistol gesture with his right hand—"they whack him." He put a calloused hand around his throat. "Then, this."

Shawn thought back to his meeting with Abbasi in the peace of his Sussex garden. He thought of shots at a pear tree, a woman in a Lexus, a kitten on a lawn. He shook his head. "Not true."

"Which bit?" asked Alfred.

"Both. Either."

Alfred shook his head. "Ye of little faith. You don't believe this, because why?"

"Because it never happened," Shawn said. "If Abbasi's dead—"

"—which, trust me, mate, he is—"

"—he wasn't killed by his own people."

"Well," Alfred said, "I don't know. It's what I heard. These days, who d'you believe? The stories you hear." He considered Shawn. "Heard one or two about you, come to that."

"Tell me," Shawn said. "I like stories."

"Might not like this one," Alfred said. "Mr. McCord's planning to pick up your girlfriend."

"You're working for him?"

"Am now," Alfred said. "Something I noticed, people stop paying you, once they're dead."

Shawn swung his chair so that he was fully facing the thickset man. "So. McCord's paying. Walking-around money, that's called. What do you do for him?"

"Now, now," Alfred said. "I don't ask you what you're doing with Miss Baptist."

"Baptiste."

"Whatever," Alfred said. "I don't ask. But when I say pick up, apropos Mr. McCord and Miss Baptist, I mean not in the sense he's asking the lady out on a date."

"I know what you mean," Shawn said. "Hasn't happened yet."

Alfred pressed large hands together: an isometric exercise. "You know why that is? I'll tell you. Because Mr. McCord has a little job for you, which he wants it done first." He turned away, then paused. "You know something?" he asked. "If I was you, which I'm glad I'm not, I wouldn't stay around this town."

"You said you hadn't been hired for a hit."

"I haven't," Alfred said. "Don't know if I'd do it, even if I was. We're getting too old for this game, you and me. You specially. Comes a time, right, when you say, okay, enough of this shit. Or your body says so. If I was you, though, and like I say, I'm glad I'm not, there's other bodies I'd be watching."

"Anyone in particular?"

Alfred bent to toss coins to an orange-robed and legless beggar scooting past them on a skateboard.

"What about the one you're living with? The bird? The one the boss wants a chat with."

Hands clasped in blessing, the beggar scooted off.

Shawn said, "You've been listening to McCord."

Alfred shrugged. "At this moment, it's my job." He reached beneath his jacket. Shawn stood and stepped back, his hand going to his own pocket.

"Relax," Alfred said. He produced an envelope and passed it over. "Last payment from Mr. Abbasi." He watched Shawn open the packet. "It's not what you settled for. Man was running short of cash. Plus, I took myself a little commission."

"You could have taken it all," Shawn said.

Alfred bared tombstone teeth. "You know what he says, whatsisface. Live outside the law, you best be honest."

Listening to the handyman, Shawn reflected on honesty, on lives cut short, on the people he knew who'd died violent deaths, at his own hand or others'. One of those others, he believed, was Alfred—who lifted one liver-spotted finger in farewell, then paused.

"Last word," he said. "I got myself a armpit of a place"—he pointed to where a gold-leafed onion dome reared above the rooftops—"right next that mosque thing there. Bitch, trying to sleep. Five in the morning, what do they do, the bastards?" He held his hands apart. "Prayer call over speakers, this near my fucking head." He yawned. "Anyway, son. You want to find me, that's where I'll be."

Shawn told him thanks for the heads-up. "No offense," he said, "but why the hell would I want to find you?"

The handyman was walking away, rolling his head to ease the muscles of his neck. "Who knows?" he asked. "This place. Fulla surprises."

34

When Shawn arrived back at the Grand Comfort Hotel, Bobby Walters was there, waiting in a veranda in a pool of shade, escaping the crowd and heat of the afternoon. Putting an arm around Shawn's shoulders, he said, "Good to see you, boy. Been a while."

"In an army chopper," Shawn said, "did you not drop into my village, two weeks back?"

"Lot goes down in two weeks," Bobby said. "Stuff happens. I came here. You came here. I want a word where no one's listening. Get your ass in the jeep."

Given orders, Shawn's instinct was to do otherwise. He'd been that way since schooldays in Turkey Forge.

Seeing this, Bobby said, "You don't do it, be a mistake. Trust me. Got a job for you."

Two buses edged past, flying the campaign flags of both political parties, together with a hundred small mirrors, hand-colored posters of Nashida Noon, and, for some reason, an image of a young and fully dressed Madonna Ciccone. Bearded men hung on the running boards and stood waving, semaphore-style, on roofs. Someone in a bus played what sounded like an off-key trumpet.

"Do I get to know where we're going?"

"The hills. Observation." Bobby—in charge of what Shawn guessed to be a hired vehicle of a certain age—peered underneath, for bombs, then sat a while adjusting the driver's seat, putting the jeep in gear; checking gas, oil, and temperature levels. He was thorough about these things. "Plus, I want a chat, where no one's listening."

Shawn thought it over, then climbed into the jeep's shotgun seat. On the edge of town, they were waved through a Pakistan army checkpoint, manned by a single nervous soldier with a submachine gun. Shawn watched until he was out of sight. A sign on the side of the road, beyond the checkpoint, read, in English and Urdu, WASH HAND BEFORE YOU PRAY.

"Is there something I should know? Some other reason for this trip?"

"Like I told you," Bobby said, "we need a chat. Plus, I want to overlook Wana and Miranshah. Get an idea of the territory. Locate ACM camps. We plan to bomb the bastards."

They were leaving Peshawar now, through the Karkhano market. The market stalls led up to the arched gate that separated Peshawar from the lawless tribal areas on both sides of the Durand Line. In one direction, the highway led through the Khyber Pass into Afghanistan. Bobby took the other fork, onto an unpaved road—a dusty track, which Shawn, in his Peshawar days, had never seen.

Gazing upward, into the mountains, he recalled the Pashtun

wedding his comrades had bombed. He wondered how Danielle would judge these latest attack plans.

To Shawn's left, along a deep defile, stood a cluster of mud-brick Pashtun dwellings, hedged with flowering ashoka trees like those under which—so his Muslim lover said—the Buddha was born.

In ascending waves of sound, a U.S. fighter-bomber passed low overhead, banked, turned, and was gone, to bring down God's wrath on southern Afghanistan. Higher and slower, an unmanned Predator circled hawklike over the mountains, seeking prey. Shawn pointed a thumb. "Still kids in Nevada flying those things?"

Bobby nodded.

"Drones based where? Helmand?"

"Here," Bobby said. "Baluchistan."

Shawn considered his colleague. "We're bombing Pakis with drones based here? In their own country? Islamabad knows?"

"Would we know if the hajjis put bombers in Iowa?" Bobby asked. "Of course they fucking know. What do they do? Throw hissy fits. Bitch about cross-border bombing. Then they name a price."

"Well," Shawn said, "some things still surprise me. Should I know what it means? ACM?"

"New jargon," Bobby said. "ACM, basically, that's ragheads. Latest designation. Pentagon's not happy, calling them insurgents." Bobby was looking to left and right, edgy now. "Insurgent, it's a term gives the wrong impression, you know what I mean." He was driving too fast for the road, swinging from side to side of the track, hurling Shawn against the door of the jeep. "Anticoalition militants. Currently approved designation." He pointed upward and eastward. "Word is, that's where they train. Someplace up there." He grinned and raised his voice, shouting at the empty land. "Wake up, guys. Smell the coffee."

The jeep was climbing through steep planes of mica schist. In declivities to right and left stood shivering windbreaks of gray-leafed poplar. Some of the trees had died; of drought, Shawn guessed.

In the distance, men led strings of hollow-ribbed camels toward flat land below.

The jeep was still climbing. As the gradient grew steeper, Bobby kicked down one gear, then another. Shawn tried to watch both sides of the track. Rafe Ramirez's killers came from these mountain villages. The only humans he saw were two men, old men, sitting motionless on the mountainside, knees drawn up to their chins. They wore thin shawls and woolen caps; their music was the belling of fat-tailed sheep. They gazed into the far distance, not turning their heads as the jeep went by.

"What's the prime minister say? She may have an opinion on what you guys plan."

"Pakistan doesn't have a prime minister. You should know that. It's election time."

Shawn thought of Danielle, reading the local Urdu news sheet. "That's not what I hear. I mean, election's over. We have a result."

"Okay," Bobby said. "Okay. As of this week, technically, yes, Pakistan has a prime minister. Nashida Noon. But come on, she's not in charge. How could she be? Transition time. She's out here in the boonies—Quetta, someplace like that." He pointed back toward the town below them. "She's coming this way. That's one of the things we need to talk about."

Shawn shook his head. "You lost me. Why would we need to do that?"

"We'll get there," Bobby said. "Tell me about your woman."

They were on the crest of the mountain, looking down on a rock-strewn plain. Glancing to his right, Shawn saw, high among the rocks, three men watching him. They carried Lee-Enfield rifles: old-fashioned, single shot, but, he knew, remarkably accurate. In Alabama, he'd trained on Lee-Enfields.

Bobby was swinging the jeep wildly, dodging holes in the road. Dust enveloped them, caking exposed skin. Bobby's normally high complexion was pale now under coats of dirt and sweat. "Who's she work for? Your girl?"

As they climbed higher, apricot trees stood, golden with fruit, in narrow terraces hacked from the stones of the mountainside. Later, the orchards gave way to sheer walls of terra-cotta rock on which nothing grew, not even weeds.

"We're fighting a fucking war here," Shawn said. He pointed down the mountain toward the distant town. "Taliban could take over Peshawar, and you want to talk about a woman I'm traveling with? Tell me something. Whose idea was it to bomb this piece of Pakistan?"

Bobby braked the jeep in a cloud of dust. He was staring into the distance, at the snow-covered peaks of the Hindu Kush. "Calvin's."

"Calvin McCord? It's his idea? The guy does get around. How'd the generals take it?"

"Pentagon?" Bobby asked. "Generals? What the fuck do they know? PR flacks. Pussies. Good war, high morale, high tech, boys home by Christmas. Afghanistan, main export, whatever the hell you want, nothing poppy related. Like some advice?"

"If it relates to women," Shawn said, "then no."

Part of the mountain road had fallen away. Bobby started driving again, hugging the cliff. Shawn leaned sideways, watching the closing gap between the jeep's wheels and what looked like a half-mile drop.

Bobby glanced across at his passenger. "I forgot. You don't like heights."

Shawn still watched the jeep's front wheels. "I'm okay with heights. It's falling off of them I don't like."

They edged past the landslip. Bobby parked at what seemed to be the mountain's highest point. He unpacked army-issue binoculars and sat silent for a time, surveying the mountains, then the desert below. "My advice, Shawn," he said finally, "do something for Uncle. We have a job for you. I'm doing this because we go back a long way, you and me." With one hand on the wheel, he put an arm around Shawn's shoulders. "Your life's gone to shit, I know that. Do this one thing, son, then get your ass out of here."

"Do what?" Shawn asked.

Bobby continued peering through glasses, seeing something, or nothing. "You're through. You know that, I know that. Screwed. Your French chick's going out the door. Forget her. Do this one thing, Shawn, we could take you back in the trade."

"Back to Langley? Back in the Company?"

Bobby nodded yes.

Before he could speak there was a distant explosion, then a high-pitched sound Shawn hadn't heard in a while. He opened the offside door and rolled out of the jeep and underneath as a shell exploded on the gradient to the east. The ground shook like a wet dog; stones flew down the slope, hitting the vehicle side with a noise like small-arms fire. Looking across the underside of the jeep, Shawn saw that Bobby, too, lay flat in the dust.

"Where the hell did that come from?" Bobby asked, speaking under the jeep. He was out of breath. "Who's shelling us?"

"Take your pick," Shawn said. "Your anti-coalition militants up ahead, Taliban over there, friendly fire from our guys. Here's a suggestion. Whoever it was, let's get the fuck out of Dodge, before they whack us again."

The two men rolled out from under the jeep. A faint echo

bounced around the mountains; then there was silence, without sign of human or animal life.

Bobby reached for his army-issue glasses.

"Let's not do this," Shawn said. "Jesus. Let's not stay parked on top of a goddamn mountain. That was a sighting shot. Next time, for Christ's sake, the bastards could nail us."

Bobby got himself behind the wheel, started the jeep, and turned it around. In the shotgun seat, Shawn was looking backward at a distant flash among the rocks.

"Go!" he shouted. "*Go!* Roll it."

Bobby accelerated, changing gear as the jeep gathered speed. Again the ground shook as a shell landed behind them, throwing up clouds of sand and rock and fragments of schist.

"Whoever he is," Shawn said, looking back through the dust, "he's got range. We hadn't moved, that would've been good night and good luck."

"We should nuke the whole fucking country," Bobby said, driving, shaking his head. "Ungrateful sons of bitches. You come in, you help them, what do they do? Try and kill you." He glanced across at Shawn. "Talking of which, this little job we have."

"Here's the deal," Shawn said. "You give me a pass to see Darius Osmani, I'll be on a plane out of here."

Bobby drove awhile in silence. After a time, he said, "I get you into the jail, you come with me to the office. We'll brief you there."

"Brief me for what?"

Bobby, driving faster now, said, "We'll get to that."

35

Bobby Walters brought the Jeep to a halt on the outskirts of Peshawar and waited for the following dust to dissipate. Back on the plain, shock set in. He sat there, trembling, checking his pulse.

Shawn, breathing hard, searched for words. "Close," he said finally. "Just fucking close. Two shells. Are you okay? You don't look—"

"Heart," Bobby said. His normally flushed face was a whiter shade of pale. "I never told you—that's my problem. Dodgy heart. Arrhythmia."

"Which is what?"

"What it sounds like." His mouth opened and closed like a fish's. "Did I tell you? I go in for checkups last year—this is D.C.—they take one look at me, throw me on a gurney, cut me open, give me a pacemaker. Keeps your heart running, theory is. You're kept alive by a damn machine. How'd you like that? You know, I know, what machines do. They go on the fucking fritz. It's like they give your dishwasher the power of life and death. Washer blows a fuse, damn thing dies, you die, too." He looked back at the mountain. "That second shell hit, sweet Jesus, my heart starts jumping around my chest like a Mexican bean. I keep thinking, what if the pacemaker goes out of whack? What if it starts running like hyperspeed? How long have I got then?"

Shawn leaned across to hug his buddy. "Oh, man," he said, "that don't sound good."

"You think?" Bobby turned to look at Shawn. "How many years have you got?"

"More'n you," Shawn said, "if that's how your heart is." He was watching the massing crowd in the streets below. "What exactly's going down here?"

Bobby unbuttoned his shirt to lay an exploratory hand on the left side of his chest. Shawn saw his lips move as he counted heartbeats. Finally Bobby sat back in his seat, looking out over the crowded square below.

"It's those moments in your life," he said, "you know—you must have had 'em—could've gone either way. Like, you know, forks in the road. That's what I think about these days. I mean, listen, I could have been in my old man's law firm, but would I? Would I hell. Told Daddy I'm not sitting behind some damn desk. I'm going off, fight for my country. Like Calvin says, God with us."

"Seeing a lot of movies, were you?"

"Bet your life." Bobby put the jeep back in gear. "Everything John Wayne ever made. What happens? I go in the navy, my sorry-ass brother goes to work for Daddy. As of now, let me tell you, Jason's got a house in Turkey Forge, you could fit my whole damn apartment, pretty much, in the downstairs john. Got his own

Gulfstream, flies to Fiji, and Jason's going to Fiji because why? Because he has his own little island, with what he calls his beach house, which, I have to tell you, it's about the same size as the spread he has in Turkey Forge. Plus, he works five months a year—doing divorce—in case his tax bill gets too big. He says to me, Bobby, bro, time to retire. Be nice to yourself. Put your feet up. I tell him, Jason, I hear you. I'd love it. Just wait while I work out what the food stamps are worth."

They sat without speaking for a couple of minutes, watching men in robes and caps pour out of tour buses, heading for the center of town.

"Okay," Shawn said. "That fork in the road thing, I understand that. I missed one or two off-ramps myself. Now, tell me what's on offer here. As background, Bobby, I'm broke. Flat broke. Chronically short of cash."

Bobby pointed at the crowd streaming down the slope. "Wait a minute. What the hell is that? We were here before, did we ever see this kind of thing?"

"You know perfectly well," Shawn said. "Nashida Noon. Victory tour."

"Sure I know," Bobby said. "How do you?"

"In the local paper."

"How d'you read that?"

"I don't," Shawn said. "I told you, I have a friend who does. This afternoon, Nashida's in town. Then she flies to whatever's the next stop. Which is, you might know where."

"I do. Classified."

"Okay," Shawn said. "What about the jail?"

"What about what jail?"

"We made a deal, remember? You've got Osmani locked up wherever it is you squeeze their balls. I have half an hour with him, I come to your office, for what I don't know, then I get the hell out of town. Out of your life."

"With the woman?"

"Danielle? She's a grown-up girl, but I'll ask her if she wants to come."

"We might discuss that," Bobby said. He looked at Shawn for what seemed a while. Then he nodded and revved up the jeep. "Okay," he said. "Let's hit the jail."

Shawn pointed. "I've been here before, remember? Time of the fire? We nearly died? Best of my memory, jail's over there."

Bobby pulled onto what would have been a sidewalk if the road had had one. He let a crowded tour bus edge down the track. On the sides of the bus were pasted full-color posters of Nashida Noon and of Imran Khan in spotless cricket gear. There was also a large close-up of a vest-clad Bruce Willis, back in the days when he still had hair.

Inside the bus, brass bands were playing.

Bobby said, "War on terror, son. Money flows. We have ourselves two jails. Like, his and hers." He pointed. "Security budget. We built our own little place, right that way. Behind the wall."

Shawn had noticed this building before, when he was out buying his pistol. He'd seen armed men at the gate and wondered just what they were guarding. Now he took in the five outsourced Pakistani guards. Three were staring up the hill behind them. Turning in their direction, Shawn saw they were watching an auto-rickshaw barreling down the hill, trailing smoke.

Then, as one man, all three ran from the jail, leaving their weapons.

Shawn leaned over, opened the driver's door of the jeep, and, lowering his shoulder, shoved his companion out. Taken by surprise, Bobby landed faceup in the dust, like an overturned turtle.

Grabbing the wheel of the jeep, Shawn swung the vehicle around. He changed gear, accelerated, and hit the side of the moving, smoking, now-driverless rickshaw, shoving it into long grass and trees at the side of the track. Then he, too, was out of the jeep, underneath it, as the rickshaw exploded. Fragments fell around him as he slid out from under the vehicle. Passengers from the bus were yelling. Above the medley of sound came Bobby's voice, high and strained.

"Shawn," he shouted. "Fuck it—there's another one—"

Shawn backed to the far side of the jeep as a second auto-rickshaw came down the hill, faster than the first, threatening to run out of control, this one still with a driver. Pouring black smoke, it slowed and came to a halt against the wall of the new jail. The driver—a small man wearing aviator shades and a gray salwar kameez—climbed out and ran down the hill.

Sheltering behind the jeep, Shawn called. "Bobby, down. Keep down."

Bobby, crawling across the track, called, "What the fuck's happening here?"

"Watch."

Moments later, the rickshaw exploded. Shawn heard Bobby say "Oh, *shit*," saw him clutch at his heart as the second blast blew away part of the jail's brick wall. A car lifted in the air and fell, stranded, on its side. Someone screamed. One of the two remaining guards, the one nearest the bomb, was gone, red-white morsels of his body scattered warm and soft about the street where Nashida Noon's followers, caught in the press of bodies, struggled away from the jail. Crowds ebbed. Bobby, hampered by being on the ground and by the size of his paunch, struggled to draw an army-issue handgun, to aim at who knew what. From the back of the parked tour bus, farther down the hill, came six robed men, moving at an easy run.

Bobby, now with Shawn, peered from behind the damaged jeep. "Shouldn't we do something?"

"Like what?" asked Shawn. He nodded at the muj squad. "Six guys, packing Uzis. You feel like John Wayne?"

The last remaining prison guard—the one who'd failed to run—still lived. He lifted himself from the dust and reached out for his Uzi, a yard away. He was shot twice through his upper body before his groping hand could touch the weapon. The man shook his head, shuddered, subsided back to the earth. Dust to dust, Shawn thought. The raiders, in a close group, entered the jail through the gap in the wall. Unaware of what was happening, or wishing to distance themselves, Nashida Noon's supporters still poured down the lower roads, toward the city square.

From inside the jail came three shots in rapid succession, then silence.

Bobby, reaching up from the ground, opened the door of the jeep. On its floor he found his radiophone. He tried to make a call. "Jesus, Bobby," Shawn whispered, "don't do this." He hauled Bobby to his feet. "Let's get the fuck out of here." He pointed. "We're going down the alley. The hajjis—they'll be coming back."

As Shawn backed into the shadows of the alley, something bright and white caught his eye. He looked up to a house whose long upper-floor windows stood open. He saw Danielle—or someone who could have been her sister—standing in shadow, staring across the road, watching raiders who now carried a burden from the jail. Still tightly grouped as they came through the ruined wall, they bore to the bus what looked like the body of a man. Shawn did not dare shout to the woman, who backed away from the window and was lost to sight. He hesitated, unsure whether it was she, unsure whether she'd seen him. Bobby gripped Shawn's arm, pointing. They turned left, down another of Peshawar's narrow and nameless side streets, Bobby now pulling Shawn with him, pushing his way through the clamoring crowd that waited for Nashida Noon.

Shawn breathed in the spreading smell of close-packed human bodies and was, for a moment, overcome by the terror he hadn't felt minutes before. He recalled the claustrophobia he'd felt when, as a kid, he'd been trapped beneath his pop's Buick as it fell from its jack. He stopped, leaning against a wall, waiting for the feeling to pass.

Bobby, breathing hard, clutching his doubtful heart, picked up a little boy lying, face upward, in the alley's dust. Hunkering down, he soothed him, brushing his face where tears made tracks through dirt. After some moments, the child's mouth twitched in what might have been the start of a smile. Then he turned fast, looked back once, and ran.

Bobby stood. He led Shawn down a narrower and quieter alley toward the Peshawar station of America's now-merged Central Intelligence Agency and Office of Special Plans.

36

When Shawn and Bobby emerged from the Peshawar alley, they fought their way through market squares now so crowded as to be nearly impassable.

Before them lay a sea of turbaned heads. On the square's periphery, women crouched over tiny braziers. Hooded, ignoring the heat, they offered cooked meats for sale. Around them swirled the scents of sweat and spice. Men milled, moving this way and that, jostling for position, reaching up, stretching to see over those in front: alert, excited, anticipatory. The crowd reminded Shawn of games he'd played in Tuscaloosa—massed fans of the Crimson Tide, tense, restless, and noisy, waiting for their team to hit the field.

Across the square, Shawn saw flag-decked floats, pulled by straining men. Bands played, competing; discordant voices were raised someplace in what might have been song. In this enclosed arena, the sheer volume of sound amazed him. If Nashida Noon planned to speak, how would anyone would hear?

Bobby, gripping Shawn's arm, pointed left, toward a four-story building. On it, a sign, in both Urdu and English, read PESHAWAR USEFUL STATIONERY SUPPLIES, PVT.

He said, "We're meeting Calvin. He's my—" Bobby paused. "My boss."

"Jesus," Shawn said. "They promoted him? Over you?"

Bobby nodded.

"Whyn't you resign?"

"I told you," Bobby said. "Cash flow. Wives. Alimony."

He used a smart card to open an electronic lock not installed, Shawn guessed, by the Useful Stationery Supplies. He struggled with the jammed door. "Pakistan," Bobby said. He was breathing hard, the effort a visible strain. "What can I tell you? Third fucking world."

The door, when it opened, revealed Calvin McCord holding an M-24 sniper rifle. In shadow stood Hassan Tarkani.

Calvin pressed the weapon into Shawn's hands. "Jesus God," he said. "You look like shit. Death on a soda cracker. What in hell is wrong with you?" Without waiting for answers, he threw an arm around Shawn's shoulders. "But good to see you, son. Your lucky day."

"What kind of luck would that be?" Shawn asked. Watching Calvin, he held up the sniper rifle, feeling its weight, checking out the sights. "What's this for?"

Bobby said to Calvin, "We were just talking about Nashida Noon. Me and Shawn here. We got interrupted. They bombed the jail."

"They what?"

"Bombed the jail. I tried stopping them." Bobby nodded toward a window looking out on the crowded intersection of Shahrah-e-Quaid and Rafique Road. "More important—I was telling Shawn here—she's on her way."

"AfPak time." Calvin wore his watch on the hand that didn't shake. "Late."

"Going to be speaking," Bobby said to Shawn, "right out there. Out that window." To Calvin he said, "Shawn here, he's up with the play. Girlfriend reads the paper."

"Local news?"

"He tells me."

"In Urdu?"

Bobby nodded.

"This is Danielle Baptiste?"

"Whoever," Bobby said. "Thing is, sonny here's up to speed. Knows about Nashida. Knows she's coming through from Quetta." Speaking directly to Shawn, he said, "Here's the plan. PM comes into town, her car stops, ragtop Lincoln, she stops"—he pointed—"right there. In the crowd. That's the plan. She speaks, five, ten minutes. You know, politicians, give them a break, run off at the mouth. Five, ten minutes, that's the plan. Then drive on."

Shawn said, "To where?"

Bobby said, "Classified."

"Airport," Calvin said. "Rawalpindi."

"I'm not Pakistani," Shawn said. "I never got a vote. I should be interested because?"

"Because," said Bobby, "we infiltrated Hezb-i-Islami. You know who they are? Hekmatyar's boys. Terrorist cell."

"Extreme crazies," Calvin said. "Out to fucking lunch."

"Bitch of a job," Bobby said. "You're Muslim, you're a double agent. Short life span, those boys."

"Useful, though," Calvin said, watching the crowd outside. "Till they fall over."

Outside the window, men fought for vantage points. The noise was deafening. Shawn shook his head. He hadn't known the town could cope with crowds like this. "What's he say, your little valley-of-the-shadow hajji?"

"I'll tell you," Bobby said. "Latest heads-up, hajji-guy says, Nashida's car stops right out there—"

"Then," said Calvin, "some crazy"—he pointed outward—"guy's likely there right now, he brings a baby to be blessed."

"Blessing?" Shawn said. "Nashida's a politician."

"Correct."

"Not a saint."

"This place," Bobby said, "ask your girlfriend, you don't have to be a saint. Politicians bless babies."

Men in the street were restless now: Through the window Shawn saw sections of the crowd stirring this way and that. Eddies in a trout stream.

Bobby was thoughtful, watching the throng. "Thing of it is, this baby that's brought to be blessed—we hear it's not a baby."

"What else would it be?" Shawn asked.

"It's a bomb."

"Okay," Shawn said, thinking it through. "Okay. This has something to do with me?"

"What we hear," Bobby said, "the bomb's wrapped like a baby. Phone detonator. Chatter we're getting, this big guy—assassin—he's going to offer the baby—"

"—the bomb—"

"—whatever the hell—offers it to Nashida, like, you know, like he wants the kid blessed. Then he tosses the thing in her car."

"If it works, then what?"

"If it works," Bobby said, "that's all she wrote. Pakistan missing a prime minister."

Calvin's phone rang. He listened, then said, "Jesus Christ. She's here." He pointed outside, to the restless crowd that was now, for a single moment, still, anticipatory. "Nashida's here."

Calvin grabbed Shawn's arm. He pointed upward. "Top floor. Move your ass."

Shawn followed Calvin and Bobby up concrete stairs. "You don't have an elevator?"

Bobby, climbing, drew a gasping breath. "On the fritz."

"Why the hell"—Shawn paused—"why didn't you get Nashida to change her route?"

Calvin was three steps ahead. "You think we didn't try? I mean, damn, not just us. Ambassador tried. She won't do it. Woman says, you know, she changes plans every time there's a death threat, she'll never leave Islamabad. So, last option, you shoot the guy."

There was a moment's silence. Shawn paused, holding the stair rail. "Say what?"

"You're a fuckup, Maguire," Calvin said, without emphasis. He was on the second flight of stairs. "Any way you slice it. Only thing you do is shoot."

"Which," Bobby said, from behind, "you do a damn sight better than the rest of us."

Calvin was climbing again, his breathing even. "It's something we can use. Guys that shoot like you."

Shawn's gut made him feel he needed a bathroom.

"Let me get this straight," he said. "You're telling me I have to kill someone? Some Pakistani out in that crowd?" He glanced down at the M-24. "That's what this is for?"

Calvin paused, staring down at Shawn. "You have a better plan?"

They were climbing again. "If I take out some father—some

father's brought his kid, his baby, to see a moment of history? What happens then?"

"You do that," Bobby said, from behind Shawn, "we put you in a chopper, so fucking fast your feet won't touch the ground. Plane waiting at Shamsi Air Base."

"Shamsi's ours?"

"It is now," said Calvin. "Don't worry about your ass. We'll get you the hell out."

"Anyway," said Bobby, breathing hard, "trust me, it's not going to happen. You'll know you got the right guy. Word is, he's tall. I mean, way tall. Like Osama."

As he reached the third floor, Shawn's mind went back to a notably tall white-robed man, working at the task of hacking the head of Rafe Ramirez from his blood-drowned neck.

Calvin, climbing slower now, pointed in the direction of the market. "Head and shoulders higher than the rest of them, is what we hear. Guy's going to hold up this bomb, looks like a baby—you know, wrapped in whatever the fuck they wrap babies in. You just have to hit him before he throws it in the car."

"Just," Shawn said.

"If you can't do it, believe me, no one can."

"She doesn't have security? Nashida?"

"Sure she does," said Calvin. He was on the fourth floor now, looking back at Shawn. "Security detail from ISI. The boys who brought us the Taliban. Are they going to protect her? You believe that? They're keeping calendar days free for the fucking funeral."

Calvin's phone rang. Still climbing, he listened, then said, "Nashida's car, moving into the square. They're going to park. Roll down the hood."

"I don't believe this," Shawn said. "Open car? In this crowd? Sitting fucking duck."

"What I been telling you," Calvin said. "Unless you get the guy first. So move."

Bobby collapsed on a concrete stair. "You guys," he called. "I'll catch you."

"Fat fuck," said Calvin. Then, to Shawn, "Through that door, east wall window, you got a great view. Whole square."

In the doorway Shawn paused. "I do this, what do I get? What's in it for me?"

"Here's the thing," said Calvin. "Do this, we take you in. You're back working. Medical, pension, all on track."

"For this, I have to kill someone?" said Shawn. Bile, acid bile, welled in his throat, and in his mouth. 'That's the deal?"

Calvin was at the window. "Don't jerk me around. It's not your first time."

"That was war," Shawn said. "I was young. You're young, you do all kind of crazy shit."

"Look at it this way," said Calvin. "You're not terminating a hajji. You're working for America. Saving the life of this woman, as of this week she's prime minister of Pakistan."

"Langley doesn't want her dead," said Calvin.

"Not here they don't."

37

Shawn, carrying the scope-sighted rifle, walked to the fifth-floor window of the stationery office building. Looking down, he saw houses and floats festooned with symbols: flags, banners of the Pakistani Democracy Party, and photos of heroes: Nashida, Sylvester Stallone, Bruce Lee. On opposite sides of the square, two amplified bands played two different martial tunes.

The prime minister's car, an armored Lincoln, edged its way through the crowd.

To Shawn's left, Calvin loaded shells in the chamber of a backup M-24.

"Little something, might interest you. Your girlfriend's guy? The missing boyfriend—Osmani?"

Shawn was adjusting the sights of his sniper rifle. He didn't look around. "Osmani's not her boyfriend. He's her husband."

"Uh-uh. Osmani, Baptiste, not married. We checked." Calvin set the second M-24 aside. "You know there's hajjis, just opened up the jail—let him loose?"

Shawn trial-sighted on the prime minister's open car. "We were there."

"Your girl organized that. We tracked a call. She has your sat-phone."

From the square below, sound swelled, breaking like ocean waves against the building.

"Bullshit."

Calvin closed the chamber of the second rifle. "Who else knew where Osmani was? We did. You did, right? Ashley told you; we know that. None of us here's going to call up Kandahar, organize a bunch of banditos, come across the border, break open a jail. We even wanted to, we can't fucking do it. The girlfriend has your phone. She could do it."

Midsquare, the prime minister's Lincoln slowed. Men sang. Band music swelled.

"Bullshit," Shawn said again, more to himself than anyone else. "Bull. Shit."

"Do you have your phone?" Bobby asked. "I mean, right now?"

Shawn shook his head. "Does it matter?"

"Does it matter, Osmani's gone? Not a lot. We leaned on him a little. Got him talking like he was on the news. Told us about A. Q. Khan. We sent some guys to look around Turquoise Mountain, see if he's right about the nukes. Which I personally doubt." Calvin, too, was watching the prime minister's car. "You want to watch that girl you're traveling with. Watch what she does." He picked up binoculars and scanned the crowd. "Like that kidnap in Cairo."

"What about it?"

"Kidnap? Give me a break. You're running around town, she's up there in al-Masri's apartment, making sure he destroys his damn laptop so we don't read the disk."

Bobby came back into the office, feeling his way along the wall, as if he were blind. His hand was on his heart. "Crazy fibrillation," he said. "Pacemaker out of whack. Bupkis."

Calvin said to Shawn, "Run-through. Paint me a picture."

"You do this for Uncle," Bobby said, still massaging his heart, "Uncle's happy. Uncle's going to write off debts."

The crowd parted before the soft-topped, slogan-painted Lincoln and closed behind it. As Shawn watched, the ragtop rolled down. From this distance, Nashida Noon, standing in the open car, looked tiny, her head covered in a Parisian Hermès scarf of blue and royal purple. Restless, expectant watchers stirred and murmured. Movement flowed through the crowd like wind through wheat. Nashida raised her arms; the bands fell silent; the crowd breathed and sighed: a collective exhalation of breath.

Someone passed the prime minister a microphone. She began to speak. From the crowd, men answered her, echoed her. Different words, Shawn thought, but what he was hearing took him back to when he was a kid: to revival meetings among pinewoods, testifying to God in white-painted wooden chapels. He scanned the square. Tremors ran through his arms to his hands. He'd never done a shot like this. Not midcrowd.

How in hell, Shawn wondered, how in hell do you shoot if you're shaking? How do you pick a single assassin from a crowd of thousands?

What does happen if you kill the wrong guy?

Shawn glanced behind him. Now only Hassan was in the room. If anything went amiss, neither Bobby or Calvin would be called to witness.

By the sound of it, by the pitch of her voice, Nashida Noon was reaching the climax of her speech. Again Shawn—staring through his rifle's sight—scanned the magnified crowd. He could see no exceptionally tall man. If this assassin stood directly behind the prime minister's Lincoln, he'd be free and clear. He could take out the woman anytime he wanted. In the confusion the man—if he lived—would walk away unharmed.

If the guy came up on *this* side, facing the prime minister—if he stood between Shawn and Nashida—

He couldn't do it, Shawn thought. He couldn't kill a man. Not a father with a baby.

Then—Jesus God—*there* he was—Shawn could see the man—unusually tall—robed in white—he looked the double of the one who murdered Rafe . . . and Shawn was aiming—

—now a red dot danced on the back of the white-robed figure, and this man—tall, loose-turbaned, bearded, head and shoulders above his neighbors—raised a baby, or something that might be a baby—raising it high in the air, thrusting the bundle toward the open car, toward Nashida—the laser dot stilled: Shawn took a breath; still himself—there was the sound of a shot, which seemed not to come from Shawn's rifle—the white garment stayed in the crosshairs, now splashed with a darker red, and—a reflex—his rifle did kick, and Shawn knew that this time he had fired—or fired again—at that same moment, someone deep in the crowd released a cage of white doves—and Shawn saw the tall figure start to sink like a holed ship, weakening, bending long legs, strength flowing out of him—and as the doves fluttered upward, the man sank in the crowd—still with the baby-bundle held high above his head as if to save it—and, as he fell, there was a woman, a hijab-shrouded woman, instinctively grabbing the baby as it went down and then—in horror, or dismay—who could say?—tossing the creature, the device, the bomb, whatever it was, away from her, backward, into the crowd—and now Nashida Noon's bulletproof car was moving on, through the crowd, the car's roof rising, people parting like the sea—and, as the crowd drew away from the fallen figure, Shawn looked left to where light glinted on glass. On top of a parked bus stood what first seemed to be a young boy, holding binoculars. As Shawn adjusted his rifle's sight, bringing the figure into focus, he saw that what he'd thought was a child was in fact a ragged-bearded dwarf, gesticulating as the crowd swirled and ebbed around the bus. Now the dwarf stared upward, his gaze fixed on the window from which Shawn had fired. The rifle's sight magnified his face. Transfixed, Shawn held the dwarf's gaze: watched as he raised a tiny arm, pointing at the window— pointing at Shawn.

Calvin was back in the whitewashed room, shouting.

"Say what?" Shawn refocused.

"I said, great shot. Now give me the damn gun. The boys are going to trash it."

Shawn passed the scope-sighted rifle to Calvin. He said, "There's a guy down there, dwarf, standing on a bus. He saw me shoot."

"Not the only one," Calvin said. He pointed to Hassan, holding a small video camera. "If our Paki friend didn't fuck up, we have us a hit movie here." He laughed. "New star—Shawn Maguire, sharp-shooter."

Shawn saw that Bobby was back in the room. There were things he wished to say to his friend, but no words came.

Bobby said, "Shawn, terrific—pick one bad guy in a crowd. Now, move." He pointed to the door. "We want you out."

"Wait a minute," Shawn said. He found his voice. He was shaking. Below him, in the square, men bent over the body of the fallen man. Beyond them, he could still see the dwarf on the bus roof, staring upward. "I have a question," he said. "The president here—he's still our guy? On the payroll?"

"Why?"

"Why am I asking?" Shawn pointed after the prime minister's vanishing motorcade. "Next week, that woman's in office."

Bobby opened a bottle of Johnnie Walker. It was all the whisky you could buy in this town. Shawn saw that his friend, too, was shaking a little. "If she lives."

In the square below, the crowd began to disperse. Men bore away a white-robed body.

"Okay," Shawn said. "The lady's in power, it's good-bye Mr. President. Is that right?" Bobby nodded. "So you lose your man? Your asset?"

Bobby nodded.

Shawn pointed to the square. "Then why not let that guy throw the damn bomb?"

Bobby said, "You know Nashida's flying to Rawalpindi."

Shawn went to the basin to wash his hands and his face in cold water. He stood there for a while, turning the tap, looking at a portrait of the president, working something out. He said, "Rawalpindi. That's ISI turf."

Bobby poured himself a drink without offering one to Shawn. "So," he said, "do the math. What's it tell you?"

"Paki intelligence assassinates Nashida—"

Bobby finished his drink fast. He stood, considering whether or not to pour another. His diet allowed one measure of alcohol per day. He said, "Go figure. President has to act. Good-bye to the invisible soldiers. Good-bye ISI. We keep him, lose them."

"And lose her," Shawn said. "Jesus—you mean we just saved

the prime minister—fuck it, *I* saved her—so ISI does a hit in Rawalpindi?"

Bobby shrugged. He made a decision; poured a second drink, calming his nerves.

"What kind of screwed-up deal is this?"

"I'll tell you what kind of deal it is," Bobby said. He came up close to Shawn, breathing whisky. "You know, I know, those guys, Inter-Service, they control nuclear production. Come on, we all know that. We leave them alone, they'll hand out warheads all down the Arab street. Picture this, son—Khan and Co. dish out nukes like blueberry fucking muffins. Sooner or later, these things'll get to al Qaeda." He crossed the room and took Shawn's arm. "We have 9/11 rerun—next time, it's nuclear. You know what I'm saying? Small device, big enough. Good-bye New York. Adios. Hasta luego. So. Here's the deal. We weigh, against the city of Manhattan, the life of one reasonably corrupt female politician who, we know, has already given nuclear secrets to North Korea. A woman who, if she lived, would have been prime minister of Pakistan. With all that implies for the U.S. of A." He placed a plump hand on Shawn's shoulder. "Moral equation, son. Above your pay grade."

"If I go public? Talk to the press? Put this fuckup on the Web?"

Calvin was listening. "Please," he said. "You know the answer. You won't be alive long. You saw inside our jails. Think Cairo—think Fes. Guys hanging from hooks? Remaining time on earth, Shawn, would be deeply unhappy."

"If I were you," said Bobby, checking the time, and breathing deeply to help his heart, "at this point I'd get my ass out of here." He pushed a small package into Shawn's jacket pocket. "Something else you can do for us," he said. "Do it for Uncle. Hold the girlfriend."

"Danielle?"

"Indeed. We don't want the lady leaving town. Not before we talk with her. Call me when you've hooked her up to something heavy."

Going downstairs, Shawn felt weaker than he had in years. Tired now, exhausted, he rubbed a wrist across the dampness of his eyes. Leaving the stationery office, he closed its red-painted door and heard the tumblers of its electronic lock fall into place. Outside, still air swam with heat.

On a cobbled street, Shawn checked the package Bobby had given him: Agency-issue plastic handcuffs, in powder blue. He was returning them to his pocket when, behind him, a man started to scream. In Shawn's head, the screams echoed, bouncing around his aching skull. He turned. At the end of the alley stood the tiny wild-bearded man he'd seen, minutes before, on a bus roof in the crowded square. Now the dwarf ran—still screaming, arms waving—at the head of a white-robed mob.

Their wild cries—*Allahu akbar*—counterpointed the midget's howl.

For a moment, Shawn considered the Makarov he carried, thought of backing into a doorway, shooting it out, and knew, in the same moment, that dog wouldn't hunt.

Not with these men, these numbers.

Turning, he ran, stumbling down a rug-lined alley, praying the crowd had cleared. Glancing back, he saw that the stump-legged dwarf moved with surprising speed, still screaming as he ran. From behind him men fired shots: .303 was Shawn's guess. Hard to be accurate when you run with a long-barreled gun. Which might not matter, Shawn thought, as he searched for an exit. In this place, there were other ways of ending a life.

Already, he was slowing, limping, his breathing hard in the heat, legs still pained from the knife attack in Fes. At this rate, within minutes, the zealots would have him, and then—Jesus God, what then? Not something you want to think about.

In the dust and humid air Shawn struggled for breath. His throat's lining burned; his lungs were on fire.

Glancing back, not watching his feet, Shawn collided with a smoking brazier. Tipping, it strewed burning coals and kebabs across the pebbled street. From somewhere, a woman wailed. Shawn turned his head toward her and fell forward into a shallow excavation: a reeking pit of Peshawar's ancient pipework.

Shawn picked himself up to run again, ducking at the sound of another shot, knowing as he did that the shot you hear is not the shot that kills you.

High over rooftops, an onion dome swam in aureoles of evening light, stirring memories of a conversation somewhere, sometime, with someone—

Then he knew. Staggering, fighting the pain in his legs, Shawn ran through a maze of unpaved paths toward the golden mosque. Gasping for air, turning down a litter-strewn alley, he collided with the solid frame of Alfred Burke.

"Hey, hey," said Alfred, stepping back. With sudden violence, he pulled Shawn through a wood-framed arch, closing nail-studded doors behind them both. "Hold your horses, son."

Shawn was listening to sounds in the alley. In silence, the handyman led the way through the empty rooms of a derelict structure that might once have been a riad. The building's walls were holed, its floors littered with shards of concrete, deep in dust. The only

domestic objects were barbells leaning against a stuffed and brindled feline on a high marble plinth. The wildcat's fur had been
eaten away by whatever eats fur. It made the thing look mangy. In
its mouth, it held a fish.

"Came with the house," said Alfred, nodding at the animal.
"It's a fishing cat."

Shawn turned to look at him.

"Does what it says on the tin. Swims rivers. Catches fish."

Alfred shoved Shawn forward when he wished to stop. In a
walled garden of dying cactus, the two men paused.

Alfred watched as Shawn tried to regain his breath. He said,
"You look like shit." He raised a thumb. "Heard what happened.
Nice bit of shooting. Take out a raghead, middle of a crowd. Seri-
ously doubt I could do that."

"He was a bomber."

Alfred nodded. "They told me. Any of these meshuggeneh see
where you're shooting from?"

Faintly now, Shawn heard high-pitched screams. "One did."
He pointed back toward the alley. "Fucking dwarf. That's him
you're hearing."

Alfred laughed. "Dwarf?" he said. "*Dwarf?* You serious?"

Shawn nodded.

"You pick 'em, don't you?" Alfred renewed his grip on Shawn's
arm. "Right, mate. Move."

Within a mud-brick outbuilding, Alfred opened the door of a
rusty dark-windowed Lada and pushed Shawn into the shotgun
seat. As his legs bent beneath him, Shawn grunted in pain.

Taking his time, the handyman eased himself into the car's
driving seat, his joints stiff. On one knee, he set an aging—but,
Shawn guessed, still functional—.38 Smith and Wesson.

Shawn's breathing slowed. He shook his head, trying to clear it. "Christ," he said. "How the hell could I do that? What the fuck possessed me?"

"Do what, exactly?"

"You know what happened. I killed a man back there."

"Well," said Alfred, "you're not the first. Cain, for instance. In the Bible."

They sat in silence awhile, listening to the distant sounds of the street.

Shawn wiped away sweat; tried to breathe deeper; tried to still the beating of his heart.

"We're driving?"

Alfred shook his head. "Not right this moment," he said. He tapped the dashboard. "You're wondering about the motor. What can I tell you? Blends in. Ragheads drive this crap." He tapped the glass and shrugged. "They like black windows. Fine. Suits me."

Shawn nodded, thinking this through.

"Let's say I forgot you lived by the mosque."

Alfred shrugged. "What's it you carry?"

"Nine-mil Makarov."

"Cap gun," said Alfred. "Water pistol." He considered Shawn. "My guess, son, you'd be brown bread by now. Bits of you messing up my street." He paused a while, then said, "Something else you want to think on. They told me, take you out."

"Who told you?"

"Who d'you suppose?" asked Alfred. He pointed east. "Your mate McCord. Didn't ask directly, mind you. Troublesome priest kind of thing." His tombstone grin. "I got the message."

Shawn was fighting sleep. He forced his eyes open, eying the pistol on Alfred's knee. "And?"

"Be honest," said Alfred, "I thought about it. Thought, no. Told you, I'm too old for this game. You, too, way you was running." He paused, then said, "Plus, I'm reading about Jesus."

"You're Jewish," Shawn said.

"Just because I don't believe he's the son of God," said Alfred, "don't mean I ignore him. I read he was dead against killing. Jesus, I mean. Not God."

"I've never been religious," Shawn said, "but that sounds right."

Alfred mused for a moment. "Owes me money," he said finally. "Mr. McCord does."

"Problem," said Shawn.

"For him," said Alfred. He was turning something over in his mind. "Being against killing don't mean I give up altogether."

They sat in silence awhile, until Alfred started the car. "Here's what we're doing," he said. "I drive you back to that shithole where you're staying. You go inside, grab an hour shuteye, so you don't go banging in the fucking furniture. Then you're out the door."

Alfred pulled the Lada from the outbuilding to the street. He drove with care along the Qissa Khawani Bazaar. Through darkened windows, he watched the thinning crowd. Men made their slow way home, awakening in Shawn memories of his own home. Memories of Martha.

"Told you," said Alfred, "didn't I? You stay here, someone sure as shit's going to slot you. Bet on it. If it's not your buddies, it's the towelheads. One or the other." He nodded at passing men. "Silly bastards out there, barking at the moon. Plus," he said, "these days, I get the feeling, whatever God these guys pray to, someone round here's about to feel His wrath."

Against his wishes, Shawn's eyes were closing. "If it was you, where would you go?"

"Like you told Mr. Abbasi," Alfred said, "before he was taken.

Spend time in Cuba. Take the bird. Miss Baptist, whatever her name is."

Catching his breath, Shawn rolled down the darkened car window.

Alfred looked across the car. "Christ. You do want to die, don't you? Roll the fucker up."

Outside the Indus Grand Comfort Hotel, the handyman pulled the Lada to the sidewalk, killing the engine.

Shawn pointed back the way they'd come. "The Agency," he said. "What'll happen?"

"To Mr. McCord?" asked Alfred. "Believe me, none of your business." He pointed toward the hotel's door. "Move your ass inside. Sleep. Then get the fuck out of town." He restarted the Lada. "Stick around here, son, you're ace of goddamn spades."

Shawn climbed the darkened stair of the Grand Comfort Hotel. He had the sense of being in a building drained of life: suddenly deserted, as if by men in flight from encroaching plague. He moved slowly, his legs still heavy. He thought of the device keeping Bobby's heart alive. His own heart beat oddly, faster than it should.

On a landing, he sat awhile on a concrete stair, wondering if he'd make it to his room. When he did, the room was hot and empty. Water ran; he guessed Danielle was in the shower. He wondered about the illness she claimed; wondered if he'd imagined her watching presence at the window overlooking the now-ruined American jail.

Sweating, Shawn shed his clothes, letting them lie where they fell, on the floor by the bed. He was too tired to care. Exhausted, drained, he fell to the bare mattress and lay on his back, watching patterns of what might be blood move on the ceiling's whitewash. He saw shapes shift, mutate, fade—now sinister, now benign. Once he saw a severed head. He closed his eyes, shutting out light, hoping sleep might erase the vision of red on a white robe; a man he'd killed sinking in a human sea. A bundle that might be a baby, or might be a bomb, tossed hand to hand, until it, too, sank in the sea.

A distant explosion shook the hotel. Flakes of ceiling plaster fell on Shawn. In his mind, the assassin's face became the face of Nashida Noon. Weeping, burning, dying, she was transformed into naked dreams of Danielle. Who came naked from the shower, standing by the bed, watching this sleeping man and then stretching on the bed beside him. Her body a blessing, a benediction.

Dazed by dreams, unwilling to wake, Shawn lay awhile in her arms, his head between her breasts. There was something in his mind; some half-remembered . . . something he should—

"Nashida," he whispered, "Nashida Noon—we ought to—" She bent close to hear him. "They might—"

Quietly then, she said it was over. "It's on the radio. Nashida's dead." She drew him closer to her naked body. "In Rawalpindi—a plane crash—"

"Jesus God. Too late."

"Did your people?" she asked. "Did they do that?"

He said something inaudible. She bent her head. "Say again?"

"I said, I love you."

Danielle raised herself, looking down at him. She kissed his closed eyes, her naked body covering his.

"Could you," he asked, "could you live with—?"

"Is this"—she bent to touch her lips on his—"is this a proposal?"

Something had changed. He sensed it. She was tender now, more loving than he'd known her; her thighs wet, her body open to his. For a time, she touched him, looking down, her nipples, expectant, brushing his chest. The scent of soap on her skin drowned in the loamy smell of her sex.

He felt the slow shift of her body above him as she leaned across the mattress, searching for something in the clothes he'd dropped. She knew he carried condoms; sex addicts do. Moments later, before he could tell what she had in mind, she fastened a plastic handcuff to his right wrist, the other link to a metal rail of the bed. Moving fast, she was away from him, pulling on underpants, buttoning a shirt.

He jerked his wrist against the cuff—the hopeless tug he'd seen in men who knew they faced darkness and death.

As he might.

Danielle took the short-barreled Makarov from his jacket. Watching him, she weighed the pistol in her hand. "You were going to give me to that man who hurt my husband."

"To Calvin?" He shook his head. "No. Never to him."

"Truly? You weren't?" She pointed at his shackled wrist. "Why carry the cuffs?"

He said nothing. What could he say? The cuffs were for her.

She checked shells in the pistol, leveled the gun. "Why would you wish to live with me? A woman who might kill you?"

He knew then how Martha had felt, facing death. "Danielle," he said, "I wanted—"

In truth, she was all he wanted.

"You just shot a man."

He wondered how she could have known.

"Would your death not make things even? Eye for eye, your Bible says. A life for a life."

Your Bible?

She put down the pistol, pulled her jeans over her hips, and slipped her feet into sneakers. She said, "I'm leaving you, Shawn. We'll take Darius somewhere safe. Someplace he'll be treated for what your friends did." She brushed hair back from her face. "He's hurt. He's ill. He may not live."

Shawn tested the strength of the handcuff. "You're not his wife."

She shook her head. "I lied. I needed him. Needed a believer. He was my operative." She was amused. "I'm the one they should have taken. Not Darius."

"What he told Calvin?"

"A mix. Truth, untruth. Nothing your people can use."

She dropped the Makarov into the pocket of her jacket, watching as he tugged again at the handcuff binding him to the bed.

She bent toward him, speaking quietly. "I'm going over the border. I have to know you won't stop me. Give me to your friends."

He felt his foolish nakedness. With one helpless hand he covered himself. The plastic cuff bit at his wrist.

"Please," he said, "Jesus, Dani, don't"—he wrenched at the handcuff—"for Christ's sake, not like this."

"Count your blessings," she said. "I'm leaving you alive. There was a time I thought I might not." She looked around, to see what else she might need. "Later, I'll call—tell the maid to check the room."

Danielle blew a light kiss and was gone.

Moments later, she was back. "One day," she said, "if I survive, I might come look for you. Your place, where Martha's buried. Think about it. Tell me if you could live with a terrorist."

With unringed fingers she made quotation marks around that final word.